本书获安徽省2017年度高校优秀青年人才支持计划重点项目
（项目编号：gxyqZD2017105）资助出版

注释对二语阅读中词汇附带习得的影响研究

Effects of Glosses on Incidental Vocabulary Acquisition in Second Language Reading

易红波 ◎著

安徽师范大学出版社
·芜湖·

图书在版编目(CIP)数据

注释对二语阅读中词汇附带习得的影响研究 / 易红波著.
— 芜湖：安徽师范大学出版社，2017.6
ISBN 978-7-5676-2910-3

Ⅰ. ①注… Ⅱ. ①易… Ⅲ. ①英语－阅读教学－教学研究 Ⅳ. ①H319.4

中国版本图书馆CIP数据核字(2017)第113966号

注释对二语阅读中词汇附带习得的影响研究　　易红波◎著

责任编辑：吴　琼
装帧设计：张培树
出版发行：安徽师范大学出版社
　　　　　芜湖市九华南路189号安徽师范大学花津校区
网　　址：http://www.ahnupress.com/
发 行 部：0553-3883578　5910327　5910310(传真)
印　　刷：虎彩印艺股份有限公司
版　　次：2017年6月第1版
印　　次：2017年6月第1次印刷
规　　格：889 mm×1194 mm　1/32
印　　张：9.625
字　　数：370千字
书　　号：ISBN 978-7-5676-2910-3
定　　价：30.00元

Abstract

Wilkins (1972: 111) holds that "without grammar very little can be conveyed, without vocabulary nothing can be conveyed." Schmitt (2015: 4) also argues that "learning vocabulary is an essential part of mastering a second language." They both emphasize the significance of vocabulary in language learning. It is generally believed that there are two ways to learn vocabulary, intentionally and incidentally. Even though the result of incidental vocabulary acquisition is not always satisfactory, nobody can deny that it is an important way to acquire vocabulary. After all, "vocabulary learning is incremental in nature." (Schmitt, 2015: 21)

The current research, which is composed of three empirical studies, aims to investigate the effects of the languages employed in glosses, the number of the options provided to glosses, and glossing positions on reading comprehension and incidental vocabulary acquisition through reading for the learners with different language proficiency. Three questions are raised in each empirical study.

1. Which type of glosses is more facilitative to learners' reading comprehension? Are there significant differences in reading

comprehension between the learners with different language proficiency under different glossing conditions?

2. Which type of glosses is more beneficial to learners' incidental vocabulary acquisition through reading? Are there significant differences in vocabulary gain and vocabulary retention between the learners with different language proficiency under different glossing conditions?

3. Are there significant differences between learners' vocabulary gain and vocabulary retention under each glossing condition? Are there significant differences between vocabulary gain and vocabulary retention for the learners with different language proficiency?

In each empirical study, the learners are divided into the group with higher language proficiency and the one with lower language proficiency, according to the results of two Vocabulary Levels Tests. Glosses of 10 target words chosen from the same text are provided in different languages, with different options and in different positions. The participants are required to take an immediate vocabulary test after finishing two reading tasks, and two weeks later, a delayed vocabulary test with the same items, but in a different order, is given to the same participants. The tests take the form of the Vocabulary Knowledge Scale. After the first vocabulary test, some participants are chosen to be interviewed about their opinions of glossing conditions. All the data collected is analyzed by means of SPSS 20.0.

The first empirical study is to investigate the effects of the languages employed in glosses on reading comprehension and incidental vocabulary acquisition through reading for the learners with different language proficiency. There are four different types of glosses, that is, Chinese glosses, English glosses, Chinese plus English glosses, as well as null glosses. It is found that there are significant differences in learners' reading comprehension under four different glossing conditions. To be exact, significant differences are found in learners' reading comprehension between four glosses, except between Chinese glosses and English glosses. There are also significant differences in reading comprehension under each glossing condition between the learners with different language proficiency. As for vocabulary gain, significant differences are found under these four glossing conditions. To be specific, significant differences in learners' vocabulary gain are found between Chinese glosses and null glosses, English glosses and Chinese plus English glosses, as well as between null glosses and Chinese plus English glosses. There are also significant differences in vocabulary gain between the learners with different language proficiency under each glossing condition, except under the condition of Chinese glosses. As to vocabulary retention, glossing conditions have a significant effect on learners' vocabulary retention. However, significant differences only exist between Chinese glosses and Chinese plus English glosses, and between null glosses and

Chinese plus English glosses. In terms of the differences between vocabulary gain and vocabulary retention, significant differences exist under each glossing condition. For the learners with higher language proficiency, there are significant differences between vocabulary gain and vocabulary retention under the condition of both Chinese plus English glosses and null glosses, while for the learners with lower language proficiency, significant differences are found under each glossing condition. In brief, glosses can greatly improve learners' reading comprehension and their incidental vocabulary acquisition through reading, especially Chinese plus English glosses.

The second empirical study is concerned with the effects of the number of the options provided to glosses on reading comprehension and incidental vocabulary acquisition for the learners with different language proficiency. There are two types of glosses involved, single Chinese plus English glosses and multiple-choice Chinese plus English glosses with two options. It is discovered that glossing conditions have a significant effect on learners' reading comprehension. And significant differences in reading comprehension also exist under two glossing conditions between the learners with different language proficiency. As to vocabulary gain, there are significant differences under two glossing conditions. To be accurate, the higher the learners' language proficiency is, the better their vocabulary gain is under two glossing conditions. As for vocabulary retention, there are not any significant differences under two glossing conditions, and neither are there between the learners with different language proficiency. With regard to the differences between vocabulary gain and vocabulary retention, it is found that there are significant differences under two glossing conditions. At the same time, significant differences between vocabulary gain and vocabulary retention also exist for the learners with different language proficiency. In short, single Chinese plus English glosses can significantly facilitate learners' reading comprehension and their incidental vocabulary acquisition through reading.

The last empirical study is involved in the effects of glossing positions on reading comprehension and incidental vocabulary acquisition through reading for the learners with different language proficiency. Four types of glosses are concerned, in-text glosses, marginal glosses, footnote glosses and endnote glosses. It is found that glossing positions have a significant effect on learners' reading comprehension. To be exact, significant differences in learners' reading comprehension exist between in-text glosses and marginal glosses, in-text glosses and endnote glosses, marginal glosses and footnote glosses, as well as between marginal glosses and endnote glosses. There are also significant differences in reading comprehension under four glossing conditions between the learners with different language proficiency. To be specific, the higher the learners' language proficiency is, the better their reading comprehension is under the condition of marginal glosses and endnote glosses. With regard to vocabulary gain, glossing positions have a significant effect on learners' vocabulary gain. Significant differences are found between four glossing positions, except between in-text glosses and footnote glosses. In addition, significant differences in vocabulary gain are found between the learners with different language proficiency. To be precise, the higher the learners' language proficiency is, the better their vocabulary gain is under the condition of marginal glosses and endnote glosses. As for vocabulary retention, glossing positions have a significant effect on learners' vocabulary retention. However, significant differences exist between in-text glosses and marginal glosses, marginal glosses and footnote glosses, as well as between marginal glosses and endnote glosses. It is also found that there are significant differences in vocabulary retention under four glossing conditions between the learners with different language proficiency. Nevertheless, significant differences only exist under the condition of marginal glosses. In terms of the differences between vocabulary gain and vocabulary retention, there are significant differences under each glossing condition. For the learners with higher language proficiency, significant differences between vocabulary gain and vocabulary retention exist under the condition of marginal glosses and endnote glosses, while for the learners with lower language proficiency, significant differences only exist under the condition of endnote glosses. In brief, marginal glosses are significantly the most beneficial to learners' reading comprehension and their incidental vocabulary acquisition through reading.

Based on the results obtained in these three empirical studies, the general conclusion is that glosses can significantly facilitate learners' reading comprehension and their incidental vocabulary acquisition through reading, especially single marginal Chinese plus English glosses. This result is partially consistent with the Involvement Load Hypothesis, which means the hypothesis needs to be revised.

The research has some implications for the compilation of English textbooks and English vocabulary teaching in practice. Theoretically, the research may throw some insights into the revision of the Involvement Load Hypothesis.

TABLE OF CONTENTS

LIST OF APPENDICES

Chapter One Introduction

Wilkins (1972: 111) once stated that without vocabulary, nothing could be conveyed. Therefore, vocabulary acquisition plays a crucially significant part in L2 learning. Reading is a critically important means to obtain the information we need. For language learners, they can acquire vocabulary through reading. While reading, the learners may try to figure out the meanings of the words with the help of the context, which gradually helps them to incidentally acquire vocabulary knowledge. Nation (1990: 130) also holds that acquiring vocabulary incidentally is one of the most important vocabulary learning strategies. Krashen (1989) even argues that the learners can acquire vocabulary best by means of incidental vocabulary acquisition. In a word, incidental vocabulary acquisition plays a vital role in vocabulary acquisition for language learners. Even so, some scholars express their doubts about the effect of incidental vocabulary acquisition through reading (Rieder, 2002). Therefore, some methods are employed to enhance the effect of incidental vocabulary acquisition, such as providing different types of glosses for the target words, setting different levels of questions, as well as increasing the reoccurrence frequencies of the target words in reading. Among these enhancement methods, providing glosses for the target words is of great significance. Consequently, the current research is to explore the effects of different types of glosses on learners' reading comprehension and their incidental vocabulary acquisition in L2 reading.

1.1 Need for the Study

There is no doubt that vocabulary is of essential importance in L2 learning. However, L2 vocabulary acquisition did not deserve attention from the scholars conducting linguistic research until the 1980s. Gradually, it has been becoming one of the foci in L2 research (Laufer, 2009).

In general, there are two common ways to acquire vocabulary, that is, intentional and incidental vocabulary acquisition. The former means that the learners acquire vocabulary knowledge consciously by means of memorizing word lists, doing relevant exercises and so on, while the latter proposed by Nagy, Herman and Anderson (1985), refers to the situation where the learners acquire vocabulary knowledge in the process of implementing tasks, which are not concerned with acquisition of the target words. In other words, language learners acquire some words in such activities as reading magazines, watching movies, and so forth. Nowadays, it has been widely agreed that the learners can acquire vocabulary incidentally while reading extensively (Huckin and Coady, 1999). Accordingly, a great number of studies have been performed to investigate the factors which influence incidental vocabulary acquisition of language learners, such as learner factors (Chang and Li, 2009; Gai, 2003; Gong, 2009; Li and Tian, 2005; Pulido, 2003, 2004b; Shao, 2006; Wang, 2009; Wu and Xu, 2009; Xu and Wu, 2007; Zhang and Qi, 2009; Zhao, 2012, etc.), text factors (Gardner, 2004; Pulido, 2004a, 2007; Rott, 1999; Zahar et al., 2001, etc.), lexicon factors (Ghafouri and Masoomi, 2016; Gu and Zang, 2011; Li and Gao, 2016; Nagy, et al., 1985; Nation, 1990, 2001; Wang et al., 2012; Zhang and Xu, 2014, etc.) and context factors (Chern, 1993; Haastrup, 1991; Li, 1988; Mondria and Wit de Boer, 1991; Wang, 2010; Xun, 2006; Zahar et al., 2001, etc.). Among these factors, glossing, one of the lexicon factors, used to improve incidental vocabulary acquisition has been becoming more and more popular.

With regard to the effects of different types of glosses on learners' incidental vocabulary acquisition through L2 reading, different scholars at home and abroad have different opinions. Some (Chen and Leung, 1989; Cheng and Good, 2009; Farvardin and Biria, 2012; Hulstijn et al., 1996; Ko, 2005; Kroll, 1993; Lv et al., 2005; Meng and Chen, 2015; Miyasako, 2002; Vela, 2015; Wu and Xu, 2009, etc.) hold that L1 glosses or L2 glosses are more facilitative to learners' incidental vocabulary acquisition, while others (Chen, 2013; Jacobs et al., 1994; Shi, 2010; Xu, 2010, etc.) argue that L1 plus L2 glosses are more conducive.

Meanwhile, some researchers (Davis, 1989; Hulstijn et al., 1996; Meng and Chen, 2015; Wu et al., 2012; Zarei and Hasani, 2011, etc.) think that marginal glosses are more helpful to learners' word knowledge retention, while others (Chen et al., 2013; Cheng and Good, 2009; Elekaei et al., 2015, Lan and Zhang 2013; etc.) consider that in-text glosses are more advantageous. What's more, some scholars (Jasteh and Akbarpour, 2011; Watanabe, 1997, etc.) believe that single glosses are more beneficial to learners' word gain and retention, while others (Cao and Song, 2014; Duan and Yan, 2004; Hulstijn, 1992; Lei, 2011; Nagata, 1999; Rott, 2005; Rott and Williams, 2003; Shi, 2010, etc.) believe that multiple-choice glosses are more conducive. In a word, which type of glosses is more profitable to learners' incidental vocabulary acquisition through L2 reading is still in doubt.

At the same time, there are some shortcomings lying in the previous studies into the effects of different types of glosses on learners' incidental vocabulary acquisition through reading. The first one is about the selection of the reading text. Too many reading texts employed in one empirical study may easily make the learners have a breakdown, and also make the research less comparable with others. The second one involves the time when the delayed vocabulary test should be given after the immediate vocabulary test has been finished, one or two weeks later, or longer than that. The third one is concerned with whether different types of glosses have an effect on learners' reading comprehension. If the results of learners' reading comprehension are wiped out from the empirical studies, how is the nature of incidental vocabulary acquisition demonstrated? The fourth one concerns how many options are contained in multiple-choice glosses. Too many options will require more involvement loads, so as to influence learners' incidental vocabulary acquisition. The fifth one is about the positions of glosses. Most of the relevant studies concern marginal glosses, with less attention to other positions. The last is that learners' language proficiency is often ignored in the related studies. These limitations will be further explored in Section 2.6.4 in detail. Therefore, the current research tries to overcome these limitations, so as to deepen the related studies.

1.2 Significance of the Study

It has been generally acknowledged that vocabulary learning plays an initial role in learners' L2 learning. Accordingly, how to strengthen learners' vocabulary acquisition is of great importance in L2 teaching. Among various ways to acquire vocabulary knowledge, incidental learning is one of the most essential manners. The current research focuses on the effects of different types of glosses on learners' reading comprehension and their incidental vocabulary acquisition through L2 reading. Its significance is demonstrated in the following.

From the perspective of methodology, the current research employs the same reading text to investigate the effects of three types of glosses on learners' reading comprehension and their incidental vocabulary acquisition through reading. With one text, the differences made by the text can be eliminated. Meanwhile, the results of learners' reading comprehension are also taken into consideration, to fully display the nature of incidental vocabulary acquisition. As for the time when the delayed vocabulary test is given, it is carefully considered, as well. These measures will help to improve the methodology taken in the research of incidental vocabulary acquisition through L2 reading.

Theoretically, the current research may help to verify the Involvement Load Hypothesis. According to this theory, the tasks with higher involvement loads will require more noting resources from the learners, resulting in deeper processing of the related information, so as to facilitate learners' incidental vocabulary acquisition through reading. However, some empirical studies (Huang, 2004; Li, 2008; Wu, 2010; Wu et al., 2010; Zhou, 2008) performed in China have thrown doubts about this hypothesis. In other words, whether the tasks with higher involvement loads can improve learners' incidental vocabulary acquisition more efficiently has not been determined. The current research will attempt to testify this hypothesis.

Pedagogically, the current research also provides some practical implications. In the textbooks published in China, most of the books only provide Chinese glosses to the unknown words; some may provide bilingual glosses, English plus Chinese glosses. As for the number of glosses provided to one target word in the textbooks, most of the textbooks only provide the single gloss. A few textbooks provide two glosses, one meaning of the word in the given context, and the other meaning which is the most common to the word. With regard to the position of glosses, almost all the books provide glosses at the end of the text. However, some reference books to English learning tend to provide marginal glosses. These three types of glosses may be of great importance in glossing arrangement for the textbooks. Therefore, the current research will provide some insights into the compilation of the textbooks.

In addition, the current research is greatly helpful to language teachers' vocabulary teaching. According to the Involvement Load Hypothesis, the tasks with different involvement loads will result in learners' different depths of processing, so as to have different effects on learners' incidental vocabulary acquisition through reading. Consequently, the teachers may choose proper tasks to facilitate learners' vocabulary learning, so as to improve their learning efficiency.

In summary, the current research will throw great implications for the related field of incidental vocabulary acquisition research.

1.3 Organization of the Thesis

The current research consists of seven chapters. Chapter One is the introduction of the thesis. It introduces the necessity of the research, its methodological, theoretical and pedagogical significance, as well as the structure of the research.

Chapter Two is the literature review of the related studies into the effects of different types of glosses on learners' incidental vocabulary acquisition through reading. To start with, some basic concepts are explicated, including the definitions of incidental vocabulary acquisition, its relationship with L2 reading, its advantages and disadvantages, as well as the category and functions of glosses. Then the ways to improve learners' incidental vocabulary acquisition are illustrated. Consequently, the factors which influence learners' incidental vocabulary acquisition through reading are discussed in detail. In the following, the relevant studies carried out at home and abroad are reviewed at length, from which some similarities and divergences are found, so as to determine what the current research should be concerned with. Next, the theoretical framework underlying the current research is presented. In the end, some limitations existing in the previous studies are elaborated. Therefore, the current research attempts to overcome these limitations within the given theoretical framework, to investigate the effects of different types of glosses on learners' reading comprehension and their incidental vocabulary acquisition through reading.

Chapter Three is involved in the research design, in which some information shared by three empirical studies is explained, including the selection of the reading material with the target words, the time for the delayed vocabulary test, the assessment of learners' language proficiency, as well as the method to evaluate learners' incidental vocabulary acquisition through reading.

Chapter Four, Chapter Five and Chapter Six are concerned with the effects of glosses in different languages, with different options and in different locations on learners' reading comprehension and their incidental vocabulary acquisition through reading. In each chapter, the methodology, the results and the discussion are presented in detail.

Chapter Sever is the conclusion of the thesis. To begin with, it summarizes the major findings of the research. In the following, the implications and the limitations of the research are explicated. Finally, some suggestions for the future research are made.

Chapter Two Literature Review

This chapter will review what has been done about the effects of different types of glosses on learners' incidental vocabulary acquisition through L2 reading. To begin with, some basic concepts will be introduced, such as the definitions of incidental vocabulary acquisition and glosses, the category and functions of glosses, as well as the relationship between incidental vocabulary acquisition and L2 reading. The following will elaborate the previous studies concerning the effects of different types of glosses on learners' incidental vocabulary acquisition through L2 reading, followed by some limitations found in these studies. Then the theoretical framework will be discussed. Finally, a brief summary of this chapter is provided.

2.1 Incidental Vocabulary Acquisition

This section is composed of three subsections. To begin with, the definitions of incidental vocabulary acquisition proposed by some scholars are presented. In addition, its advantages and disadvantages are discussed. Finally, a brief summary of this section is made.

2.1.1 Definitions of Incidental Vocabulary Acquisition

There are two types of vocabulary acquisition that are distinguished, intentionally and incidentally. "Intentional" means "deliberate", or "by conscious purpose". Therefore, intentional vocabulary acquisition means that the learners are required to or take the initiative to do certain exercises or participate in some activities to learn some target words, in the process of which the learners' noticing resources concentrate on the target words. It is a way to "commit lexical information to memory" (Laufer, 2003). This is the most common vocabulary learning method in a L2 classroom. The disadvantage is that the learners will have to spend much time on vocabulary learning, easily resulting in learning burnout. However, for language beginners, this method obviously helps them to gain a larger vocabulary in a short time.

Opposite to intentional vocabulary acquisition, the concept of incidental vocabulary acquisition is first put forward by Nagy, Herman and Anderson (1985), based on their research in children's native language learning. They hold that for children, their vocabulary growth during school years mainly originates from incidental learning. According to their investigation, they put forward the Incidental Vocabulary Acquisition Hypothesis, which consists of four components. The first is the noticing assumption. When the learners come across an unknown word during their reading, they will allocate some noticing resources to the word. This is the beginning of vocabulary learning. The next is the guessing ability assumption. The learners will employ some learning strategies they have developed to figure out the meaning of the unfamiliar word. The hypothesis assumes that it is common for the learners to get the correct word meaning with the aid of the context. The following is involved in the guessing-retention link assumption. After the learners have worked out the word meaning, they are inclined to carry out some necessary processing for the word, resulting in memorizing the word. The last is concerned with the cumulative gain assumption. It may be quite difficult for the learners to memorize the word which only appears once in the text. With the increase of its reoccurrence frequency, it will get easier for the learners to memorize the word. The learners may only memorize a couple of words through one reading. However, continuous reading may help the learners acquire more word knowledge. Vocabulary learning is of a cumulative process (Schmitt, 2015: 21). Huckin and Coady (1999) also state that for L2 language learning, the vast majority of words are acquired incidentally, except for some frequently used words. Since then, different scholars have held different opinions about incidental vocabulary acquisition.

Gass (1999: 320) thinks that in incidental vocabulary acquisition research, the core is to thoroughly understand every word in this term. Without a unified definition acknowledged by most scholars, the relevant research would be greatly doubted. Singleton (1999: 161) also holds that what should be done first is to determine what is included in this term. To be simple, they believe that before the research, the first is to have a better understanding of the definition.

Incidental vocabulary acquisition means that the learners don't exploit their noticing resources to the target words in such activities as reading passages, watching movies, listening to music or chatting with others, while in this course, they acquire some vocabulary knowledge (Nation, 1990: 2-3). This definition focuses on the word "incidental".

Paribakht and Wesche (1993: 18) consider that incidental vocabulary acquisition will take place "when the learners focused on comprehending meaning rather than on the explicit goal of learning new words". This definition emphasizes the condition of incidental vocabulary acquisition. Similarly, Huckin and Coady (1999: 187) define incidental vocabulary acquisition as "a by-product of a meaning-focused communicative activity, such as reading, listening and interaction. It occurs through multiple exposures to a word in different context."

Nation (2001) holds that incidental vocabulary acquisition is a kind of unconscious vocabulary learning, in which language learners' noticing resources concentrate on the meanings expressed in the context, rather than on the words themselves. This definition may stem from Schmitt's (1994) and Joe's (1998) points of view. Schmitt (1994) considers vocabulary learning as an activity without the intention to learn. The learners may put all their noticing resources to other activities, such as communicating in the target language, while in this process they acquire some vocabulary knowledge. Similarly, Joe (1998) argues that in the course of reading, the learners may pay more attention to the tasks of reading comprehension, not to the vocabulary learning. However, as a matter of course, they can also acquire some vocabulary knowledge. Nation's (2001) definition stresses which aspect language learners' noticing resources are directed at, the meanings or the words.

To sum up, even though there is not a uniform definition of incidental vocabulary acquisition, it is universally agreed that incidental vocabulary acquisition lays the stress on the incidental nature of vocabulary acquisition, in the process of which the learners don't intend to acquire vocabulary knowledge in the proceeding activities related to the target language. However, they actually acquire some vocabulary knowledge, as a result. In the current research, incidental vocabulary acquisition refers to vocabulary acquisition through reading, in the process of which the learners are required to finish some tasks related to reading comprehension, while they acquire some vocabulary knowledge, at the same time.

2.1.2 Advantages and Disadvantages of Incidental Vocabulary Acquisition

In the field of L2 language teaching and learning, incidental vocabulary acquisition is significantly important, because a large amount of vocabulary is acquired in this way (Huckin and Coady, 1999; Nation, 2001). Huckin and Coady (1999) have summarized some advantages resulting from incidental vocabulary acquisition.

First of all, incidental vocabulary acquisition is closely connected with the context, from which the learners may guess the meaning of the target word, and also learn how to use the word. This way of vocabulary acquisition is more interesting and efficient. In the classroom, it is a common practice that the teacher tells the learners the pronunciation of the word, and its usage by providing some examples. Because of the absence of the context, it may be easy for the learners to get bored, leading to the learners' demotivation.

Furthermore, to some extent, incidental vocabulary acquisition is efficient in learning, because two or more different tasks can be performed at the same time. The learners may acquire some vocabulary from extensive reading, for example. They can also acquire vocabulary knowledge in the speaking class, in the course of which learners' listening and speaking skills may be improved, and they may acquire some vocabulary, as well. The learners who get accustomed to acquiring vocabulary incidentally will be inclined to become multitaskers, so as to raise learning efficiency.

Additionally, incidental vocabulary acquisition emphasizes its personal nature of learning. The learners may choose whatever they are interested in, and process what they want to. They may choose to learn vocabulary knowledge by means of watching movies, listening to music, or even quarreling with others. No matter what manners the learners may choose, they are the ones language learners prefer. During performing the tasks they like to do, they acquire some vocabulary knowledge. In other words, language learners can pick out any methods they like to acquire vocabulary knowledge, making vocabulary acquisition much more personal and interesting, so as to facilitate their vocabulary acquisition.

Apart from the above three advantages, incidental vocabulary acquisition helps to increase the opportunities of using vocabulary knowledge (Krashen, 1989). The vocabulary acquisition process is closely related to other language activities. It will be easy for the learners to integrate what has been learnt into the interlanguage system, so as to use the vocabulary in the actual situation.

Every coin has two sides. Incidental vocabulary acquisition also has some disadvantages. First, word-guessing is not always right. Whether incidental vocabulary acquisition is successful or not is decided by whether the learners can figure out the meaning of the target word in the context. However, sometimes it is difficult for the learners to get the accurate meaning, resulting in the failure of precise understanding of the text (Grabe and Stoller, 1997; Parry, 1993, 1997). In this process, much time is wasted, and it will also have a negative influence on learners' vocabulary acquisition, because of not having a better understanding of the unfamiliar word.

In addition, the learners need enough time to work out the meanings of the target words, which will influence the completion of other related tasks. Meanwhile, word-guessing is inseparable from the full understanding of the context. The learners must know the rest words, and make full use of the contextual clues and some other background information. At times, certain learning strategies are in great need. However, learning strategies are what L2 learners lack greatly.

Moreover, the effect of incidental vocabulary acquisition is barely satisfactory. Vocabulary knowledge acquired from a reading passage is limited. The learners may center on the meaning of the target word. Other aspects of the word are likely to be neglected. To be precise, the learners only get to know the specific meaning of the word in the context, without knowing how to use the word in other contexts. At times, they may not know how to pronounce the word correctly, let alone its collocation with other words. In addition, limited exposure to the target word may also result in moderate difficulty for the learners to memorize the word.

Finally, the learners may have great difficulty in acquiring some vocabulary knowledge of idioms, and set phrases (Arnaud and Savignon, 1997). It may be quite easy for the learners to figure out the meaning of a single word in the context. However, guessing the meanings of some idioms and set phrases will be greatly difficult. For most of the idioms and set phrases, their meanings are not always equal to the ones of the combination of the composite words. For example, two persons are talking with each other and one says, "Are you really a bad sailor?" What is the meaning of the "bad sailor"? Of course, here the word "sailor" does not refer to the person who works on a ship. In fact, it refers to the person who always feels dizzy when he or she travels by ship. It is quite obvious that this kind of vocabulary knowledge can only be given in class.

Even if there are some disadvantages of incidental vocabulary acquisition, there is no denying that it is an important means to acquire vocabulary knowledge in L2 learning.

To conclude, the way of acquiring vocabulary incidentally may help to motivate learners' language learning, improve their learning efficiency and exert their personality. The disadvantage is that the learning effect is not always satisfactory, as a result of the difficulty caused by the time limitation and the incorrect inference of the word meanings. At the same time, it is of great difficulty to incidentally acquire idioms and set phrases.

2.1.3 Summary

In this section, first of all, some definitions of incidental vocabulary acquisition are reviewed. Then based on the review, the working definition of incidental vocabulary acquisition is given. In the current research incidental vocabulary acquisition is limited to vocabulary knowledge acquisition through reading. Next, the advantages and disadvantages of incidental vocabulary acquisition are discussed in detail. First of all, it is closely related to the context, which adds some interest to language learning. Moreover, it is highly efficient, because the readers may perform two or more tasks at the same time. What's more, it has a good sense of individuality, giving the learners more freedom to choose what to read and how to read the text. Finally, it brings more opportunities to the learners to use what they may learn about the vocabulary knowledge, so as to improve the development of their interlanguage system. Of course, the disadvantages are also quite obvious. To begin with, the learning result is not always well pleasing. The wrong inference of the word meanings will result in misunderstanding of the text. In order to figure out the meanings of the unknown words, the learners may slow down their reading, influencing the completion of the given tasks. At the same time, the learning efficiency is not always satisfactory, because the learners may pay more attention to the meanings of the unknown words, ignoring other aspects of the words. Finally, it may be difficult for language learners to incidentally acquire some idioms and set phrases.

2.2 Incidental Vocabulary Acquisition and L2 Reading

Studies on vocabulary acquisition in earlier days concentrate on how vocabulary is acquired in an intentional way. At present, incidental vocabulary acquisition has been becoming the focus of vocabulary acquisition in L2 learning, especially from the perspective of L2 reading (Wang, 2013: 68).

This section is made up of three subsections. The first subsection is involved in the relationship between incidental vocabulary acquisition and L2 reading. The following is to present the advantages and disadvantages of incidental vocabulary acquisition through reading. In the end, a brief summary is to be made.

2.2.1 Incidental Vocabulary Acquisition through L2 Reading

It is generally held that there are two common purposes to read, either for reading only or for completing some tasks through reading (Paribakht and Wesche, 1997). In the process of reading only, readers only need to comprehend what they have read, including understanding the words they encounter. If they meet with some unknown word, they will choose how to deal with it, guessing the meaning of the word or skipping it, according to its importance in reading comprehension. If the unknown word has little or nothing to do with text comprehension, they may choose to ignore it. Otherwise, they will make full use of the contextual clues or their general knowledge to figure out the meaning of the word. During this process, the learners may acquire some word knowledge incidentally. Of course, the readers can only acquire the words related to the topic of the reading material. More than half of the unfamiliar words which are not involved in the text comprehension will be ignored.

Judd (1978) holds that "extensive reading potentially provides the learners with the opportunity to process an unfamiliar word in its various natural contexts in order to acquire the complex properties of lexical items, such as its polysemic and registerial aspects." From this, it may be easily concluded that extensive reading is of great significance for incidental vocabulary acquisition. Shelton and Newhouse (1981) find that as for the same target words in extensive reading, the learners better acquire word knowledge in an incidental way. Their result is supported by Gass (1999). Therefore, Stanovich (1986) states in extensive reading, the learners may greatly exploit the contextual information to figure out the meanings of the unfamiliar words, in order to comprehend the text, resulting in better vocabulary acquisition.

Based on the analysis of 144 relevant studies, Krashen (1989) concludes that the Comprehensible Input Hypothesis can be employed to explain incidental vocabulary acquisition through reading. However, in fact, among 144 studies, only two are involved in L2 reading. The rest are concerned with L1 acquisition through reading. Even so, his opinion has been agreed by most of L2 acquisition researchers. It is generally believed that vocabulary acquisition through reading may be influenced by various factors, such as contextual clues, learners' noticing resources, learners' knowledge about the topic of the reading, task demands, and so forth. Wang (2013: 69) claims that in extensive reading, the learners may put all their heart into comprehension of the reading material. That is to say, they may more center on the meanings of the words, and ignore their spellings. In other words, incidental vocabulary acquisition through reading may take place on condition that the learners can combine word meanings and their corresponding forms together. Only in this way may incidental vocabulary acquisition through reading be greatly improved.

Paribakht and Wesche (1997) employ the terms of search, evaluation and lexical inference to explain the route of incidental vocabulary acquisition through reading only and reading for finishing given tasks. Search means that the learners attempt to work out the meanings of the unknown words, with the help of the dictionaries, glosses, the wordlist, or inquiry of the teachers or other learners. Generally speaking, it is quite easy for the learners to get the meanings of the unfamiliar words through glosses, as well as reference to the dictionaries and the teachers. However, without help, the learners would have to figure out the meanings of the unfamiliar words with the aid of the contextual information. In the process of reading only, the learners only need to infer the meanings of the words, while in the course of reading for completing tasks, they have to finish the given tasks, besides lexical inference. In other words, they have to process the words deeper. Only the words which are processed deeper can be stored in the long-term memory. With enough practice, the words can be related to other words stored in the long-term memory, so as to retrieve them easily in the daily communication. Evaluation occurs after search and lexical inference. The unknown words may have various meanings. Nevertheless, within the given context, the meanings of the words are definite. Therefore, the learners have to evaluate which meaning is appropriate in the given context.

What is worthy to be mentioned is that not all the reading materials can benefit language learners' incidental vocabulary acquisition. According to Krashen's Comprehensible Input Hypothesis (1985), the reading material should be in accordance with the principle of "i+1". To be exact, it should be neither too hard nor too easy, but just be moderately difficult. This type of reading material will bring the moderate challenge to the learners. It means that the learners with proper efforts are still able to comprehend the text, without feeling overwhelmed. At the same time, the reading material may greatly arouse the learners' interest, which makes reading interesting, but not boring. Only in this way will reading help the learners to raise their self - confidence and reduce reading anxiety, so as to promote learners' incidental vocabulary acquisition through reading.

To sum up, the effect of incidental vocabulary acquisition through reading is determined by how the target words are processed while reading. Whether the words are processed is decided by what reading purposes the learners have, in turn. In short, different reading purposes decide how the learners process the unfamiliar words, which determines whether incidental vocabulary acquisition may take place, accordingly. Meanwhile, whether the reading material is proper or not also has a considerable impact.

2.2.2 Advantages and Disadvantages of Incidental Vocabulary Acquisition through L2 Reading

Nowadays, nobody will deny the fact that incidental

vocabulary acquisition is an important approach to learning vocabulary, even though it is incremental with small quantities. Ma (2013: 47 - 50) generalizes some advantages of incidental vocabulary acquisition through L2 reading.

First of all, incidental vocabulary acquisition through reading helps to greatly enlarge learners' vocabulary. It is estimated that the receptive vocabulary of an educated native speakers can reach up to 100,000 to 200,000 words, most of which are acquired through extensive reading (Nation, 2001). Krashen (1989) also finds that the learners who read or watch movies in class can acquire 5 to 10 words per hour. In L2 learning context, some similar results have been found, as well. In a word, the learners may guess the meanings of the unfamiliar words with the help of the contextual information in reading, so as to facilitate vocabulary acquisition, resulting in enormously enlarging their vocabulary.

In addition, the way vocabulary is acquired incidentally through reading can greatly facilitate learners' vocabulary acquisition. In the process of reading, almost every word does not appear alone, always accompanied by a certain context. The word in a certain context always has a specific meaning. In order to work out the meaning of an unfamiliar word, the learners may use the information provided by the formation process of the word, such as the prefix, the stem, as well as the suffix. Another important clue to guess the meaning of the unfamiliar word is to exploit the context, in which the word appears. In English, many words may have different meanings. However, a word in the specific context may have one definite meaning. That is, the context helps to eliminate the ambiguity of the word. In a word, the learners may make full use of the linguistic and non-linguistic information, in order to get the meaning of the target word. In this process, the word is processed deeper than the one taught in the regular classroom, which means the learners will have a better understanding of the word, so as to improve learners' vocabulary acquisition. Therefore, Hatch and Brown (2001: 365) state that "the best internalization of vocabulary comes from encounters (comprehension or production) with words within the context of surrounding discourse, rather than from isolated words or dictionary definition."

Finally, the way of incidental vocabulary acquisition through reading may help to improve learners' learning strategies. Oxford (1990) distinguishes six learning strategies, that is, memory strategies, cognitive strategies, compensation strategies, metacognitive strategies, affective strategies and social strategies. Ellis (1999: 539) regards this classification as the most comprehensible one of learning strategies to date. Memory strategies are mainly involved in how to memorize words. Different learners may have different ways to memorize new words. While reading, the learners may use different resources to figure out the meanings of the unknown words. At the same time, they may acquire some other aspects of the words, such as pronunciation and collocation of the words. After the long-term practice, the learners may develop good vocabulary learning strategies, which help to greatly improve their vocabulary acquisition.

Even though the learners may acquire more vocabulary knowledge incidentally through reading, there are some disadvantages of incidental vocabulary acquisition, as well. First of all, incidental vocabulary acquisition cannot happen without restrictions. In other words, only if some requirements are satisfied, incidental vocabulary acquisition will take place. In the first place, the learners have to possess a certain amount of vocabulary. Huckin and Coady (1999) hold that the learners have to master at least 3,000 word families in order to acquire vocabulary knowledge through reading. Meanwhile, the unfamiliar words in the reading material should not be more than 5% of the total words (Nation, 2001). In a word, incidental vocabulary acquisition will not happen, if the learners have a limited vocabulary, or when they have to read something with too many unfamiliar words. To put it another way, language beginners are not likely to acquire vocabulary knowledge incidentally through reading a rather difficult text.

Moreover, the learners have to master some learning strategies, in order to incidentally acquire some vocabulary knowledge through reading. It has been mentioned several times that the learners have to figure out the meanings of the unknown words, with the help of the linguistic and non - linguistic information. They should know some general principles on how the words are formed. At the same time, they have to know how to use the contextual information to guess the meanings of the words. All these knowledge is closely related to learning strategies. Therefore, Nagy (1997) identifies three types of knowledge employed to guess the meanings of the unknown words, that is to say, linguistic knowledge, world knowledge and strategic knowledge. If we say that the former two kinds of knowledge serve as the basis of word meaning inference, the strategic knowledge will be involved in how to use the basic knowledge. Without proper strategies, it would be quite difficult for the learners to acquire vocabulary incidentally. Therefore, the learners should be trained on how to work out the meanings of the target words in reading. In other words, appropriate strategy instruction will be of great need, so as to improve the probability of word meaning inference, resulting in better vocabulary acquisition through reading.

Finally, Ma (2013: 55) holds that one disadvantage of incidental vocabulary acquisition through reading is that it may not necessarily always take place as a result of some influence from other factors. The first factor is about the context. It is generally known that the context is crucial in working out the meanings of the unfamiliar words. Sometimes, the contextual information is quite direct, or close to the unfamiliar words, which will help the learners easily infer the meanings. However, at times, the contextual information is indirect, or a little far from the target words, which may result in great difficulty for the learners to work out the meanings. Another important factor that affects incidental vocabulary acquisition is the reading tasks. Different tasks may require the learners to process the target words differently, resulting in different acquisition effects of vocabulary knowledge. Generally speaking, compared with the tasks of filling in the blanks with proper forms of the target words, or choosing proper meanings of the target words, the tasks of reading comprehension in the multiple-choice format may not facilitate learners' incidental vocabulary acquisition. The last factor is concerned with the choice of reading materials. The reading material should comply with the "i + 1" principle. That is to say, the learners may feel it fairly difficult, but they are not overwhelmed. If they can make full use of different types of knowledge they have learnt before, they can infer the meanings of the target words, even with greater efforts. Of course, whether the reading material is familiar to the learners is also of great importance. If the learners are not familiar with the topic of the reading material, it will be quite difficult for them to figure out the meanings of the target words, even with greater efforts.

To sum up, incidental vocabulary acquisition through reading is a significantly important way to acquire vocabulary knowledge. It helps to enlarge learners' vocabulary, better memorize the words so as to retrieve them easily, and improve learners' language learning strategies. However, it also has some disadvantages. The learners have to possess a certain amount of vocabulary and the unfamiliar words in the reading text should not be more than 5% of the total words. Meanwhile, learning strategies also have an important effect on incidental vocabulary acquisition through reading. Some other factors also influence incidental vocabulary acquisition through reading, as well.

2.2.3 Summary

In this section, the relationship between incidental vocabulary acquisition and L2 reading is examined. To be short, different reading purposes determine how language learners deal with the unknown words, resulting in different depths of processing the words, so as to have a different influence on learners' incidental vocabulary acquisition through reading. After that, the advantages and disadvantages of incidental vocabulary acquisition through reading are explicated in detail. Incidental vocabulary acquisition through reading may help the learners to enlarge their vocabulary size, facilitate their L2 acquisition, and improve their learning strategies. However, one of the disadvantages is that whether incidental vocabulary acquisition takes place or not is initially determined by the vocabulary size of language learners. At the same time, some requisite learning strategies are of great need. This means that if the learners have a small vocabulary size, or are lacking in necessary learning strategies, it will be quite difficult for their incidental vocabulary acquisition to occur in reading. Finally, apart from these two disadvantages, incidental vocabulary acquisition through reading may not always take place as expected, because some other important factors need to be considered, such as the context in which the target words appear, the reading tasks that the learners are given, as well as the readability of the reading material.

2.3 Factors Influencing Incidental Vocabulary Acquisition through L2 Reading

Generally speaking, four factors will be touched upon, concerning the factors influencing incidental vocabulary acquisition of L2 learners (Yi and Mu, 2013). One is involved in the learners themselves. Another is concerned with the media that the learners are exposed to. In the current research, the media refers to the reading text handed to the participants. The third is related with the lexicon, which means how the words are presented, besides their reoccurrence frequencies. The last factor affecting learners' incidental vocabulary acquisition is closely connected with the context in which the target words appear.

2.3.1 Learner Factors

Learner factors consist of learners' vocabulary size, overall language proficiency, learning strategies employed in reading, reading ability, as well as reading intentions. The first learner factor is how many words the learners have mastered. It is generally acknowledged that mastering 3,000 word families is the threshold of incidental vocabulary acquisition through reading (Huckin and Coady, 1999). In other words, in order to have a better understanding of a text, the learners must know 95% of the words in the text, with only 5% unfamiliar words. Of course, in reading the larger vocabulary the learners have, the better the text will be understood. Gai (2003) finds that the learners with a larger vocabulary can incidentally acquire more words through reading, and keep them longer.

Another learner factor related with learners' vocabulary acquisition is learners' overall language proficiency. Some researchers (Wang, 2009; Wu and Xu, 2009; Xu and Wu, 2007) have discovered that the learners with higher language proficiency can incidentally acquire more words through reading. However, some minor differences can also be found. In Xu and Wu's (2007) research, it is found that there are significant differences between learners' overall language proficiency and the semantic acquisition of the target words, while language proficiency does not significantly affect learners' morphological acquisition of the target words. The result gets confirmed by Gong (2009). Nevertheless, Zhang and Qi (2009) find that in the task that requires the learners to pay more attention to the meanings, morphological acquisition of vocabulary is significantly better than its semantic acquisition, however, semantic acquisition will be significantly improved and kept longer, as time goes on.

The learners' ability to infer the meanings of the unfamiliar words in the text is also of great significance in their incidental vocabulary acquisition. Li and Tian (2005) have proved that the learners who excel in working out the meanings of the unknown words perform better in incidental vocabulary acquisition through reading. However, Zhao (2012) holds that the words whose meanings are inferred from the text cannot be acquired, and even though acquired, they cannot be kept in the long-term memory for a relatively longer time. Huckin and Bloch (1993) hold that some learners have innate abilities to guess meanings of the unknown words, but for other learners, the skill may be acquired with being trained. Kern (1989) discovers that the learners who have received relevant training can acquire significantly more words incidentally through reading. It has also been found that the strategy of guessing meanings of the unfamiliar words is the most frequently used one by L2 learners (Rubin, 1987; Zhang, 2004). However, what is worth mentioning is that Chinese learners still believe that memorizing is the best way to acquire the unknown words.

Strategies employed in the process of reading may also influence learners' incidental vocabulary acquisition, such as learning strategies, and metacognitive strategies. Chang and Li

(2009) find out that the learners who more frequently use problem-solving strategies in reading can significantly acquire more word knowledge. Nevertheless, this result is opposite to that of the research carried out by Gai (2003). In her empirical study, she confirms that learning strategies do not exert any significant effects on learners' vocabulary acquisition through reading.

The learners' reading ability also plays an important role in their incidental vocabulary acquisition through reading. The learners' reading ability is quite complex, which is closely related with the learners' vocabulary, as well as overall language proficiency. Of course, some other factors are also concerned, such as learning strategies, background knowledge, and general knowledge about the world. Pulido (2003, 2004b) holds that reading abilities have a positive effect on learners' incidental vocabulary acquisition. Those with greater reading abilities can figure out the meanings of the unfamiliar words, and they also know which words are important for reading, and where they can find some clues to infer the meanings of the unknown words. Therefore, the learners with greater reading abilities can incidentally acquire more words than those with weaker reading abilities.

The realization of reading intentions is based on the completion of the reading tasks (Shao, 2006). Different reading intentions may result in different processing of information exposed to language learners, therefore, impacting their incidental vocabulary acquisition through reading. Gai (2003) distinguishes two different types of reading intentions, answering questions after reading and retelling the text after reading. The results demonstrate that retelling the text after reading can be significantly more facilitative to learners' incidental vocabulary acquisition through reading.

To sum up, learner factors affecting incidental vocabulary acquisition are involved in learners' vocabulary size, overall language proficiency, learners' ability to infer the meanings of the unknown words, reading strategies, reading ability, as well as learners' reading intentions.

2.3.2 Text Factors

The first text factor is whether the learners are familiar with the subject of the text. Pulido (2007) required 35 adult Spanish learners to read two narrative clips. One was from "The Trip to the Supermarket", and the other from "Publishing an Article". Each story had 8 target words, which were replaced with non-words. According to the learners' evaluation, the first story was quite close to their daily lives. Therefore, they were familiar with it. However, the second one was unfamiliar to them. After reading, they were asked to take a sight vocabulary test. And one week later, the same test was provided again. The results indicated that the more familiar the learners were with the topic of the text, the better the retention of the target words would be. In other words, familiarity with the topic of the text can greatly facilitate language learners' incidental vocabulary acquisition through reading.

The other factor is about the style of the text. Gardner (2004) employed 28 narrative texts and 28 expository texts from children's books to investigate the effect of text styles on elementary - school learners' incidental vocabulary acquisition. The results indicated that narrative texts were more facilitative to learners' vocabulary acquisition through reading. In other words, the more interesting the text is, the more helpful it is to learners' incidental vocabulary acquisition (Wang, 2013: 74).

In summary, text factors are mainly concerned with the familiarity of the text and the text style.

2.3.3 Lexicon Factors

There is no doubt that lexicon factors are closely connected with learners' incidental vocabulary acquisition. The first is involved in the part of speech of the word. Nation (2001) argues that the words expressing familiar concepts, such as verbs and nouns, may better facilitate learners' incidental vocabulary acquisition. Compared with adjectives, nouns and verbs which are more related to other words may greatly help the learners to infer their meanings. Under the similar circumstances, adjectives and adverbs are more difficult for the learners to acquire incidentally (Schmitt et al., 2001). To put it another way, words with different parts of speech may have different effects on learners' incidental vocabulary acquisition.

Another lexicon factor is involved in the reoccurrence frequency of the word. Nation (1990) argues that the word which appears 5 to 16 times will be easier to be acquired incidentally. Chinese scholars Zhang and Qi (2009) used three simplified texts originating from classical English novels to examine the effect of the reoccurrence frequencies of the target words on learners' incidental vocabulary acquisition through reading. It was found out that the higher reoccurrence frequency the target word had, the more facilitative it would be to learners' incidental vocabulary acquisition, especially to semantic acquisition of the word. Moreover, it was also discovered that the word acquired best needed to reoccur in the text 4 to 5 times. However, Xu and Wu (2007) discovered that the word with higher reoccurrence frequency was not only conducive to learners' semantic acquisition, but also to their morphological acquisition of the word. Nevertheless, the target word should appear in the text 10 to 17 times. Another scholar Gong (2009) found out that more contact with the target word will significantly help the learners to acquire its meaning incidentally through reading, but it does not exert any significant effects on the morphological or collocational acquisition of the word. He also discovered that the word appearing once in the text was not likely to be incidentally acquired through reading. Nagy et al. (1985) argued that the learners could incidentally acquire the word that appeared once in the text with the probability of 5%, while Nation (1990) held that the learners could incidentally acquire such a word with the probability of 10% to 15%. No matter what the reoccurrence frequency of the target word has, it is quite definite that it has an important influence on learners' incidental vocabulary acquisition through reading.

The lexicon factor is also concerned with the modality of the input words. According to Gu (2007: 3), modality refers to the ways of reaction between human senses, such as sight, smell, touch, vision and so on, and the surroundings, such as characters, animals and events. In Ghafouri and Masoomi's (2016) research, 75 Iranian university students majoring in English language teaching were asked to receive the auditory and visual input. The immediate and delayed vocabulary tests showed that both input enhancement methods were significantly efficient to learners' vocabulary development. Chinese scholars Gu and Zang (2011) had different findings. 99 second - year English majors were required to receive the test material input in the auditory form, the visual form and in the audiovisual form. Two vocabulary tests' results indicated that the learners who received the audiovisual material could better understand the text than those received the auditory material. What's more, the learners who received the audiovisual material and the visual material significantly acquired more words than those received the auditory material, however, there were not any significant differences between the audiovisual group and the auditory group. The findings are contrary to those of the research performed by Wang et al. (2012). In their investigation, 140 first-year non-English majors were asked to receive the test material with 15 target words. The material was presented either in the reading form or in the auditory form. The results displayed that the learners who were presented with the auditory material significantly acquired more words than those with reading material. In addition to the visual and auditory modes, Liu and Qin (2014) also found that the words presented in the mode of "pictures plus comics plus videos" could significantly improve learners' incidental vocabulary acquisition. Zhang and Xu (2014) also had similar findings. Liu (2011) and Li and Gao (2016) found that the target words provided in the mode of multimedia had a significant influence on learners' vocabulary acquisition. In short, different ways the target words are presented have different effects on learners' incidental vocabulary acquisition.

The last lexicon factor is involved in how the target words are glossed. In other words, the target words are glossed in L1, L2 or L1 plus L2. The number of glosses provided is also concerned. To be exact, glosses are provided in the single form or in the multiple-choice form. Moreover, the locations of glosses are involved, as well. Glosses may appear on the marginal side of the text, at the end of the page, or at the end of the text, or just beside the target words. For this point, it will be illustrated in detail in Section 2.6.1 to 2.6.3.

2.3.4 Context Factors

In the course of L2 reading, it is quite common for the readers to encounter some unfamiliar words. Sometimes, their meanings can be easily inferred. However, it may be quite difficult for the readers to figure out meanings of some words at times. Under this situation, the context counts. The contextual information plays an important part in inferring the meanings of the unknown words. Its function is determined by three aspects. One is that whether the contextual information is available. Another one is involved in the nature of the contextual information. The other one is concerned with the distance between the target word and its corresponding contextual information. Xun (2006) thinks that two points can account for the reason why the meaning of a certain word in the text can be figured out. The first reason is that there is adequate contextual information provided to the target word. The other is that the learners may have greater ability to guess the meaning of the target word.

Chern (1993) holds that the learners tend to make full use of the textual context and their general knowledge to work out the meanings of the target words without any instruction, but the learners with lower language proficiency need necessary guidance. Wang (2013: 75) considers that the unknown words will not always appear with the contextual information, because the function of the context is not prepared for inferring the meanings of the unfamiliar words, but for conveying some extra information to the readers who are quite familiar with the target language. Therefore, Zahar et al. (2001) claim that the contextual information is of limited help to learners' incidental vocabulary acquisition.

Li (1988) distinguished two types of contextual information. The first type provided adequate clues to the target words, while the other type supplied inadequate clues. It was discovered that the target words occurring in the first type of contextual information could be significantly beneficial to learners' inferring the meanings of the words and their incidental vocabulary acquisition than those in the second type of contextual information. On the contrary, Mondria and Wit de Boer (1991) had different opinions. The pregnant context and the non-pregnant context were identified in their research. These two contexts were similar to the two types of contextual information mentioned above in Li's (1988) research. They found out that the learners could easily work out the meanings of the words appearing in the pregnant context, but they had greater difficulty in memorizing these words. In a word, the rich contextual information may help the learners to figure out the meanings of the unfamiliar words, but it is not conducive to learners' memorization of the words. The findings get confirmed by Haastrup (1991). In conclusion, the greater difficulty the learners have in working out the meanings of the target words, the greater efforts they will make, resulting in better acquisition of the words. To be simple, the words whose meanings are easily figured out do not guarantee that they can be acquired, which means the nature of the context counts, but not the quantity of the context.

As for the location of the contextual information, it is generally held that the closer the context is to the target word, the more helpful it will be to the inference of the word meaning. It simply results from the fact that the contextual information closer to the target word is easier to be found by the readers. As a result, it will greatly help the readers to figure out the meaning of the unknown word, so as to facilitate readers' incidental vocabulary acquisition through reading.

In a word, the nature, the quantity, as well as the location of the contextual information have a crucial influence on learners' incidental vocabulary acquisition through reading.

2.3.5 Summary

This section is mainly involved in the factors that influence learners' incidental vocabulary acquisition through reading. Generally speaking, there are four factors, that is to say, learner factors, text factors, lexicon factors, as well as context factors. Learner factors are involved in learners' vocabulary size, overall language proficiency, word meaning inferring ability, learning strategies, reading ability and reading intentions. Text factors mainly concern learners' familiarity with the theme of the text and the style of the text. Lexicon factors are concerned with the word class and reoccurrence frequency of the target word, and the modality of the input target word, as well as how the target word is glossed. And context factors involve the nature and the quantity of the context, as well as the distance between the target word and its corresponding context.

2.4 Ways to Enhance Incidental Vocabulary Acquisition

From what has been mentioned above, it is known that there are so many factors influencing learners' incidental vocabulary acquisition through reading. Meanwhile, because of its incremental nature, the retention of word meanings in the process of reading is rather dissatisfactory. Some ways must be employed to enhance learners' incidental vocabulary acquisition. Wang (2013: 71) summarizes three enhancement methods.

The first one is to provide glosses to the target words in reading. Glosses may eliminate learners' misunderstanding of the unfamiliar words, assisting them to figure out the word meanings. Meanwhile, glosses also supply comprehensible input, not only facilitating vocabulary acquisition, but also aiding the learners to comprehend the reading text. The learners with higher language proficiency also benefit from glosses in reading (Davis, 1989; Jacobs, 1994). There is no doubt that the learners may refer to the dictionary, in order to figure out the word meanings. However, it is a waste of time, to some extent, because this will interrupt the learners' reading process. Glosses may offer accurate word meanings in accordance with the context, so that learners' reading can continue and they can focus their attention on reading comprehension (Lomicka, 1998). At the same time, glosses may provide word meanings more accurately than dictionaries (Hulstijn et al., 1996). Of course, the learners may make their own decisions on whether they need to look up the words in the dictionary (Ko, 2005). Other researchers (Chun and Plass, 1996; Laufer and Hill, 2000) agree that glosses presented on the Internet will be more beneficial to learners' incidental vocabulary acquisition through reading than those provided in some common ways.

Another method is to set different tasks for reading. In common reading, the readers only need to know the general idea of the text. It is not necessary for them to spend too much time in figuring out the meanings of some unknown words, which means that the words are not processed deeply. Reading only is not conducive to learners' incidental vocabulary acquisition. Nevertheless, if such tasks as filling in the blanks, or making up sentences with the target words are required in reading, the readers may center on the deep processing of the target words. They have to guess the word meanings and know how to use them correctly. In this way, words are processed much deeper, which will not only help to enlarge learners' vocabulary, but also deepen their vocabulary knowledge (Gai, 2003; Laufer, 2003; Xu, 2010). Xu (2010) divided 125 first-year university English learners of China into four groups, according to the scores in the national entrance exam. Each group was assigned different tasks of reading comprehension for the same text including 10 target words, which were explained with glosses, sentences accompanied by annotated target words, glosses and the help of dictionaries, as well as no extra aid. It was found that the learners had significantly better word retention in the task requiring higher involvement loads. This research confirms that reading tasks can be employed to foster language learners' incidental vocabulary acquisition through reading.

The input enhancement is also used to improve learners' incidental vocabulary acquisition. The target words may be underlined or presented in boldface. At the same time, increasing the reoccurrence frequencies of the target words also helps the learners to acquire vocabulary incidentally. As science and technology has been developing fast, the target words may be presented in the auditory, visual and audiovisual manner. With the help of the input enhancement, the learners may easily notice the target words, and perform necessary processing, so as to facilitate their incidental vocabulary acquisition. Shahrokni (2009) investigated the effect of how the target words were presented on learners' incidental vocabulary acquisition. 90 English learners of Iran were divided into 3 groups, according to their scores of the English placement test. Each group with 30 learners was asked to read the same passage with 25 target words, which were presented with glosses in three different means. Glosses were offered in the form of the texts, the pictures, as well as the textual and pictorial combination. It was discovered that the learners could significantly acquire more word knowledge with the help of glosses presented with the combination of pictorial and textual information. Even though in the research, only male English learners with lower language proficiency are involved, it indirectly proves that the ways in which the target words are presented have an important influence on learners' incidental vocabulary acquisition through reading.

In summary, glosses, the reading tasks and the input enhancement can be exploited to improve learners' incidental vocabulary acquisition. Among them, glosses are significantly important, which not only help to strengthen the salience of the target words, but also facilitate learners' comprehension of the reading text, so as to improve learners' incidental vocabulary acquisition through reading. Therefore, in the current research the approach to enhancing incidental vocabulary acquisition through reading is to provide different types of glosses to the target words.

2.5 Glosses

Glosses, according to the explanation provided by Oxford Advanced Learners' English-Chinese Dictionary, are defined as a way of explaining something to make it more acceptable (2009: 867). From this explanation, glosses provide accurate elaboration of the word meanings in the context, mainly to help the learners reduce the difficulty of inferring the word meanings from reading, so as to comprehend the reading text better.

This section consists of four subsections. To start with, the definitions of glosses are presented. Next, types of glosses are introduced. In addition, the functions of glosses are briefly discussed. Finally, a brief summary of this section is made.

2.5.1 Definitions of Glosses

The concept of glosses can date back to the Middle Age (Hüllen, 1989). In order to understand the foreign literature better, the learners write some notes about explanations of the unknown words. Later, the notes gradually develop into glossaries and even dictionaries, which show the instructional significance of glosses. That is to say, glosses are initially used to help the learners understand the word meanings.

Lomicka (1998: 41) holds that glosses "typically located in

the side or bottom margins … are most often supplied for unfamiliar words, which may help to limit continual dictionary consultation that may hinder and interrupt second language reading comprehension process”. In other words, glosses are primarily used to help the learners continue reading the text, without referring to the dictionary.

Nation (2001: 173) defines glosses as “a brief definition … of the unknown words provided in text”, either in L1 or L2. And glosses may be supplied in the single or multiple-choice format. This definition emphasizes the language and the form glosses may employ.

Segler et al. (2002) regard glosses as brief explanations for difficult texts. They may be presented in the form of pictures, texts and aural information with either pictures or texts. This definition stresses the modality glosses may take. To put it another way, it is concerned with how the target words are presented to language learners.

From the definitions mentioned above, glosses are principally used to help the learners to read the text without difficulty, and they may be presented in different languages, and in various modes. In the current research, glosses are defined as the explanatory information for the unknown words, to help the learners figure out the meanings of the target words, so as to improve learners’ understanding of the reading text without interruption and their incidental vocabulary acquisition through reading.

2.5.2 Types of Glosses

According to what has been described above, glosses can be categorized into different types. Meanwhile, different types of glosses may have different effects on learners' incidental vocabulary acquisition through reading.

According to different reading purposes, glosses may be provided by different people. They may be language learners, the professionals, the teachers or the textbook developers (Widdowson, 1978). Glosses supplied by the professionals are named priming glossaries (Widdowson, 1978: 82), which precede the reading passage, while glosses that the learners may refer to are termed promoting glossaries (Widdowson, 1978: 86). Furthermore, Widdowson (1978) makes a distinction between signification glosses and value glosses. The former glosses are originally dictionary definitions, which offer the definitions of the words, while the latter glosses offer the meanings of the words in the context, that is, the pragmatic meanings of the words. The relationship between two different types of classification is that the priming glossary may take the form of signification glosses or value glosses, while the promoting glossary is usually composed of value glosses.

In terms of the languages glosses may use, the target words may be glossed in L1, L2 or L1 plus L2 (Roby, 1999).

From the perspective of the positions where glosses may appear, glosses can be divided into marginal glosses, footnote glosses and endnote glosses (Holley and King, 1971). Marginal glosses appear either on the right or left side of the text. Footnote glosses refer to the glosses which are shown at the end of the same page where the unfamiliar words are located. And endnote glosses always appear at the end of the whole text. It is also called the wordlist or the glossary. There is also another type of glosses, called in-text glosses, which occur between the lines of the text, just following the unfamiliar words.

On the basis of the effects of glosses on reading comprehension and vocabulary retention, Stewart and Cross (1991) distinguish elaboration glosses and bridging glosses. The former glosses usually employ statements, questions or both of them to clarify the text, while the latter glosses always function as a bridge between what has been learnt before and what will be learnt in the future. These two types of glosses are closely connected with the situation model put forward by Lomicka (1998), who names them informational glosses.

According to the number of glosses provided to the unfamiliar words, glosses may be classified into single glosses, double glosses, multiple-choice glosses and null glosses. In this classification, one or more than one language may be used. As for double and multiple - choice glosses, the learners may be required to make a choice on which is the proper meaning of the unknown word in the given context. At times, these two types of glosses may also be presented with the pictures or the examples, in addition to the textual information.

In the light of the modality employed to present the target words, glosses can be presented by the multimedia equipment with or without the pictures, or in the traditional form, that is, on the paper (Lomicka, 1998). If glosses are provided by the multimedia equipment, it may be presented in the form of the sound or the vision. Moreover, the vision may take the form of the image, the symbol and the video with or without the sound.

In the current research, glosses may be presented in different languages, in L1, L2 and L1 plus L2, with different numbers, single glosses and multiple - choice glosses with two options, as well as in different positions, in the interline position, on the marginal side of the text, at the bottom of the page and at the end of the text, as well.

2.5.3 Functions of Glosses

Roby (1999) believes that glossing is an efficient way to help the learners comprehend the text. To be specific, there are four functions of glosses in reading.

To begin with, glosses provide the accurate and proper explanations for the unknown words, avoiding incorrect inference of the word meanings by the learners (Nation, 2001). Because of the deficiency of learning strategies, and limited vocabulary knowledge, some learners may find it difficult to figure out the meanings of the unfamiliar words. With the help of glosses, the learners may easily get the correct word meanings.

In addition, glosses may help the learners to read the text smoothly, without being interrupted by the unknown words (Ko, 2005; Nation, 1990). From our common reading habit, it is generally known that if we don't know the meaning of a give word in the text, we may stop reading and try to work out the proper meaning, either from referring to the dictionary or from the teacher, resulting in the pause of reading. With glosses, the learners do not need to spend time guessing the word meaning, so that reading with the difficult word may continue.

Moreover, glosses help to bridge the gap between what has been learnt by the learners and what is new in the text (Ko, 2005). In order to figure out the meanings of the unknown words, the learners have to retrieve something closely related to the target words, and then relate it to the information provided in the text. The interaction between the target words and the text may help the learners to better comprehend the text information and process the words. In this course, some words may be kept in the long-term memory for the future use.

Finally, glosses help the learners to develop an autonomous learning habit. While reading, the learners may make full use of glosses provided to figure out the meanings of the unknown words, making them get accustomed to less depending on the dictionaries or language teachers. In casual reading, even though reading is only to get the main idea of the text, the encounter with some unfamiliar words in the text also serves as a large obstacle to continuing with reading. With the help of glosses provided, the learners may easily get the approximate meanings of the unknown words, without making greater efforts. In this situation, the learners may experience the joy brought by reading, on one hand. On the other hand, learners' learning confidence may be greatly raised, because of autonomous reading. This is especially true for learners' time-limited reading, as well.

From what has been mentioned above, because of the convenience and the efficiency, glosses have been becoming an important input enhancement method employed to facilitate learners' incidental vocabulary acquisition, especially in L2 reading.

2.5.4 Summary

This section is mainly about the concept of glosses. To begin with, the working definition of glosses is introduced, based on a brief review of the definitions given to glosses. Next is involved in the category of glosses, from which glosses in the current research are divided into three types, according to the languages they employ, the options they provide to the target words and the positions they appear. Finally, the basic functions of glosses are discussed. Glosses are employed to help the learners read the text without interruption and form an autonomous learning habit, so as to improve their target language learning, especially their vocabulary learning.

2.6 Previous Studies on Effects of Glosses on Incidental Vocabulary Acquisition through Reading

Glosses may take different forms because of different purposes. In the current research, glosses are classified into three types, according to the languages glosses use, the number of glosses, as well as the locations where glosses appear. The following is the review of previous studies on the effects of different types of glosses on incidental vocabulary acquisition through reading.

2.6.1 Effects of Glosses in Different Languages on Incidental Vocabulary Acquisition

Just as glosses provided in textbooks, some provide L1 glosses, some L2 glosses, and others L1 plus L2 glosses. In the field of incidental vocabulary acquisition through reading, some researchers have performed various studies into the effects of vocabulary acquisition caused by glosses in different languages.

Jacobs et al. (1994) investigated the effects of L1 glosses

and L2 glosses on learners' incidental vocabulary acquisition through reading. 85 Spanish learners of English were asked to read a Spanish text with 613 words. L1 glosses, L2 glosses and null glosses were provided to explain the target words. After reading, the learners were required to take an immediate vocabulary test, as well as a delayed vocabulary test without being told in advance four weeks later. The results in two vocabulary tests indicated that L1 glosses and L2 glosses were more beneficial to learners' incidental vocabulary acquisition through reading than null glosses. Nevertheless, there were not any significant differences in learners' incidental vocabulary acquisition under the condition of these three types of glosses. The results get support from Ko's (2012) research, which showed that there were not any significant differences between L1 glosses and L2 glosses. That is, the learners are more likely to acquire the words with glosses. The results of these two studies are consistent with the findings discovered by Rott (2005), who also found out there were not any significant differences among four types of glosses, that is, L1 glosses, L2 glosses, L1 plus L2 glosses, and null glosses. The research result is confirmed by Yoshii (2006).

Xu (2010) also had similar findings. 103 freshmen from Qingdao University of Science and Technology were requested to read a 774 - word passage with 18 target words, which were explained with Chinese glosses, English glosses and Chinese plus

English glosses. After reading the passage, the participants were asked to take an immediate vocabulary test and a delayed test one week later. The results showed that Chinese plus English glosses were more helpful to learners' vocabulary gain and vocabulary retention. This result gets confirmed by Shi (2010), who also found out that Chinese plus English glosses were more beneficial to learners' incidental vocabulary acquisition.

Chinese scholars Cao and Song (2014) also have similar findings. The subjects were 60 freshmen in a college. They were required to read two texts, either of which were about 200 words with 10 target words, respectively. The target words were explained with Chinese glosses, English glosses or English glosses with two options, one of which was correct. Having finished reading, the learners were asked to take an immediate vocabulary test and a delayed one. It was found that English glosses with two options were more beneficial to learners' incidental vocabulary acquisition through reading in the immediate vocabulary test. However, in the delayed vocabulary test, there were not any significant differences under these three glossing conditions. In other words, we cannot conclude that L1 glosses or L2 glosses are more efficient. The research results support Aljabri's (2011) empirical study.

However, other researchers have different findings. Miyasako (2002) divided glosses into five types, that is to say, single L1 glosses, single L2 glosses, multiple-choice L1 glosses, multiple-choice L2 glosses, as well as null glosses. 187 Japanese senior middle school students were required to read a text of 504 words with 20 target words. Having finished reading the text, the learners had to take an immediate vocabulary test in the form of multiple-choice questions, and a delayed vocabulary test 18 days later. It was found out that L2 glosses were more likely to facilitate learners' incidental vocabulary acquisition through reading than L1 glosses, no matter which form glosses might take, the single or multiple-choice form. As for the differences between the learners with different language proficiency, the learners with higher language proficiency tended to benefit more from L2 glosses, while those with lower language proficiency tended to benefit more from L1 glosses.

Ko (2005) used quantitative and qualitative methods to investigate the effects of different types of glosses on learners' incidental vocabulary acquisition. 106 Korean undergraduates at a university were involved in the research. They were asked to read a text of 931 words with 22 target words. After reading, the subjects were requested to take a multiple-choice test with four answers, among which only one was correct, and fill in a questionnaire about learners' attitudes towards the presence of glosses and their preference for these three types of glosses, that is to say, L1 glosses, L2 glosses, as well as null glosses. It was discovered that L2 glosses have a significant effect on learners' incidental vocabulary acquisition through reading. Meanwhile, most of the subjects preferred to have glosses and 62% of them favored L2 glosses.

Farvardin and Biria (2012) classified glosses into three types, that is to say, single L1 glosses, single L2 glosses, and multiple-choice L2 glosses. 120 Irian students at Azad University of Najafabad were chosen as the subjects, who were asked to read a passage of 901 words with 30 target words. Having finished reading, the learners were required to take two vocabulary tests, one of which was performed immediately after reading, and the other of which was preformed three weeks later, and a reading comprehension test. The results indicated that L2 glosses were more facilitative to learners' reading comprehension and their incidental vocabulary acquisition through reading.

The above three studies are in favor of Chen and Leung's (1989), and Kroll's (1993) research. In other words, the learners incidentally acquire vocabulary significantly better under the condition of L2 glosses.

However, other researchers have found that L1 glosses are more effective. Lv et al. (2005) investigated 50 senior middle school English learners' incidental vocabulary acquisition through reading. There were three texts, each of which was about 600 words. Each text had 11 target words, respectively, which were explained with L1 glosses or L2 glosses. After reading, the learners were required to take an immediate vocabulary test, and a delayed test two weeks later, both of which were composed of three tests, that is, explaining the target words, making up sentences with the target words, as well as a writing task. The results indicated that L1 glosses were significantly more beneficial to learners' incidental vocabulary acquisition through reading, especially for those with lower language proficiency. This research partially supports Miyasako's (2002) study.

The findings are supported by Meng and Chen (2015). They took 223 non-English majors as the subjects. A text of 887 words with 25 target words was involved. The words were explained with five types of glosses, that is, null glosses, marginal Chinese glosses, marginal English glosses, endnote Chinese glosses, and endnote English glosses. After reading, 3 tests were provided, that is, a reading comprehension test, an immediate vocabulary test, and a delayed one. It was found that marginal Chinese glosses were more beneficial to learners' reading comprehension and the retention of the target words. In two vocabulary tests, the learners performed better in vocabulary acquisition under glossing conditions. In other words, L1 glosses are more facilitative.

Wu and Xu (2009) utilized the story of "The Seven Ravens" with 936 words from Grimm's Fairy Tales to examine the effects of different types of glosses on learners' incidental vocabulary acquisition through reading. 104 freshmen of non-English majors were asked to read a passage with 24 target words which were glossed in Chinese, English, Chinese plus pictures, as well as English plus pictures. Two tests were involved, an immediate test and a delayed test two weeks later. In either of the tests, the learners were requested to identify Chinese or English meanings of the target words and fill in the blanks with the target words. The results indicated that in terms of the languages glosses used, Chinese glosses were more beneficial; with regard to the use of pictures, Chinese glosses plus pictures were more facilitative to learners' incidental vocabulary acquisition. Concerning learners' language proficiency, the learners with higher language proficiency were better at employing glosses in incidental vocabulary acquisition. In a word, L1 glosses are more conducive. This result gets support from Cheng and Good's (2009) research. However, they also found that glosses did not have any significant effects on learners' reading comprehension.

Vela (2015) employed two texts to investigate 60 learners' incidental vocabulary acquisition through reading. Three types of glosses were involved, that is to say, null glosses, L1 glosses and L2 glosses. After reading, the learners had to take a multiple-choice reading comprehension test, as well as a vocabulary test. The research results demonstrated that the learners with lower language proficiency benefited more from L1 glosses, while those with higher language proficiency profited more from L1 glosses and L2 glosses. In other words, L1 glosses are more effective in learners' incidental vocabulary acquisition through reading. This research confirms the studies conducted by Lv et al. (2005), and Meng and Chen (2015).

With the popularity of the multimedia employed in L2 teaching and learning, some scholars have carried out some studies, in which the target words with glosses in different languages are presented with the help of the computer. Wang (2005) required 182 English majors (92 learners with lower language proficiency and 90 with higher language proficiency) to watch a documentary clip of "Panama Wild" about 16 minutes with L1 and L2 captions from the program of "National Geographic". Having finished watching the clip, the learners were asked to finish two tests, one of which was composed of the word recognition, the word spelling and the word meaning, and the other of which was involved in the multiple-choice reading comprehension. The results showed that the captions had a significant effect on learners' vocabulary gain and vocabulary retention. To be exact, L2 captions helped to foster learners' word spelling and word recognition, while L1 captions were more beneficial to learners' word meaning memorization. As for the effects of learners' language proficiency, L1 captions were more facilitative to vocabulary acquisition for the learners with lower language proficiency, however, significant differences were not found for the learners with higher language proficiency under the condition of these two glossing conditions. In a word, different glossing conditions have different effects on learners' vocabulary acquisition. The findings are partially consistent with those of the study performed by Chen (2013). She discovered that under the situation of CALL (Computer-aided Language Learning), L1 plus L2 glosses were more conducive to learners' vocabulary retention. Nevertheless, Rouhi and Mohebbi (2012), and Taylor (2006) found that computer - aided L1 glosses had a significant influence on learners' reading comprehension. In summary, in the field of the multimedia, the findings are quite mixed. However, it is obvious that L1 glosses are more beneficial to learners' vocabulary acquisition.

From what has been mentioned above, it is easily found out that some researchers (Aljabri, 2011; Cao and Song, 2014; Jacobs et al., 1994; Ko, 2012; Rott, 2005; Yoshii, 2006) find that there are not any significant differences in learners' incidental vocabulary acquisition between L1 glosses and L2 glosses. Some scholars (Chen and Leung, 1989; Farvardin and Biria, 2012; Ko, 2005; Kroll, 1993; Miyasako, 2002) hold that L2 glosses are more facilitative to learners' incidental vocabulary acquisition through reading. Some researchers (Cheng and Good, 2009; Hulstijn et al., 1996; Lv et al., 2005; Meng and Chen, 2015; Rouhi and Mohebbi, 2012; Taylor, 2006; Vela, 2015; Wu and Xu, 2009) find that L1 glosses are more conducive. Some scholars (Chen, 2013; Shi, 2010; Xu, 2010) discover that L1 plus L2 glosses are more helpful to learners' incidental vocabulary acquisition through reading. In a word, there is not a consensus about whether L1 glosses, L2 glosses or L1 plus L2 glosses are more beneficial to learners' incidental vocabulary acquisition through reading.

As for the effects of language proficiency on learners' incidental vocabulary acquisition through reading, it is generally thought that the learners with lower language proficiency benefit more from L1 glosses (Lv et al., 2005; Miyasako, 2002; Vela, 2015; Wang, 2005), while for the learners with higher language proficiency, there is a different story. Vela (2015) holds that the learners with higher language proficiency profit more from both L1 glosses and L2 glosses, while Miyasako (2002) believes that L2 glosses are more beneficial to them. As is mentioned by Gao and Liu (2009), the effects of language proficiency on learners' incidental vocabulary acquisition through reading needs to be further explored.

2.6.2 Effects of Glosses with Different Numbers on Incidental Vocabulary Acquisition

It has been mentioned above that glosses may be provided in L1, L2, or L1 plus L2, and they may also have different numbers. Of course, their effects are quite different on learners' reading comprehension and their incidental vocabulary acquisition through reading. In addition, some scholars have performed related studies into the effects of the number of glosses provided on learners' incidental vocabulary acquisition through reading. In other words, for some unfamiliar words, more than one gloss may be provided.

Glosses in the text make the learners look through the target words and the text back and forth, therefore, giving them more chances to encounter the target words, and increasing the opportunities of memorizing them for the learners (Watanabe, 1997). However, single glosses deprive the learners of more encounters with the target words. In order to overcome the inherent shortcomings of single glosses, Hulstijn (1992) proposed to use multiple-choice glosses to replace single glosses with only the exact meanings of the unfamiliar words. It was considered that multiple - choice glosses provided the learners with more chances to search and evaluate glosses, from which the best meaning was chosen to fit in with the context. Hulstijn (1992) carried out a study into the effects of single glosses and multiple-choice glosses on learners' incidental vocabulary acquisition through reading. 45 Dutch learners were required to read a passage with the target words glossed under two conditions, that is, single glosses which were given in the form of the synonyms of the target words, as well as multiple-choice glosses, in which only one was correct and the rest three acted as the distracters. After reading, the learners were requested to finish a reading comprehension task and a vocabulary retention test without being told in advance. The results revealed that the learners with multiple-choice glosses performed better than those with single glosses, in terms of incidental vocabulary acquisition through reading. However, a fact that cannot be ignored is that in multiple - choice glosses, 30% of the answers inferred from glosses were wrong.

For the sake of solving higher proportions of incorrect inferring, Nagata (1999) employed a computer program to enhance learners' vocabulary acquisition through reading. 26 English learners of Japanese were asked to read a passage with the target words explained with single glosses and multiple-choice glosses with two options. After reading, the participants were provided with a vocabulary test and a grammar test. Having completed these two tests, they were offered correct meanings of the target words with the help of the computer program. One month later, a delayed vocabulary test was given to the participants. The results manifested that the learners with multiple-choice glosses outperformed those with single glosses in vocabulary retention, and it was found out that there were significant differences between single glosses and multiple-choice glosses. The results support Hulstijn's (1992) opinion that for multiple - choice glosses, two options would be better, one providing the correct word meaning, and the other acting as the distracter. However, it was unconvincing in that the computer program helped the learners to get the correct meanings of the unfamiliar words, which might effectively facilitate learners' vocabulary retention.

Rott and Williams (2003) carried out a study to investigate the effects of multiple - choice glosses and periodic text reconstruction on learners' vocabulary retention through reading. 14 Germany English learners, who were learning in an American public university, were required to read a passage with the target words explained with multiple - choice glosses, or null glosses. After reading, they were requested to complete an immediate word gain test and a delayed word recognition test. Meanwhile, a think - aloud method was exploited to explore how the learners processed information. The results indicated that multiple-choice glosses were more helpful to learners' vocabulary retention through reading. However, the results were based on the comparison between multiple-choice glosses and null glosses. It may be safe to get the conclusion that glosses are more beneficial to learners' vocabulary retention. It will be doubtful to conclude that the learners with multiple - choice glosses can do better in vocabulary retention. What's more, even though they claimed that 14 learners were concerned, in fact only 12 participants were involved in the research. These two factors make it uncertain to say that multiple-choice glosses are more conducive to learners' incidental vocabulary acquisition through reading.

Two years later, with some conditions modified, Rott (2005) performed another study to probe into the effects of single glosses and multiple - choice glosses on learners' incidental vocabulary acquisition through reading. 10 German learners of

English in an American public university were required to read a passage with the target words explained with single glosses and multiple - choice glosses. What was different from the former research was that glosses of the target words would appear three more times after the first appearance. After reading, the learners were asked to complete a reading comprehension task, an immediate vocabulary test and a delayed vocabulary test four weeks later, both of which were concerned with vocabulary knowledge scale and vocabulary recognition. The think - aloud technique was also used in this research. The results indicated that the learners with multiple-choice glosses performed better in vocabulary retention. Even though the learners under these two types of glossing conditions were approximately equal in the text comprehension, it was quite obvious that the learners with multiple-choice glosses performed better. Therefore, it is apparent to draw a conclusion that multiple - choice glosses are more beneficial to learners' incidental vocabulary acquisition through reading. However, what is bothered is that it is difficult to determine whether the result is caused by the reoccurrence frequencies of the target words. The other problem lying in the research is that there are a few participants involved, which lowers the reliability of the results.

However, there are also some different stories. In order to further explore the effects of single glosses and multiple-choice glosses on learners' incidental vocabulary acquisition, Watanabe

(1997) performed a rather complicated study, in which 231 English learners of Japanese were asked to read a 500 - word passage with 16 target words that were explained in terms of single marginal glosses, multiple - choice marginal glosses with two options, appositive glosses, as well as null glosses. After reading, the participants were required to complete a comprehension task and a cloze test. In addition, two vocabulary tests were offered, as well, one of which was an immediate test, and the other of which was a delayed test one week later. The results demonstrated even though the learners with single glosses did better than those with multiple-choice glosses, there were not any significant differences between single glosses and multiple-choice glosses for learners' vocabulary retention. It was also found out that the learners with single marginal glosses and multiple - choice glosses outperformed those with appositive glosses and null glosses. However, the learners with multiple-choice glosses made more mistakes in inferring word meanings. Therefore, Hulstijn (1992) put forward that the multiple - choice glosses had better be provided with only two options, one of which was correct and the other of which worked as the distracter. Two options may help to reduce learners' cognitive burden in working out the meanings of the unfamiliar words, so as to increase the opportunity of correct inferring. Nevertheless, Ke (2003) argued that glosses with four options were more helpful to learners' correctly inferring the word meanings, while glosses with two options could greatly facilitate learners' incidental vocabulary acquisition through reading.

Jasteh and Akbarpour (2011) required 101 English learners with intermediate language proficiency to read a passage with the target words glossed in the single format and multiple - choice format, in which three options were involved. The control group was provided with the text without any glosses to the target words, but they were encouraged to look up the unfamiliar words in the dictionaries. After reading, the participants were asked to take two tests, one of which was a vocabulary retention test, and the other of which was a vocabulary production test. The results indicated that the learners with glosses did better than those referring to the dictionaries in the tests of vocabulary retention and vocabulary production. Meanwhile, even though significant differences were not found between the learners with single glosses and those with multiple - choice glosses, the participants who received the text with single glosses performed better than those with multiple-choice glosses. This result is consistent with that of Watanabe (1997), but contrary to those of Hulstijn (1992), Nagata (1999), Rott (2005), as well as Rott and Williams (2003), who all argue that multiple-choice glosses are more facilitative to learners' incidental vocabulary acquisition through reading.

Some Chinese scholars have also carried out some research to explore the relationship between single glosses and multiple-choice glosses in Chinese foreign language learning context.

Duan and Yan (2004) asked 89 freshmen who were English majors to read a passage about 570 words with 11 target words, which were explained in the format of single glosses, multiple-choice glosses with three options and null glosses. What should be mentioned was that in multiple - choice glosses, the right glosses were marked in certain positions of the text. After reading, the learners were required to take an immediate test and a delayed test one week later, both of which were about vocabulary retention. The items in these two tests were the same. However, the order was quite different. The results indicated that the learners with glosses did better in the vocabulary retention test than those with null glosses. At the same time, the learners with multiple - choice glosses performed better than those with single glosses. It was also found out that the learners with a larger vocabulary size kept the words longer. The research partially supports the empirical study carried out by Shi (2010), who found that double glosses were significantly conducive to learners' vocabulary gain and vocabulary retention. However, there were not any significant differences between single glosses and multiple-choice glosses, as well as between single glosses and null glosses. Nevertheless, in Duan and Yan's (2004) research, the right definitions of the target words were marked in certain locations of the passage. Whether the results were influenced by this factor or not could not be determined.

Lei (2011) compared the effects of single glosses, multiple-choice glosses and null glosses on English learners' incidental vocabulary acquisition through reading. 108 participants were divided into three groups, one of which was not involved in the experiment. After having read the two passages, the learners were asked to take three tests, one of which was a vocabulary test, another a cloze test, the other a translation test. The results indicated that the participants with glosses did better than those with null glosses, and the learners with multiple-choice glosses outperformed those with single glosses, even though there were not any significant differences between these two types of glosses. What's more, the learners with higher language proficiency significantly performed better than those with lower language proficiency. The results support the research conducted by Shi (2010), who holds that multiple-choice glosses are more beneficial to learners' incidental vocabulary acquisition, even though there are not any significant differences between single glosses and multiple-choice glosses. Later Cao and Song (2014) also found that multiple-choice glosses could greatly foster learners' vocabulary retention through reading.

From what has been discussed above, most of the scholars (Cao and Song, 2014; Duan and Yan, 2004; Hulstijn, 1992; Lei, 2011; Nagata, 1999; Rott, 2005; Rott and Williams, 2003; Shi, 2010) at home and abroad have found that multiple-choice glosses are more conducive to learners' incidental vocabulary acquisition through reading. However, other scholars (Jasteh and

Akbarpour, 2011; Watanabe, 1997) have also found out that single glosses are more beneficial. However, there are also some differences among these studies. Some (Jasteh and Akbarpour, 2011; Lei, 2011; Shi, 2010; Watanabe, 1997) have found that there are not any significant differences between single glosses and multiple - choice glosses, while Duan and Yan (2004), and Nagata (1999) have claimed that there are significant differences between these two types of glossing. It is also found that the studies mentioned above are seldom involved in the relationship between different types of glosses and language proficiency of L2 learners, except the study performed by Lei (2011). With regard to multiple - choice glosses, some provide four options (Hulstijn, 1992); some offer three options (Duan and Yan, 2004; Jasteh and Akbarpour, 2011); some supply two options (Nagata, 1999; Watanabe, 1997). Different numbers of the options may demand different noticing resources from the learners, resulting in different depths of information processing, so as to influence the results of the studies, accordingly.

2.6.3 Effects of Glosses in Different Positions on Incidental Vocabulary Acquisition

Glosses may be provided in different languages and with different options. At the same time, they may appear in different locations in the text, that is to say, on the side of the page, at the bottom of the page, at the end of the text or between the lines of the text. Different locations where glosses appear in the text may have different effects on learners' allocation of noticing resources, resulting in different results of learners' incidental vocabulary acquisition through reading.

Holley and King (1971) employed three types of glosses, that is to say, marginal glosses, endnote glosses, as well as glosses on a separate page. A revised story with 750 words was used as the reading material to examine 110 Germany learners' incidental vocabulary acquisition through reading. Two tests were performed. One was a multiple - choice vocabulary test, and the other was a reading comprehension test. The results indicated that glosses neither facilitated nor hampered learners' vocabulary acquisition through reading. Meanwhile, there were no significant differences among three types of glosses. In other words, glossing positions do not exert any influences on learners' incidental vocabulary acquisition through reading. The result is consistent with that of the research carried by Johnson (1982).

However, some researchers find that marginal glosses are more beneficial. Davis (1989) carried out a study to check whether marginal glosses could be helpful to foreign language learners' incidental vocabulary acquisition through reading. 71 French learners from America were required to write about what they remembered after reading. The research results showed that marginal glosses might be more beneficial to learners' incidental vocabulary acquisition through reading. However, there is only one type of gloss positioning in the research, not involved in other glossing locations, which is similar to Meng and Chen's (2015). The findings are confirmed by Hulstijn et al. (1996), who examined different effects of glosses in different positions on learners' vocabulary acquisition. In their research, marginal L1 glosses, bilingual dictionary use, as well as null glosses or no dictionary use were involved. It was found out that marginal L1 glosses were more effective.

Zarei and Hasani (2011) exploited 158 English B. A. freshmen of Persian to investigate the effects of four types of glosses on learners' incidental vocabulary acquisition, that is to say, in-text glosses, marginal glosses, pre-text glosses as well as post-text glosses. The learners were divided into eight groups, four of whom were given the text with interlingual glosses, and four of whom with intralingual glosses. After reading, the learners were requested to complete a vocabulary recognition test with 30 items in the multiple-choice format and a recall vocabulary test with 30 items in the form of filling in the blanks with the target words. The results indicated that there were not any significant differences among these four different types of glosses on learners' incidental vocabulary acquisition in the intralingual glossing groups, while in the interlingual glossing groups, marginal groups and pre-text groups did significantly better than post-text groups in vocabulary recognition. However, in the vocabulary recall test, in-text glosses were more facilitative. The results partially support Davis' (1989) research.

Chinese scholars Wu et al. (2012) employed a story of 1,411 words with 16 target words to investigate 115 freshmen's incidental vocabulary acquisition through reading. The words were glossed on the side of the page, at the bottom of the page and on a separate page. After reading, two tests were concerned. One was a multiple-choice reading comprehension test, and the other was a vocabulary test, involved in cued recall, that is to say, explaining the target words in Chinese or English. The results indicated that marginal glosses were more facilitative to learners' vocabulary acquisition through reading, while positions of different types of glosses did not have any significant effects on learners' reading comprehension. In a word, as for the effects of glossing conditions on learners' incidental vocabulary acquisition, the research supports the studies performed by Davis (1989), Hulstijn et al. (1996), as well as Meng and Chen (2015). However, as to the effects of glossing conditions on learners' reading comprehension, the result is consistent with that of Holley and King's (1971) research.

However, other scholars have different findings as for the effects of glosses in different positions on learners' incidental vocabulary acquisition through reading. Cheng and Good (2009) compared the effects of four types of glosses on learners' reading comprehension and vocabulary retention, that is, L1 glosses plus L2 examples, in-text L1 glosses, marginal L1 glosses, as well as null glosses. 135 participants were undergraduate students majoring in business and engineering. After reading, they were requested to finish a reading comprehension task and three vocabulary retention tests concerning the given 16 target words in the reading passage. One was an immediate test, and the other two delayed tests were carried out one week later and two weeks later. The items in the vocabulary tests were the same, but in a different order. The results showed that glosses greatly helped to promote learners' incidental vocabulary acquisition. However, glossing types did not have any significant effects on learners' reading comprehension, This result is consistent with those discovered by Holley and King (1971) and Wu et al. (2012). Among four different types of glosses, L1 glosses plus L2 examples were the most profitable to learners' vocabulary acquisition. As for positions of glosses, in - text glosses were significantly more facilitative than marginal glosses. This result gets confirmed by Elekaei et al. (2015).

Elekaei et al. (2015) selected 140 English learners of Iran to investigate the effects of glossing types on learners' reading comprehension and vocabulary retention. A reading passage with 28 target words was given to the participants. The words were glossed at the bottom of the page, within the text, on the marginal side of the page, as well as in the form of the wordlist. After reading, the participants were required to complete two reading comprehension tasks and take two tests, that is, the immediate vocabulary test and the delayed one. With regard to the reading tasks, the participants with the target words glossed within the text significantly exceeded those in the other three groups. In the delayed test taking the multiple-choice form, the learners with target words explained within the text significantly outperformed those in the other three groups, in terms of both vocabulary gain and vocabulary retention. In other words, among four different types of glosses, in-text glosses are the most conducive to learners' reading comprehension and vocabulary gain and vocabulary retention.

Chinese scholars Chen et al. (2013) also have similar findings. Their participants were 79 non-English sophomores in Chongqing University. They were requested to read 7 passages, each of which was about 400 words. In total, 21 target words were involved. Four different types of glosses were presented by computers, that is, marginal glosses, glosses at the bottom of the webpage, in-text glosses, as well as null glosses. The results demonstrated that in-text glosses were the most beneficial to learners' incidental vocabulary acquisition through reading. This result also gets support from the research performed by Lan and Zhang (2013).

From what has been discussed, it is generally acknowledged that some scholars (Holley and King, 1971; Johnson, 1982; Zarei and Hasani, 2011) hold that glossing positions do not have any significant effects on learners' incidental vocabulary acquisition through reading; some scholars (Davis, 1989; Hulstijn et al., 1996; Meng and Chen, 2015; Wu et al., 2012) argue that marginal glosses were more facilitative to learners' vocabulary acquisition; other researchers (Chen et al., 2013; Cheng and Good, 2009; Elekaei et al., 2015; Lan and Zhang, 2013; Zarei and Hasani, 2011) consider that in-text glosses are more beneficial to learners' vocabulary acquisition. Meanwhile, some contradictory results are also revealed. Chen et al. (2013), Elekaei et al. (2015), Farvardin and Biria (2012), Lan and Zhang (2013), Meng and Chen (2015), and Taylor (2006) hold that glosses are beneficial to learners' reading comprehension and vocabulary acquisition, while Holley and King (1971), Johnson (1982) and Wu et al. (2012) argue that glosses are not facilitative to learners' reading comprehension. At the same time, Cheng and Good (2009) think glosses are conducive to learners' vocabulary acquisition, but not to their reading comprehension.

There are only a few related studies performed at home and abroad to investigate the effects of glosses in different positons on learners' incidental vocabulary acquisition through reading (Wu et al., 2012). From what has been known in the teaching practice, the unfamiliar words in most of the textbooks in China are glossed at the end of the text. As for the languages employed, most of glosses only use Chinese language, and only some of them use both Chinese and English languages. However, even though some scholars (Chen et al, 2013; Cheng and Good, 2009;

Lan and Zhang, 2013; Wu et al., 2012) have proved that either marginal glosses or in - text glosses are more beneficial to learners' incidental vocabulary acquisition through reading, their results are not displayed in the arrangement of glosses in the textbooks designed for the English learners in middle schools or in colleges. Besides, there are only a few studies concerning the locations of glosses. Therefore, more studies are in great need to investigate the effects of different glossing locations on learners' incidental vocabulary acquisition through reading.

2.6.4 Limitations of the Previous Studies

In the field of incidental vocabulary acquisition through reading, scholars at home and abroad have carried out varieties of studies to investigate the effects of glosses in different languages, with different numbers as well as in different positions on learners' vocabulary acquisition. What's more, fruitful results have been obtained. However, there are some limitations, as well, which will be explicated in the following.

The first limitation is concerned with the selection of the reading material. To begin with, only one reading passage is involved in some of the studies mentioned above (Elekaei et al., 2015; Farvardin and Biria, 2012; Jacobs et al., 1994; Meng and Chen, 2015; Miyasako, 2002; Wang, 2005; Xu, 2010, etc.). However, there are some studies (Cao and Song, 2014; Huang, 2004; Lv et al., 2005; Vela, 2015; Wu, 2010; Zhang and Qi,

2009; Zhou, 2008, etc.) employing more than one reading passage to investigate the effects of different types of glosses on learners' incidental vocabulary acquisition through reading. If more than one text is involved, it will be hard to determine whether the results are caused by the difficulty of the texts or by the types of glosses. Next is about the time given to read the text. This is also a quite obvious problem, especially in some empirical studies carried out in China. For example, In Gong's (2009) research, the text is about 4,330 words, and the time given to finish reading the text is about 50 minutes. Therefore, the average reading speed for first-year English majors is 86.600 words per minute. However, in Gai's (2003) investigation, the text is about 500 words, and the reading time is about 10 minutes, so the reading speed for second-year English majors is about 50.000 words per minute. It means that first-year English majors can read faster than second-year English majors. Therefore, the reading time should be given according to a certain standard. What's more, the long text will easily make the participants tired, so as to influence the research results (Chen et al., 2013). For example, in Zhang and Qi's (2009) research, the reading texts are four simplified version of English classics with more than 2.1 million words. And the time lasts for about 6 months. The reading task is really challenging enough, even for language teachers themselves, let alone English learners. They may be easily overwhelmed, making the results of the research full of doubts.

The second limitation is involved in the time set for the delayed vocabulary test. In order to investigate the effects of different types of glosses on learners' vocabulary retention, the delayed test is of great necessity. It is given one week later after reading in most of the studies (Cheng and Good, 2009; Duan and Yan, 2004; Shi, 2010; Watanabe, 1997; Xu, 2010, etc.). Some researchers (Cheng and Good, 2009; Lv et al., 2005; Miyasako, 2002; Wu and Xu, 2009, etc.) set the delayed vocabulary test two weeks later after reading. Others (Farvardin and Biria, 2012; Jacobs et al., 1994; Nagata, 1999; Rott, 2005) even set it more than three weeks later. From what has been mentioned above, it can be concluded that most of the studies set the delayed test one or two weeks later after the learners finishing reading the text. It is generally known that the longer the interval is between the immediate test and the delayed test, the worse learners' vocabulary retention will be. Therefore, whether the result is caused by the time factor or by different types of glosses is still in doubt.

The third limitation is that the results of reading comprehension are seldom touched upon. As one of the advantages of incidental vocabulary acquisition through reading mentioned in Section 2.2.2, learning vocabulary knowledge through reading is efficient, because language learners can perform two tasks at the same time, reading for comprehending the given text and for completing some other tasks, such as making up sentences and filling in the blanks with the target words. If reading comprehension is deleted from the research, how is the efficiency of incidental vocabulary acquisition through reading demonstrated? However, the fact is that only some of the studies (Cheng and Good, 2009; Elekaei et al., 2015; Farvardin and Biria, 2012; Holley and King, 1971; Meng and Chen, 2015; Rott, 2005; Taylor, 2006; Wu et al., 2012, etc.) are concerned with the effects of glossing types on learners' reading comprehension. Most of the studies (Cao and Song, 2014; Chen et al., 2013; Hulstijn, 1992; Jasteh and Akbarpour, 2011; Lan and Zhang, 2013; Shi, 2010, etc.) only pay attention to the effects of glossing types on learners' incidental vocabulary acquisition, without concerning the effects of glossing types on learners' reading comprehension.

The fourth limitation is the number of the options in multiple-choice glosses. Some researchers (Cao and Song, 2014; Nagata, 1999; Shi, 2010; Watanabe, 1997, etc.) provide two options. Some (Duan and Yan, 2004; Jasteh and Akbarpour, 2011, etc.) provide three options. And others (Hulstijn, 1992) provide four options. From what has been mentioned above, it can be seen clearly that two or three options are quite common for multiple-choice glosses. The more options multiple-choice glosses provide, the more noticing resources the learners will allocate to glosses of the target words. It means that the words will be processed deeper, because more information related to the words needs to be dealt with. This may result in the intentional learning of the target words, deviating from the incidental characteristic of vocabulary acquisition.

The fifth limitation lies in the studies concerning the effects of glossing locations on learners' incidental vocabulary acquisition through reading. The relevant studies (Chen et al., 2013; Cheng and Good, 2009; Davis, 1989; Elekaei et al., 2015; Holley and King, 1971; Hustijn et al., 1996; Wu et al., 2012; Zarei and Hasani, 2011, etc.) mainly focus on marginal glosses. Some (Chen et al., 2013; Elekaei et al., 2015; Holley and King, 1971; Wu et al., 2012; Zarei and Hasani, 2011, etc.) are related to endnote glosses. Some (Chen et al., 2013; Cheng and Good, 2009; Elekaei et al., 2015; Zarei and Hasani, 2011, etc.) are involved in in-text glosses. Others (Elekaei et al., 2015; Holley and King, 1971; Wu et al., 2012; Zarei and Hasani, 2011, etc.) use the separate wordlist format. From what has been mentioned above, it can be summarized that most of the studies are concerned with marginal glosses. Other types of glosses with regard to the positions need to be further explored.

The last limitation is about the effects of learners' language proficiency on their incidental vocabulary acquisition through reading. Only some related studies (Duan and Yan, 2004; Lei, 2011; Lv et al., 2005; Miyasako, 2002; Vela, 2015; Wang, 2005, etc.) are concerned with learners' language proficiency. Among these studies, the effects of learners' language proficiency are quite complicated, even including some contradictory results. For example, Miyasako (2002) finds that the learners with higher language proficiency benefit more from L2 glosses, while Vela (2015) discovers that both L1 glosses and L2 glosses are more beneficial to these learners. Therefore, the effects of learners' language proficiency on incidental vocabulary acquisition through reading need to be reconsidered.

2.6.5 Summary

This section is mainly about the review of what has been done about the effects of different types of glosses on learners' incidental vocabulary acquisition through reading, to be exact, the effects of glosses in different languages, with different numbers, as well as in different locations in the text. Among these studies, there are both similarities and differences, and even some paradoxical results. At the end of this section, the limitations lying in the previous relevant studies are discussed in detail. Therefore, the current research attempts to avoid these limitations discovered in the previous studies performed at home and abroad, so as to deepen the empirical studies conducted in the field of incidental vocabulary acquisition through reading.

2.7 Theoretical Framework

With more and more attention received in the field of incidental vocabulary acquisition research, different scholars have employed different theories to explain how vocabulary is acquired incidentally through reading. In the following, five theories closely related to incidental vocabulary acquisition will be introduced, to be exact, the Theory of Depth Processing, the Involvement Load Hypothesis, the Noticing Hypothesis, the Input Hypothesis, as well as the Output Hypothesis.

2.7.1 Theory of Depth Processing

The Theory of Depth Processing proposed by Craik and Lockhart (1972) is a powerful reaction against the Information Processing Theory. The theory focuses on information processing related to memory. The central concept of this theory is that retention of memory is dependent on different depths of processing. It means that the deeper the information is processed, the longer it will be kept in memory. In general, there are three ways to process information that is received, that is, structural processing, phonemic processing, and semantic processing, illustrated in Figure 2.1. The former two ways belong to shallow processing, while semantic processing belongs to deep processing.

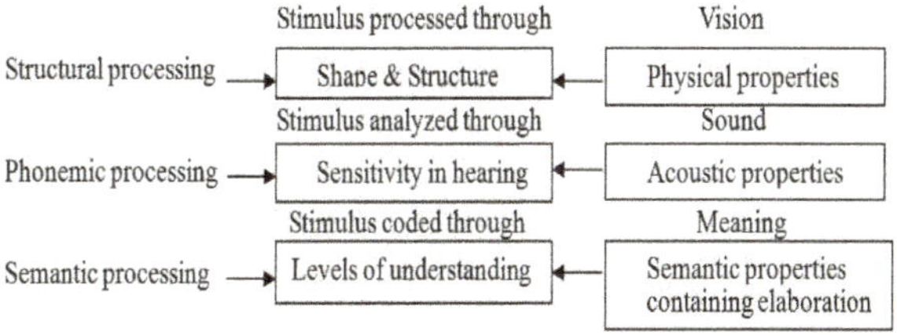

Figure 2.1 Theory of Depth Processing (Craik and Lockhart, 1972)

As is shown in the above figure, structural processing decodes the physical properties of the information, such as what the word looks like and how the word is spelt. Phonemic processing is used to decode the acoustic properties of the information, such as how the word is pronounced. These two ways of shallow processing help to keep information in short-term memory. Semantic processing is responsible for decoding the meaning of a certain word, and then the learners relate it with other similar words. Deep processing is involved in the more meaningful analysis of the given information, leading to the better retrieval of the target word. In a word, how the information is processed has an impact on the way it is to be memorized. In other words, whether the new information can be kept in long-term memory depends on the depths of processing, that is to say, the deeper the information is processed, the better it will be retained.

In incidental vocabulary acquisition research, the learners may encounter an unfamiliar word in L2 reading. First of all, they may catch a glimpse of its appearance, knowing whether the word is written in small letters or capitalized letters. The next step is to figure out whether they can pronounce the word. Finally, they will try to guess the meaning of the word in a certain context, employing all the vocabulary knowledge that has been learnt before. In this process, all the words similar to the target word may be activated. The word processed in this way will be kept in memory longer than the one processed in the former two ways.

The main idea of the theory has been confirmed in Li and Tian's (2005) research, with the conclusion that the deeper the target word is processed, the better learners' incidental vocabulary acquisition through reading will be. In the current research, the learners may notice different aspects of the target words, which may result in different levels of processing, leading to different acquisition effects.

However, there are two serious defects lying in this theory. One defect is what the vocabulary processing level is composed of; the other one is how to identify the depths of information processing (Zhang and Ren, 2013). The depths of processing can be not quantified, which results in some practical problems.

2.7.2 Involvement Load Hypothesis

In order to solve the practical problems resting in the Depth of Processing Theory, Laufer and Hulstijn (2001), from the perspective of affective-cognitive construct of involvement, put forward the Involvement Load Hypothesis, which makes possible the quantitative analysis of incidental vocabulary acquisition through reading. Based on this theory, it is believed that reading tasks can facilitate incidental vocabulary acquisition through reading. The Involvement Load Hypothesis elaborates thoroughly the depths of information processing, which means different types of reading tasks demand different depths of processing. In turn, language learners are required to make various efforts to accomplish reading tasks with different involvement loads. To be simple, the more involvement loads reading tasks demand, the greater efforts language learners are supposed to make. Therefore, the tasks will greatly improve incidental vocabulary acquisition through reading. Three components are identified in the Involvement Load Hypothesis, that is, need, search, as well as evaluation.

Need, a type of affect factors, is closely related to learners' language learning motivation. When the learners encounter an unknown word in reading, which influences their comprehension, they need to infer the meaning of the word. Need may originate from both outside and inside factors. Accordingly, Laufer and Hulstijn (2001) distinguish two types of need, moderate need and strong need. The former is imposed by external factors. For instance, the learners are required to produce a sentence using the target word. Nevertheless, strong need is imposed by the learners themselves. They voluntarily learn the target word. Search and evaluation, as cognitive factors, refer to the process of information processing. Search is the effort the learners make to work out the meaning of the target word, by means of using a dictionary or with the help of the teacher. Evaluation is meant to compare the target word with other words in terms of word meanings, so as to make a decision on which meaning is appropriate in the context. If evaluation is concerned with comparing differences of the target word in terms of different word forms or senses, the evaluation is moderate. On the contrary, strong evaluation is involved in the actual use of the target word with other words in sentences.

Vocabulary learning tasks are differentiated with regard to involvement loads. Greater involvement loads are required when there are higher degrees of need, more searching resources exploited to figure out the word meaning, and strong evaluation of the target word and the context, as well. In a specific learning task, these three components can be labeled as present or absent (+/-), and moderate (+) or strong (++), which can be illustrated in the following table.

Table 2.1 Involvement loads of different tasks (Laufer and Hulstijn, 2001)

Task	Need	Search	Evaluation
1. Reading comprehension (unrelated to target words)	-	-	-
2. Reading comprehension (related to target words)	+	-	-
3. Reading comprehension and filling in blanks (related to target words)	+	-	+
4. Making up sentences (related to target words)	+	-	++
5. Writing (related to target words)	+	-	++
6. Writing (unlimited to target words)	++	+	++

It is clearly displayed in the above table that different tasks require different involvement loads. To be accurate, the greater involvement loads there are in these three components, the better effects incidental acquisition of the target words will have. To put it another way, the words processed with greater involvement loads tend to be acquired better.

Studies have shown that the Involvement Load Hypothesis can be employed to improve vocabulary acquisition under the situation of vocabulary enhancement. Therefore, the teachers can assign different levels of reading tasks to language learners, according to their individual learning stages and language proficiency (Duan and Yan, 2004; Huang, 2004; Li, 2014; Wu and Xu, 2009). In other words, the teachers should make full use of the allocation of the amount of need, search and evaluation to interfere learners' vocabulary learning.

However, some Chinese scholars have carried out some empirical studies to verify the Involvement Load Hypothesis. Huang (2004) investigated the effects of three different reading tasks with different involvement loads on learners' incidental vocabulary acquisition through reading. The results partially support this theory. She holds that some quantified indicators in the theory need to be revised. For example, the effects of the given time and learners' language proficiency on the reading tasks should be taken into consideration. In addition, the processing purposes of the reading tasks should be contained in the theory, as well (Li, 2008). Zhou's (2008) empirical study indicates that there are significant differences in learners' incidental vocabulary acquisition through reading between two reading tasks with the same involvement loads. According to the theory, the tasks with the same involvement loads should be processed in the same way, resulting in the same results. He argues that the result is caused by the fact that even though there are the same involvement loads for the reading tasks, three components, need, search and evaluation take up different proportions. Meanwhile, Wu et al. (2010) consider that the task with higher involvement loads is identified by the component of search. Wu (2010) also thinks that the reason why the results of the studies mentioned above deviate from the Involvement Load Hypothesis is that it is based on two conditions, which cannot be satisfied. One is concerned with the degree to which the involvement load can be measured. The other involves how the involvement load influences the learners.

To sum up, from the aspects of learners' affect and cognitive factors, the Involvement Load Hypothesis exploits three components to evaluate the quality of incidental vocabulary acquisition through reading. Even though it has been found that there are some defects lying in this theory, there is no doubt that it has exerted a positive influence on learners' incidental vocabulary acquisition in the field of L2 teaching and learning.

2.7.3 Noticing Hypothesis

From our language learning experience, it may be easily found out that if we pay too much attention to passage comprehension in L2 reading, we will reduce our attention to language forms of some certain words. This phenomenon is caused by our limited capacity of noticing resources. It may be difficult for us to complete two different tasks at the same time, because of the noticing limitation.

From the perspective of cognition, Schmidt (1990) proposes the Noticing Hypothesis, based on the analysis of his own Portuguese learning journals. There are six factors that may have an effect on noticing, that is to say, frequency, expectation, perceptual salience, skill levels, task demands, and processing capacity of the learners, as well (Schmidt, 1990). Frequency refers to the times of reoccurrence of the target words in reading. The higher frequency the given word has, the more noticing it will receive. Expectation is to predict which input can be noticed by the learners, and whether noticing the input has received is proper in the context. Of course, in this process, teachers' instructions may increase the opportunities of learners' noticing the input. Perceptual salience indicates the significance of the language forms. Supposing that all the input is equal, the one that is more outstanding than the others is more likely to be noticed. Skill levels represent the automatic degrees of learners' processing ability, which is employed to deal with the input. In other words, the learners with higher degrees of automaticity of processing capacity tend to handle the input more efficiently, and are more likely to notice the target words. Task demands suggest the expected results of the behavior that language learners intend to perform. Processing capacity of the learners refers to learners' ability to handle the input. In a word, Schmidt holds the opinion that if the learners can focus on the input being processed, incidental vocabulary acquisition through reading is quite possible.

Schmidt (1995) thinks that noticing is confined to the elements of the surface structure of utterances in the input. It contains analysis and comparison of the input, as well as learners' ability to test hypothesis. He distinguishes attention from noticing. Noticing is the necessary and sufficient condition for the learners to transfer input to intake. That is, provided that the learners notice certain language forms, intake will be likely to take place.

Some L2 researchers have doubts about the Noticing Hypothesis proposed by Schmidt (1990, 1995). For example, Tomlin and Villa (1994) believe that without noticing, language acquisition is also possible. With perception, language knowledge can also be acquired. Truscott (1998) considers that the Noticing Hypothesis is an empty theory, with a weak basis both in theory and in practice. It does not illustrate which features of the input can be noticed and acquired, and it doesn't obtain support from cognitive scientific experiments, either.

Confronted with other scholars' criticisms, Schmidt (2001) makes some compromises. He holds the point of view that noticing is not the absolute condition for language acquisition. However, there is no doubt that noticing can facilitate language acquisition. Be that as it may, he still believes that learning without noticing will not bring potential benefits to the learners.

Different learners have different learning habits. It implies that the learners may notice different aspects of the target language in L2 learning, so as to produce different acquisition results. In the current research, the learners may notice different aspects of the target words, so as to obtain different acquisition results.

2.7.4 Input Hypothesis

The Input Hypothesis, one of the five hypotheses in L2 acquisition, proposed by Krashen (1985) is aimed to explain how L2 is acquired by the learners. He makes a distinction between acquisition and learning. The former is natural and unconscious, while the latter is conscious. The Input Hypothesis is only related to acquisition.

According to the Input Hypothesis, acquisition is likely to take place because of learners' understanding the comprehensible input, which is a little beyond their current level. If we suppose that the learners' current level is "i", the comprehensible input should be at the level of "i + 1". Only in this way can the learners acquire language knowledge along the "natural order", that is, moving from "i" to "i + 1".

Later, Krashen employs the Input Hypothesis in L2 vocabulary acquisition. It is found that the learners can incidentally acquire vocabulary in a most effective way through reading (Krashen, 1989). The best approach to vocabulary acquisition is to guess the meanings of unknown words from the corresponding contexts. Even though vocabulary is acquired incidentally, the effect is the best. This concept gets support from Lee and VanPatten (1995).

The implication of the Input Hypothesis for our current research is that the material we choose to examine learners' incidental vocabulary acquisition should be a little beyond their current level, that is, neither too difficult to get them overwhelmed, nor too easy to make it less challenging. To make it simple, the chosen reading material should be in accordance with the requirement of the comprehensible input.

2.7.5 Output Hypothesis

The Input Hypothesis acknowledges the importance of language input. However, output has been ignored. Based on his long - time research into immersion instruction of French in Canada, Swain (1985) finds out that the learners under this instruction can receive enough comprehensible input. According to Krashen's Input Hypothesis (1985, 1989), the learners should have a better understanding of the target language. Nevertheless, the story is not always true. The learners' performance in listening and reading is almost the same as that of the natives, while their performance in writing and speaking is inferior to that of the natives. The results make Swain puzzled, causing him to throw doubts about the Input Hypothesis, which leads to the emergence of the Output Hypothesis.

The basic concept of the Output Hypothesis (Swain, 1985) is that output is also an important method to enhance learners' language acquisition. Nobody will deny the fact that the comprehensible input is of great importance in language acquisition. But language output will make the learners more aware of their problems in language learning. They may exploit what has been learnt to complete the output tasks in hand, so as to facilitate language acquisition.

It is thought that there are three functions of language output, that is to say, noticing function, hypothesis testing function, as well as meta-linguistic function (Swain, 1995). When asked to produce some aspects of the target language, the learners may be trapped in the situation, under which they want to convey something, but some unknown words may prevent them from expressing themselves in the target language. In order to accomplish the given task, the learners may notice the problems they are confronted with, and employ their interlanguage system. In this process, the learners may exploit what they have learnt to test what they intend to produce. The receiver of the information may also provide some necessary feedback. After that, the learners will use language knowledge that has been learnt to modulate their L2 learning, so as to further facilitate L2 acquisition.

In summary, the output plays a significant part in learners' L2 learning. In the course of producing language output, the learners have to trigger their interlanguage system and notice the current problems they are facing. In the present research, the learners will be asked to accomplish two reading tasks related to the target words. They have to exploit different noticing resources, trying to guess the meanings of the target words and use them precisely. Consequently, learners' language acquisition will be improved in this way.

2.7.6 Summary

This section introduces the theoretical framework underlying the current research. The first three theories, that is, the Theory of Depth Processing, the Involvement Load Hypothesis and the Noticing Hypothesis lay psychological foundations for the current research, while the latter two, to be exact, the Input Hypothesis and the Output Hypothesis serve as the linguistic basis for the current research. Actually, the Theory of Depth

Processing is identical to the Involvement Load Hypothesis, with different perspectives to explicate that how the information is processed influences learners' incidental vocabulary acquisition (Gan and He, 2015). In other words, the deeper the information is processed, the greater involvement loads it will require, resulting in better gain and retention of vocabulary knowledge.

2.8 Summary

This chapter is composed of seven sections. The first section mainly introduces the definitions of incidental vocabulary acquisition and its advantages and disadvantages. The second section chiefly discusses the relationship between incidental vocabulary acquisition and L2 reading. The third section is about the factors which influence incidental vocabulary acquisition. The fourth section is involved in the ways to enhance the effects of learners' incidental vocabulary acquisition through L2 reading. The fifth section is concerned with the definitions, the classification, as well as the functions of glosses. The sixth section is of great significance. It reviews the previous studies into the effects of different types of glosses on learners' incidental vocabulary acquisition through reading. The last section presents the theoretical framework related to the current research.

Chapter Three Research Design

The current empirical research is composed of three empirical studies. One is to investigate the effects of glosses in different languages on learners' reading comprehension and their incidental vocabulary acquisition through reading. Another one is to check the effects of glosses with different options. The other one is to examine the effects of glosses in different positions in the text. Therefore, in this chapter, some information shared by these three experiments is presented in detail.

3.1 Reading Material

In the current research, the same reading text is used to examine the effects of different types of glosses on learners' reading comprehension and their incidental vocabulary acquisition through reading. The text is taken from one of the reading exercises in the reading textbook edited by Pasternak and Wrangell (2008), which is designed for the foreign English learners with intermediate language proficiency. The exercises are provided in the form of the worksheet. The title of the reading text is "Surviving the Sahara" with 513 words, from which 31 unfamiliar words were chosen by the researcher, and the teachers who were teaching English in the classes the participants belonged to. However, in the current three empirical studies, the learners who were in the same classes as the participants identified 23, 22 and 24 unknown words respectively, which they considered to be important. It means that the learners know 95.322% to 95.712% of the total words in the text, which demonstrates that the difficulty of the text is proper for the learners. Among these unfamiliar words, 10 target words were chosen in each empirical study. They were different from each other in each empirical study. Meanwhile, reading comprehension tasks were prepared. One was involved in 10 multiple-choice questions with four options, among which only one was the right answer. The other was to tell true or false for five statements. In total, there are 15 questions with 15 points.

According to the reading speed required by the CET Band Four, the average speed is 27.500 to 32.500 words per minute. The participants are all from first-year non-English majors. With the suggestions made by their English teachers, in the current research, the time for reading the text with two reading tasks is set to 20 minutes. In other words, the average reading speed is 25.650 words per minute, slightly slower than that required by the CET Band Four.

Concerning the teachers' comments on the reading material, the learners' current language proficiency, as well as the reading speed required to finish the reading tasks in three empirical studies, it may be concluded that the chosen reading text is proper, in accordance with the principle of "i+1" by Krashen (1985).

3.2 Time for the Delayed Vocabulary Test

As mentioned in Section 2.6.4, most of the scholars (Cheng and Good, 2009; Duan and Yan, 2004; Lv et al., 2005; Miyasako, 2002; Shi, 2010; Watanabe, 1997; Wu and Xu, 2009; Xu, 2010, etc.) investigating learners' incidental vocabulary acquisition set the delayed vocabulary test one or two weeks later after the immediate test. Some (Farvardin and Biria, 2012; Jacobs et al., 1994; Nagata, 1999; Rott, 2005, etc.) even provide the delayed test three weeks later, or longer than that. As to when the learners should take the delayed test, there is not a consensus.

Hermann Ebbinghaus (1913), based on his empirical investigation, puts forward the world - known "Ebbinghaus' Forgetting Curve", which is demonstrated in Figure 3.1. From the figure, it is clearly seen that as time goes on, the effect of the retention is becoming worse and worse. 6 days after the first learning, the learners can only memorize 25% of what they have learned. What's more, 31 days later, only 21% is kept in memory. It means that within the day of learning, the learners forget most of the information. However, one day later, the memory of the learners keeps relatively stable, with the memory loss becoming less and less. It is quite obvious that the memory loss between one week later and two weeks later does not differ too much.

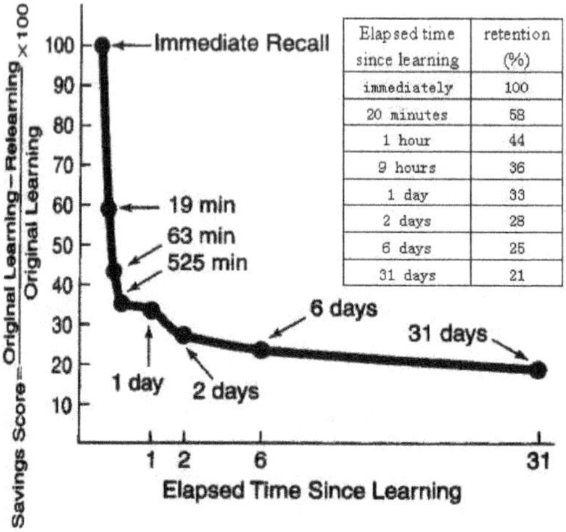

Elapsed time since learning	retention (%)
immediately	100
20 minutes	58
1 hour	44
9 hours	36
1 day	33
2 days	28
6 days	25
31 days	21

Figure 3.1 Ebbinghaus' Forgetting Curve (1913: 22)

Therefore, concerning the rule of forgetting, as well as the interval between the immediate vocabulary test and the delayed test in the previous studies, the delayed vocabulary test in the current research is set two weeks later. The vocabulary items in these two tests are the same, but in a different order.

3.3 Evaluation of Learners' Language Proficiency

In the current research, learners' language proficiency is evaluated by means of the Vocabulary Levels Test, which is "perhaps the most widely used vocabulary size test in the ESL context" (Schmitt, 2015: 219). This test is used for two purposes. One purpose is to check whether the participants have reached the vocabulary threshold required by incidental vocabulary acquisition. The other one is to help divide the participants into two groups, one group with higher language proficiency and the other with lower language proficiency, according to their vocabulary size.

The Vocabulary Levels Test, designed by Nation (1983, 1990), centers on vocabulary at four different frequency levels: 2,000, 3,000, 5,000 and 10,000. In the current research, the version adapted by Schmitt et al. (2001) is employed. Based on the form-recognition matching format, the test is composed of the definitions and the options for the target words. In each vocabulary level, there are 10 sections, each of which consists of 6 options and 3 definitions. The learners are required to match 3 options out of 6 with their corresponding definitions. Below is an example (cited from Schmitt, 2015: 312):

1. birth		
2. dust		
3. operation	5	game
4. row	6	winning
5. sport	1	being born
6. victory		

In the current research, two levels of the vocabulary test are employed, the 3,000 word level and the 5,000 word level. It is thought that the learners at the 3,000 word level have the initial access to reading the authentic materials, and that those at the 5, 000 word level are able to read these materials independently. The total score in these two tests is 60 points. According to Qin's (2003: 37) method, the learners are divided into two groups with different language proficiency, based on their scores in the tests.

3.4 Assessment of Incidental Vocabulary Acquisition

In order to evaluate the results of learners' incidental vocabulary acquisition, some means must be taken. In the current research, the Vocabulary Knowledge Scale is employed, because it is "the best known and most widely-used depth-of-knowledge scale" (Schmitt, 2015: 243).

The Vocabulary Knowledge Scale (shortened as VKS), designed to demonstrate learners' knowledge development of some given words at a specific period of time under the experimental or instructional situation, provides a relatively effective method to track the changes in the receptive and initial productive knowledge of some specific words, arising from instructional activities, such as reading and vocabulary exercises (Wesche and Paribakht, 1996). It is composed of five categories, employing a five-level rating scale (Paribakht and Wesche, 1997: 180), ranging from complete unfamiliarity with the word, and recognition of the word form and its specific meaning to the capability to use the word with grammatical accuracy and semantic appropriateness in the given sentence.

I. I don't remember having seen this word before.

II. I have seen this word before, but I don't know what it means.

III. I have seen this word before, and I think it means ______. (synonym or translation)

IV. I know this word. It means ________. (synonym or translation)

V. I can use this word in a sentence: ________. (Write a sentence.) (If you do this section, please also do Section IV.)

From the statement in each category mentioned above, Category I means that the learners do not know the word completely. Category II indicates that the learners only know the word form, but don't know what it actually means. Category III shows that the learners can recognize the word form, but they are not sure about the word meaning. Category IV requires the learners not only to know the word and its meaning, but also to prove their claims by means of writing its synonym or translating the word. Category V is the highest level, at which the learners should be able to use the word in a sentence with grammatical accuracy and semantic appropriateness. The first four categories are mainly concerned with the receptive knowledge of the word, from the word form to the word meaning. The last category is used to evaluate learners' productive knowledge of the word. To reach this level, the learners have to go through the former four categories. This concept also illustrates the incremental nature of vocabulary learning.

However, the most serious defect of the Vocabulary Knowledge Scale is that the first two categories are based on the learners' self-report. In order to make it more practical and more quantitative, another scale is introduced, which is illustrated in the following table.

Table 3.1 VKS Scoring Scale (Paribakht and Wesche, 1997: 181)

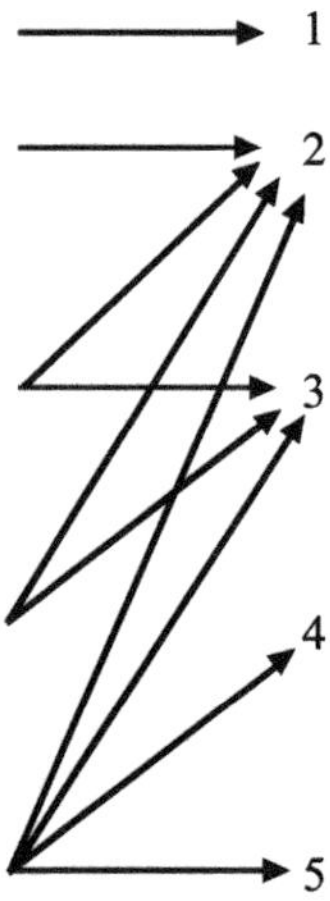

Self-report categories	Possible scores	Meaning of scores
Ⅰ	1	The word is not familiar at all.
Ⅱ	2	The word is familiar, but its meaning is not known.
Ⅲ	3	A correct synonym or translation is given.
Ⅳ	4	The word is used with semantic appropriateness in a sentence.
Ⅴ	5	The word is used with semantic appropriateness and grammatical accuracy in a sentence.

From the above table, it is manifest that the learners' self-report vocabulary knowledge level is identical with their corresponding response to each word. To be exact, Category I corresponds to the score of 1 (the word is not familiar at all) and Category II to the score of 2 (the word is familiar, but its meaning is not known). Categories III and IV result in the score of 3, if the learners can give a correct synonym for the target word, or a Chinese equivalent of the given word, or the score of 2, as a result of the learners failing to do so. As to Category V, it is rather complicated. It may be in response to the scores of 2, 3, 4 or 5. If the learners are able to use the given word with semantic appropriateness in the sentence, but with grammatical inaccuracy, they will be awarded with the score of 4. The learners will get the score of 5, if they are capable of using the word with grammatical accuracy and semantic appropriateness in the sentence. Category V may be likely to result in the score of 2 or 3, if the learners cannot provide an acceptable synonym or translation for the given word, or if they can only use the word with semantic appropriateness, but with grammatical inaccuracy. Accordingly, it is safe to conclude that there is not a one-to-one relationship between the learners' self-report category and the score. Therefore, during the administration of the current research, the participants are told that the self-report category is only employed as a means of self-evaluation, and that their actual performance in vocabulary knowledge tests is more important. There are 10 target words for each empirical research. Accordingly, the total score for each participant in each vocabulary test after reading is 50 points.

3.5 Summary

This chapter introduces some information shared in three empirical studies. To begin with, how the reading text is chosen, as well as how the target words are identified is explicated. Then the way to set the time for the delayed vocabulary test is illustrated. After that, the method taken to evaluate language proficiency of the participants is introduced. Finally, how to assess the results of learners' incidental vocabulary acquisition through reading is elaborated.

Chapter Four　Empirical Study I

This chapter is concerned with the first empirical study in the current research. To be specific, it centers on how glosses in different languages influence learners' reading comprehension and their incidental vocabulary acquisition through reading. In the following, how the study is carried out will be explicated in detail. The results and some discussion will be presented, as well.

4.1 Methodology

This section is concerned about the introduction of the methodology involved in the first empirical study. To start with, the research questions are addressed. What is followed is how the participants are chosen, as well as how they are divided into groups, according to their language proficiency. Finally, how the date is collected is presented.

4.1.1 Research Questions

This empirical study attempts to explore the relationship between glosses in different languages and learners' reading comprehension, together with their incidental vocabulary acquisition through reading. Therefore, the following questions are addressed.

1. Which type of glosses is more facilitative to learners' reading comprehension? Are there significant differences in reading comprehension between the learners with different language proficiency under different glossing conditions?

2. Which type of glosses is more beneficial to learners' incidental vocabulary acquisition through reading? Are there significant differences in vocabulary gain and vocabulary retention between the learners with different language proficiency under different glossing conditions?

3. Are there significant differences between learners' vocabulary gain and vocabulary retention under each glossing condition? Are there significant differences between vocabulary gain and vocabulary retention for the learners with different language proficiency?

4.1.2 Participants

The participants were 253 first-year non-English majors in 4 classes. They were required to take two vocabulary tests with the 3,000 and 5,000 word levels at the same time. Their scores were ranked in order from the highest to the lowest. According to Qin's (2003: 37) method, the participants whose scores were equal or higher than 42 belonged to the higher language proficiency group, while those whose scores were equal or lower than 36 belonged to the lower language proficiency group. Each group had 63 learners. Concerning the fact that the target words were glossed in four different ways, 60 participants were chosen in each group. The two groups were then subdivided into 4 subgroups, each of which was composed of 15 higher language proficiency learners and 15 lower language proficiency learners.

Table 4.1 Differences between the learners of four groups

Group	Proficiency	N	Mean	SD	t	Sig.(2-tailed)
CG	HLP	15	46.267	4.527	11.011	.000
	LLP	15	32.333	1.877		
EG	HLP	15	46.400	3.795	13.168	.000
	LLP	15	32.800	1.265		
CEG	HLP	15	46.200	4.313	11.632	.000
	LLP	15	32.267	1.710		
NG	HLP	15	46.133	2.850	17.431	.000
	LLP	15	32.133	1.246		
Total	HLP	60	46.250	3.825	26.071	.000
	LLP	60	32.383	1.530		

Note: CG: Chinese glosses; EG: English glosses; CEG: Chinese plus English glosses; NG: null glosses; HLP: higher language proficiency; LLP: lower language proficiency.

From the above table, it is clearly seen that there are significant differences between the participants with higher language proficiency and those with lower language proficiency ($t=26.071$, $p=.000<.01$). It is also found that significant differences exist between the learners with different language proficiency under each glossing condition (under the condition of Chinese glosses, $t=11.011$, $p=.000<.01$; under English glosses, $t=13.168$, $p=.000<.01$; under Chinese plus English glosses, $t=11.632$, $p=.000<.01$; under null glosses, $t=17.431$, $p=.000<.01$).

4.1.3 Target Words

As mentioned above, 120 learners out of 253 were chosen to participate in the study. The rest 133 learners identified 23 unfamiliar words. In the end, 10 target words were chosen, to be exact, 4 adjectives (equivalent, grueling, disoriented and blazing), 4 nouns (testament, mosque, urine and verge), and 2 verbs (combat and dehydrate). These unfamiliar words were glossed in Chinese, English, as well as Chinese plus English. The learners in the control group received the text with null glosses. What's more, the grammatical categories of the target words were provided, as well, to help the learners use the words correctly. The given glosses referred to Oxford Advanced Learners' English-Chinese Dictionary (2009). Glosses were provided on a separate paper (refer to Appendix Ⅱ to Ⅴ).

4.1.4 Date Collection

The reading text with glosses in Chinese, English, as well as Chinese plus English or with null glosses was handed to the participants, together with two reading comprehension tasks. They were required to finish the reading tasks within 20 minutes. After having handed in the papers, they would be given an immediate vocabulary test for the 10 target words with the format of the Vocabulary Knowledge Scale 10 minutes later, to assess the results of learners' vocabulary gain. In each group, 10 participants (5 with higher language proficiency and 5 with lower language proficiency) were required to have a semi - structured interview about their attitudes toward English reading and their opinions about glosses provided in reading. In total, 40 participants joined in the interview. Two weeks later, a delayed vocabulary test with the same items as the immediate vocabulary test, but in a different order, would be offered to the participants. All the participants didn't know that two vocabulary tests would be given in advance.

All the data collected was analyzed by means of SPSS 20.0.

4.2 Data Analysis and Results

In this part, the results of learners' reading comprehension, as well as their vocabulary gain and vocabulary retention will be presented. Meanwhile, the effects of language proficiency on learners' reading comprehension under the condition of glosses in different languages, and on their vocabulary gain and vocabulary retention through reading will also be demonstrated. The differences are compared between vocabulary gain and vocabulary retention for the learners with different language proficiency, as well.

4.2.1 Relationship between Learners' Language Proficiency and Reading Comprehension

This section is composed of two subsections. One is to introduce the results of learners' performance in reading comprehension under four different glossing conditions, that is to say, Chinese glosses, English glosses, Chinese plus English glosses, as well as null glosses. The other is to present the effects of learners' language proficiency on their reading comprehension under these four different glossing conditions.

4.2.1.1 Reading Comprehension under Four Glossing Conditions

The following table shows the results of learners' reading comprehension under four glossing conditions, Chinese glosses, English glosses, Chinese plus English glosses, as well as null glosses.

Table 4.2 Results of learners' reading comprehension under four glossing conditions

Group	N	Minimum	Maximum	Mean	SD
CG	30	7.000	14.000	10.667	2.073
EG	30	6.000	15.000	10.867	2.515
CEG	30	9.000	15.000	12.334	1.988
NG	30	7.000	13.000	8.767	1.654
Total	120	6.000	15.000	10.659	2.417

From the mean scores of learners' reading comprehension under four glossing conditions displayed in the above table, it can be concluded that Chinese plus English glosses are the most helpful to learners' reading comprehension (Mean=12.334), followed by English glosses (Mean=10.867) and Chinese glosses (M=10.667), while null glosses are the least facilitative (M= 8.767). Meanwhile, the mean score of all the participants' reading comprehension is 10.659, which may indicate that the learners do not have a good understanding of the reading text, even with the help of glosses. One possible reason may be that the learners who read the text without any glosses did not perform well in their reading comprehension, making the total score lower. According to the raw data provided by the learners who read the text with null glosses, more than half of the learners (18 participants out of 30) failed in their reading comprehension under this glossing condition. The above table also demonstrates that in this group, the highest score is 13, and that the lowest score is 7. The mean score in this group is 8.767, the lowest score among four groups.

The above analysis is mainly based on the mean score of each group under each glossing condition. Further analysis is needed to examine whether there are significant differences in learners' reading comprehension under four different types of glosses. The following table indicates that glossing conditions have a significant effect on learners' reading comprehension ($F=14.847$, $p=.000<.01$).

Table 4.3 Differences in learners' reading comprehension under four glossing conditions

	Sum of Squares	df	Mean Square	F	Sig.
Between Groups	192.825	3	64.275	14.847	.000
Within Groups	502.167	116	4.329		
Total	694.992	119			

The differences between four glossing conditions are illustrated in the following table. To begin with, it is obviously seen that there are significant differences in learners' reading comprehension between Chinese glosses and null glosses (Mean Difference=1.900, $p=.003<.01$), between English glosses and null glosses (Mean Difference=2.100, $p=.001<.01$), as well as between Chinese plus English glosses and null glosses (Mean Difference=3.567, $p=.000<.01$). Concerning the mean scores provided in Table 4.2, it can be concluded that glosses can significantly improve learners' reading comprehension, no matter what languages are employed in glosses. This result is consistent with the findings obtained by Davis (1989), Elekaei et al. (2015), Farvardin and Biria (2012), Meng and Chen (2015), and Rott (2005), while it is contrary to the findings discovered by Cheng and Good (2009), Holley and King (1971), Johnson (1982), as well as Wu et al. (2012), who all argue that glosses do not have any help to the learners in their reading comprehension.

Table 4.4 Differences in learners' reading comprehension between four glossing conditions

(I) Group	(J) Group	Mean Difference (I-J)	Std. Error	Sig.	95% Confidence Interval Lower Bound	95% Confidence Interval Upper Bound
CG	EG	-.200	.537	.982	-1.600	1.200
	CEG	-1.667*	.537	.013	-3.067	-.266
	NG	1.900**	.537	.003	.500	3.300
EG	CG	.200	.537	.982	-1.200	1.600
	CEG	-1.467*	.537	.036	-2.867	-.066
	NG	2.100**	.537	.001	.700	3.500
CEG	CG	1.667*	.537	.013	.266	3.067
	EG	1.467*	.537	.036	.066	2.867
	NG	3.567**	.537	.000	2.166	4.967
NG	CG	-1.900**	.537	.003	-3.300	-.500
	EG	-2.100**	.537	.001	-3.500	-.700
	CEG	-3.567**	.537	.000	-4.967	-2.166

Note: *<.05; **<.01

Concerning the relationship between glossing types and learners' reading comprehension, it is easily found that there are significant differences between Chinese plus English glosses and Chinese glosses (Mean Difference=1.667, $p=.013<.05$), and between Chinese plus English glosses and English glosses (Mean Difference=1.467, p=.036<.05). Taking into account the mean scores porivided in Table 4.2, it means that Chinese plus English glosses can significantly facilitate learners' reading comprehension. Nevertheless, Farvardin and Biria (2012) hold that L2 glosses are more conducive to learners' reading comprehension. Meanwhile, Meng and Chen (2015) argue that L1 glosses are more facilitative to learners' reading comprehension.

However, with regard to learners' reading comprehension under four glossing conditions, there are not any significant differences between Chinese glosses and English glosses (Mean Difference=.200, p=.982>.05).

In summary, the learners perform significantly differently under four different glossing conditions. To be exact, significant differenes in learners' reading comprehension are found between Chinese plus English glosses and Chinese glosses, English glosses, and null glosses. There are also significant differnces between Chinese glosses and null glosses, and between English glosses and null glosses. However, there are not any significant differences in learners' reading comprehenion between Chinese glosses and English glosses. In a word, glosses can be exploited to significantly facilitate learners' reading comprehension, espeicially Chinese plus English glosses .

4.2.1.2 Effects of Learners' Language Proficiency on Reading Comprehension

The following table shows the effects of learners' language proficiency on their reading comprehension under four different glossing conditions.

Table 4.5 Proficiency differences in learners' reading comprehension under four glossing conditions

Group	Proficiency	N	Mean	SD	F	t	Sig.
CG	HLP	15	12.200	1.320	.124	6.040	.000
	LLP	15	9.133	1.457			
EG	HLP	15	12.867	1.302	.925	7.276	.000
	LLP	15	8.867	1.685			
CEG	HLP	15	13.400	1.183	8.795	3.445	.002
	LLP	15	11.267	2.986			
NG	HLP	15	9.667	1.839	11.573	17.431	.002
	LLP	15	7.867	.743			
Total	HLP	60	12.034	2.008	.002	.968	.000
	LLP	60	9.284	1.975			

From the above table, it is manifest that there are significant differences in reading comprehension between the learners with higher language proficiency and those with lower language proficiency under four glossing conditions (F=.002, t=.968, p=.000<.01). Under each glossing condition, significant differences in reading comprehension are also found between the learners with different language proficiency (under the condition of Chinese glosses, F=.124, t=6.040, t=.000<.01; under English glosses, F=.925, t=7.276, t=.000<.01; under Chinese plus English glosses, F=8.795, t=3.445, t=.002<.01; under null glosses, F= 11.573, t=17.431, t=.002<.01). In a word, the learners with higher language proficiency perform significantly better than those with lower language proficiency, no matter what languages are used in glosses (for the learners with higher language proficiency, M=12.034; for the learners with lower language proficiency, M=9.284). To be detailed, for the learners with higher language proficiency, the mean score of reading comprehension is the highest under the condition of Chinese plus English glosses (M=13.400), followed by English glosses (M= 12.867) and Chinese glosses (M=12.200), while the lowest score is 9.667 under null glosses. Likewise, for the learners with lower language proficiency, the highest mean score of reading comprehension is 11.267 under the condition of Chinese plus English glosses, followed by Chinese glosses (M=9.133) and English glosses (M=8.867), while the lowest score is 7.867 under the condition of null glosses. The similarity between the mean scores of the reading comprehension for the learners with different language proficiency under each glossing condition is that null glosses are significantly the least conducive. Compared with the mean scores of learners' reading comprehension under each glossing condition, it is evident that Chinese plus English glosses are significantly the most facilitative to learners' reading comprehension, while null glosses are significantly the least beneficial.

In summary, glosses can significantly improve learners' reading comprehension, especially Chinese plus English glosses. As for the effects of learners' language proficiency, the learners with higher language proficiency significantly outperform those with lower language proficiency under each glossing condition.

4.2.2 Relationship between Learners' Language Proficiency and Incidental Vocabulary Acquisition

This section is mainly to report the results of learners' vocabulary gain and vocabulary retention through reading, based on the scores of the immediate vocabulary test and the delayed vocabulary test two weeks later after reading. The effects of learners' language proficiency on their vocabulary gain and vocabulary retention are provided, as well.

4.2.2.1 Results of the Immediate Vocabulary Test

The following table shows the results of learners' vocabulary gain under four glossing conditions. It is evident that the learners under the condition of Chinese plus English glosses get the best vocabulary gain (M=32.534), followed by Chinese glosses (M=31.034) and English glosses (M=29.834), while the worst vocabulary gain comes from reading under null glosses (M=28.734). What's more, the average score of the learners under four different glossing conditions is 30.534, just beyond the passing score.

Table 4.6 Results of learners' vocabulary gain

Group	N	Minimum	Maximum	Mean	SD
CG	30	27.000	34.000	31.034	1.921
EG	30	25.000	38.000	29.834	2.780
CEG	30	25.000	42.000	32.534	3.848
NG	30	25.000	35.000	28.734	2.900
Total	120	25.000	42.000	30.534	3.233

The table below demonstrates that under four glossing conditions, learners' vocabulary gain is significantly different (F=

9.216, p=.000<.01). It means that the languages employed in glosses have a significant effect on learners' vocabulary gain through reading.

Table 4.7 Differences in learners' vocabulary gain under four glossing conditions

	Sum of Squares	df	Mean Square	F	Sig.
Between Groups	239.400	3	79.800	9.216	.000
Within Groups	1004.467	116	8.659		
Total	1243.867	119			

The following table shows the differences of learners' vocabulary gain through reading between four different glossing conditions. From the data revealed in the table, it is obvious that there are not any significant differences in learners' vocabulary gain between Chinese glosses and English glosses (Mean Difference=1.200, p=.394>.05), and between Chinese plus English glosses and Chinese glosses (Mean Difference=1.500, p=.204>.05). In addition, significant differences are not found in learners' vocabulary gain, either, between English glosses and null glosses (Mean Difference=1.100, p=.472>.05).

Table 4.8 Differences in learners' vocabulary gain between four glossing conditions

(I) Group	(J) Group	Mean Difference (I-J)	Std. Error	Sig.	95% Confidence Interval Lower Bound	Upper Bound
CG	EG	1.200	.760	.394	-.781	3.181
	CEG	-1.500	.760	.204	-3.481	.481
	NG	2.300*	.760	.016	.320	4.281
EG	CG	-1.200	.760	.394	-3.181	.781
	CEG	-2.700**	.760	.003	-4.681	-.720
	NG	1.100	.760	.472	-.881	3.081
CEG	CG	1.500	.760	.204	-.481	3.481
	EG	2.700**	.760	.003	.720	4.681
	NG	3.800**	.760	.000	1.820	5.781
NG	CG	-2.300*	.760	.016	-4.281	-.320
	EG	-1.100	.760	.472	-3.081	.881
	CEG	-3.800**	.760	.000	-5.781	-1.820

Note: *<.05; **<.01

However, Table 4.8 clearly indicates that there are significant differences in learners' vocabulary gain through reading between Chinese glosses and null glosses (Mean

Difference=2.300, p=.016<.05). There also exist significant differences in learners' vocabulary gain between Chinese plus English glosses and English glosses (Mean Difference=2.700, p=.003<.01), and between Chinese plus English glosses and null glosses (Mean Difference=3.800, p=.000<.01).

Concerning the mean scores of learners' vocabulary gain under each glossing condition provided in Table 4.6, it can be concluded that among four glossing conditions, Chinese plus English glosses, as well as Chinese glosses can significantly facilitate learners' vocabulary gain through reading. This result confirms the studies conducted by Chen (2013), Shi (2010) and Xu (2010), who hold that Chinese plus English glosses are more facilitative to learners' vocabulary gain through reading. However, Cao and Song (2014), and Ko (2005) believe that L2 glosses are more helpful. In addition, Jacobs et al. (1994), Lv et al. (2005) and Miyasako (2002) argue that both L1 glosses and L2 glosses are conducive to learners' vocabulary gain.

The following table demonstrates that there are significant differences in vocabulary gain through reading between the learners with different language proficiency under four different glossing conditions (F=1.494, t=5.801, p=.000<.01). To be exact, significant differences exist in vocabulary gain between the learners with different language proficiency under the condition of English glosses (F=.728, t=3.943, p=.000<.01), Chinese plus English glosses (F=1.057, t=4.145, t=.000<.01), as well as null glosses (F=1.797, t=5.968, p=.000<.01). However, significant differences are not found in vocabulary gain between the learners with different language proficiency under Chinese glosses (F= 1.073, t=-.093, t=.926>.05).

Table 4.9 Proficiency differences in learners' vocabulary gain under four glossing conditions

Group	Proficiency	N	Mean	SD	F	t	Sig.(2-tailed)
CG	HLP	15	31.000	1.732	1.073	-.093	.926
	LLP	15	31.067	2.154			
EG	HLP	15	31.467	2.615	.728	3.943	.000
	LLP	15	28.200	1.860			
CEG	HLP	15	34.867	2.973	1.057	4.145	.000
	LLP	15	30.200	3.190			
NG	HLP	15	30.867	2.326	1.797	5.968	.000
	LLP	15	26.600	1.502			
Total	HLP	60	32.050	2.908	1.494	5.801	.000
	LLP	60	29.017	2.820			

It is seen clearly from the above table that the learners with higher language proficiency (M=32.050) perform significantly better than those with lower language proficiency (M=29.107).

To be specific, for the learners with higher language proficiency, the highest mean score of vocabulary gain is 34.867 under the condition of Chinese plus English glosses, followed by English glosses (M=31.467) and Chinese glosses (M=31.000), while the lowest mean score is 30.867 under null glosses. Meanwhile, for those with lower language proficiency, the highest mean score of vocabulary gain is 31.067 under the condition of Chinese glosses, followed by Chinese plus English glosses (M=30.200) and English glosses (M=28.200), while the lowest score is 26.600 under null glosses. The similarity between the mean scores of vocabulary gain for the learners with different language proficiency is that null glosses are significantly the least facilitative. For the learners with higher language proficiency, Chinese plus English glosses are significantly the most beneficial to learners' vocabulary gain. Even though for those with lower language proficiency, they perform better in vocabulary gain under the condition of Chinese glosses, significant differences are not found between the learners with different language proficiency. Therefore, it is safe to draw a conclusion that Chinese plus English glosses are significantly the most facilitative to learners' vocabulary gain through reading.

In summary, under four different glossing conditions, learners' vocabulary gain is significantly different. Chinese plus English glosses are the most conducive to learners' vocabulary gain, while null glosses are the least facilitative. With regard to glossing conditions, there are significant differences in learners' vocabulary gain between Chinese glosses and null glosses, as well as between Chinese plus English glosses and English glosses, and null glosses. As for the effects of learners' language proficiency, the learners with higher language proficiency perform significantly better in vocabulary gain through reading, especially under the condition of English glosses, Chinese plus English glosses, as well as null glosses, while under Chinese glosses, significant differences are not found between the learners with different language proficiency. In a word, Chinese plus English glosses are significantly the most facilitative to learners' vocabulary gain through reading, while null glosses are the least beneficial. However, what is worth mentioning is that under the condition of Chinese glosses, the learners with lower language proficiency perform slightly better in vocabulary gain than those with higher language proficiency, even though significant differences are not found between the learners under this glossing condition.

4.2.2.2 Results of the Delayed Vocabulary Test

Two weeks later, the participants were required to take a delayed vocabulary test to examine their vocabulary retention through reading. The following table demonstrates the results of learners' vocabulary retention through reading.

Table 4.10 Results of learners' vocabulary retention

Group	N	Minimum	Maximum	Mean	SD
CG	30	21.000	34.000	27.400	3.517
EG	30	21.000	33.000	27.367	3.908
CEG	30	24.000	32.000	29.067	2.463
NG	30	22.000	32.000	25.567	2.394
Total	120	21.000	34.000	27.350	3.284

From the table, it is easily found that the average score of learners' vocabulary retention is 27.350, lower than the required passing score. Learners' vocabulary retention through reading under the condition of Chinese plus English glosses is the best (Mean=29.067), while under null glosses, learners' vocabulary retention is the worst (Mean=25.567). Learners' vocabulary retention under Chinese glosses (Mean=27.400) and English glosses (Mean=27.367) is just in between.

Table 4.11 shows that under four different glossing conditions, learners' vocabulary retention through reading is significantly different (F=4.716, p=.004<.01). Taking into consideration the mean scores of learners' vocabulary retention under each glossing condition, it is evident that Chinese plus English glosses are significantly the most facilitative to learners' vocabulary retention through reading, while null glosses are the least conducive.

Table 4.11 Differences in learners' vocabulary retention under four glossing conditions

	Sum of Squares	df	Mean Square	F	Sig.
Between Groups	139.500	3	46.500	4.716	.004
Within Groups	1143.800	116	9.860		
Total	1283.300	119			

The above table displays that different glossing conditions have a significant effect on learners' vocabulary retention through reading. According to Table 4.12, to be specific, significant differences in learners' vocabulary retention through reading are not found between English glosses and Chinese glosses (Mean Difference=.567, $p=.897>.05$), null glosses and Chinese glosses (Mean Difference=.633, $p=.863>.05$), Chinese plus English glosses and English glosses (Mean Difference=1.700, $p=.160>.05$), as well as between English glosses and null glosses

(Mean Difference=1.200, p=.453>.05). However, there are significant differences in learners' vocabulary retention between Chinese plus English glosses and Chinese glosses (Mean Difference=2.267, p=.030<.05), and between Chinese plus English glosses and null glosses (Mean Difference=2.900, p=.003<.01). Concerning the mean scores of learners' vocabulary retention through reading provided in Table 4.10, the results indicate that Chinese plus English glosses are significantly the most beneficial to learners' vocabulary retention through reading. This result is consistent with the findings discovered by Chen (2013), Shi (2010) and Xu (2010), who all hold that Chinese plus English glosses are more facilitative to learners' vocabulary retention through reading. However, the result is against the findings obtained by Meng and Chen (2015), who argue that Chinese glosses are more helpful to learners' vocabulary retention. In addition, Jocobs et al. (1994), and Lv et al. (2005) think that both L1 glosses and L2 glosses are significantly facilitative to learners' vocabulary retention.

Table 4.12 Differences in learners' vocabulary retention between four glossing conditions

(I) Group	(J) Group	Mean Difference (I-J)	Std. Error	Sig.	95% Confidence Interval	
					Lower Bound	Upper Bound
CG	EG	-.567	.811	.897	-2.680	1.547
	CEG	-2.267*	.811	.030	-4.380	-.153
	NG	-.633	.811	.863	-1.480	2.747
EG	CG	.567	.811	.897	-1.547	2.680
	CEG	-1.700	.811	.160	-3.813	.413
	NG	1.200	.811	.453	-.913	3.313
CEG	CG	2.267*	.811	.030	.153	4.380
	EG	1.700	.811	.160	-.413	3.813
	NG	2.900**	.811	.003	.787	5.013
NG	CG	.633	.811	.863	-2.747	1.480
	EG	-1.200	.811	.453	-3.313	.913
	CEG	-2.900**	.811	.003	-5.013	-.787

Note: *<.05; **<.01

Table 4.13 reveals proficiency differences in learners' vocabulary retention through reading under four different glossing conditions. There are significant differences in vocabulary retention between the learners with higher language proficiency and those with lower language proficiency (F=.207, t=13.955, p=.000<.01). What's more, significant differences in vocabulary retention are also found between the learners with different language proficiency under each glossing condition (under the condition of Chinese glosses, F=4.189, t=10.151, p=.000<.01; under English glosses, F=.088, t=15.371, p=.000<.01; under Chinese plus English glosses, F=6.540, t= 7.755, p=.000<.01; under null glosses, F=5.375, t=5.101, p=.000<.01).

Taking into consideration the mean scores of vocabulary retention under each glossing condition, for the learners with higher language proficiency, Chinese plus English glosses are the most beneficial to learners' vocabulary retention (M=31.067), followed by English glosses (M=31.000) and Chinese glosses (M=29.867), while null glosses are the least conducive (M= 27.800). For the learners with lower language proficiency, Chinese plus English glosses are the most facilitative to learners' vocabulary retention (M=27.067), followed by Chinese glosses (M=24.933) and English glosses (M=23.733), while null glosses are the least helpful (M=23.333). To be simple, no matter what language proficiency the learners have, Chinese plus English glosses are significantly the most facilitative to learners' vocabulary retention through reading, while null glosses are the least beneficial. In addition, the learners with higher language proficiency (M=29.934) perform significantly better in vocabulary retention under four glossing conditions than those with lower language proficiency (M=24.767).

Table 4.13 Proficiency differences in learners' vocabulary retention under four glossing conditions

Group	Proficiency	N	Mean	SD	F	t	Sig.(2-tailed)
CG	HLP	15	29.867	1.995	4.189	10.151	.000
	LLP	15	24.933	1.223			
EG	HLP	15	31.000	1.309	.088	15.371	.000
	LLP	15	23.733	1.280			
CEG	HLP	15	31.067	.799	6.540	7.755	.000
	LLP	15	27.067	1.831			
NG	HLP	15	27.800	2.111	5.375	5.101	.000
	LLP	15	23.333	1.302			
Total	HLP	60	29.934	2.082	.207	13.955	.000
	LLP	60	24.767	1.960			

In summary, under four different glossing conditions in the delayed vocabulary test, learners' vocabulary retention through reading is significantly different. To be exact, learners' vocabulary retention through reading is significantly different between Chinese plus English glosses and Chinese glosses, and between Chinese plus English glosses and null glosses. It indicates that Chinese plus English glosses can significantly improve learners' vocabulary retention through reading. As for the effects of language proficiency, the learners with different language proficiency perform significantly differently under four different glossing conditions. Considering the mean scores of learners' vocabulary retention, it is also obvious that Chinese plus English glosses are significantly the most beneficial to learners' vocabulary retention.

4.2.2.3 Differences between Two Vocabulary Tests

The following table indicates that there are significant differences between learners' vocabulary gain and vocabulary retention under four different glossing conditions ($t=11.020$, $df=119$, $p=.000<.01$). Significant differences are also found between these two vocabulary tests under each glossing condition (under the condition of Chinese glosses, $t=5.822$, $df=29$, $p=.000<.01$; under English glosses, $t=4.762$, $df=29$, $p=.000<.01$; under Chinese plus English glosses, $t=6.526$, $df=29$, $p=.000<.01$; under null glosses $t=5.444$, $df=29$, $p=.000<.01$). Under the condition of Chinese glosses, the mean score of vocabulary gain ($M=31.034$) is higher than that of vocabulary retention ($M=27.400$); under English glosses, the mean score of vocabulary gain ($M=29.834$) is higher than that of vocabulary retention ($M=27.367$); under

Chinese plus English glosses, the mean score of vocabulary gain (M=32.534) is higher than that of vocabulary retention (M=29.067); under null glosses, the mean score of vocabulary gain (M=28.734) is also higher than that of vocabulary retention (M=25.567). In a word, learners' performance in vocabulary gain (M=30.534) is significantly better than theirs in vocabulary retention (M=27.350).

Based on the mean scores of learners' vocabulary gain and vocabulary retention from Table 4.14, we may come to a conclusion that Chinese plus English glosses are significantly the most beneficial to learners' incidental vocabulary acquisition through reading. This result is consistent with the findings obtained by Chen (2013), Shi (2010) and Xu (2010), who all argue that Chinese plus English glosses are the most facilitative to learners' incidental vocabulary acquisition through reading. However, some scholars (Cheng and Good, 2009; Hulstijn et al., 1996; Lv et al., 2005; Meng and Chen, 2015; Vela, 2015; Wu and Xu, 2009) hold that L1 glosses are more helpful. Other researchers (Chen and Leung, 1989; Farvardin and Biria, 2012; Ko, 2005; Kroll, 1993; Miyasako, 2002) think that L2 glosses are more conducive.

Table 4.14 Differences between learners' vocabulary gain and vocabulary retention under four glossing conditions

Group	Test	N	Mean	SD	t	df	Sig.(2-tailed)
CG	IVT	30	31.034	1.921	5.822	29	.000
	DVT	30	27.400	3.517			
EG	IVT	30	29.834	2.780	4.762	29	.000
	DVT	30	27.367	3.908			
CEG	IVT	30	32.534	3.848	6.526	29	.000
	DVT	30	29.067	2.463			
NG	IVT	30	28.734	2.900	5.444	29	.000
	DVT	30	25.567	2.394			
Total	IVT	120	30.534	3.233	11.020	119	.000
	DVT	120	27.350	3.284			

Note: IVT: the immediate vocabulary test; DVT: the delayed vocabulary test

Table 4.15 demonstrates the differences in vocabulary acquisition for the learners with higher language proficiency between these two vocabulary tests. Between these two vocabulary tests, there are significant differences in vocabulary acquisition for the learners with higher language proficiency (t=5.511, df=59, p=.000<.01). To be specific, for learners' vocabulary acquisition, significant differences are found between these two vocabulary tests under the condition of Chinese plus English glosses (t=5.442, df=14, p=.000<.01) and null glosses (t=3.570, df=14, p=.003<.01), while significant differences are not found under either Chinese glosses (t=1.839, df=14, p=.087>.05) or English glosses (t=.788, df=14, p=.444>.05).

Taking into account the mean scores of vocabulary acquisition for the learners with higher language proficiency, under the condition of Chinese plus English glosses, the mean score of vocabulary gain (M=34.867) is higher than that of vocabulary retention (M=31.067); under null glosses, the mean score of vocabulary gain (M=30.867) is also higher than that of vocabulary retention (M=27.800). This result not only shows that Chinese plus English glosses are significantly the most beneficial to learners' incidental vocabulary acquisition through reading, but also illustrates that for the learners with higher language proficiency, their performance in vocabulary gain (M=32.050) is significantly better than theirs in vocabulary retention (M=29.934).

Table 4.15 Differences between vocabulary gain and vocabulary retention for the learners with higher language proficiency

Group	Test	N	Mean	SD	t	df	Sig.(2-tailed)
CG	IVT	15	31.000	1.732	1.839	14	.087
	DVT	15	29.867	1.995			
EG	IVT	15	31.467	2.615	.788	14	.444
	DVT	15	31.000	1.309			
CEG	IVT	15	34.867	2.973	5.442	14	.000
	DVT	15	31.067	.799			
NG	IVT	15	30.867	2.326	3.570	14	.003
	DVT	15	27.800	2.111			
Total	IVT	60	32.050	2.908	5.511	59	.000
	DVT	60	29.934	2.082			

Table 4.16 indicates that there are significant differences in vocabulary acquisition for the learners with lower language proficiency under four different glossing conditions ($t=11.294$, $df=59$, $p=.000<.01$). To be exact, significant differences exist between these two vocabulary tests under the condition of Chinese glosses ($t=11.043$, $df=14$, $p=.000<.01$), English glosses

(t=10.269, df=14, p=.000<.01), Chinese plus English glosses (t=3.841, df=14, p=.002<.01), as well as null glosses (t=5.385, df=14, p=.000<.01). Considering the mean scores of learners' vocabulary gain and vocabulary retention, it is safe to conclude that the learners with lower language proficiency perform significantly better in their vocabulary gain (M=29.017) than in vocabulary retention (M=24.767).

Table 4.16　Differences between vocabulary gain and vocabulary retention for the learners with lower language proficiency

Group	Test	N	Mean	SD	t	df	Sig.(2-tailed)
CG	IVT	15	31.067	2.154	11.043	14	.000
	DVT	15	24.933	1.223			
EG	IVT	15	28.200	1.860	10.269	14	.000
	DVT	15	23.733	1.280			
CEG	IVT	15	30.200	3.190	3.841	14	.002
	DVT	15	27.067	1.831			
NG	IVT	15	26.600	1.502	5.385	14	.000
	DVT	15	23.333	1.302			
Total	IVT	60	29.017	2.820	11.294	59	.000
	DVT	60	24.767	1.960			

Taking into consideration the mean scores of learners' vocabulary gain and vocabulary retention under each glossing condition, under the condition of Chinese glosses, the mean score of vocabulary gain (M=31.067) is higher than that of vocabulary retention (M=24.933); under English glosses, the mean score of vocabulary gain (M=28.200) is higher than that of vocabulary retention (M=23.733); under Chinese plus English glosses, the mean score of vocabulary gain (M=30.200) is higher than that of vocabulary retention (M=27.067); under null glosses, the mean score of vocabulary gain (M=26.600) is also higher than that of vocabulary retention (M=23.333). Even though the mean score of learners' vocabulary gain under Chinese glosses (M=31.067) is higher than that under Chinese plus English glosses (M=30.200), the mean score of learners' vocabulary retention under Chinese plus English glosses (M=27.067) is much higher than that under Chinese glosses (M=24.933). Therefore, it is safe to conclude that for the learners with lower language proficiency, Chinese plus English glosses are significantly the most facilitative to learners' incidental vocabulary acquisition through reading.

From Table 4.15 and Table 4.16, it may be safe to conclude that for the learners with higher or lower language proficiency, Chinese plus English glosses are the most facilitative to their incidental vocabulary acquisition through reading. This result is inconsistent with the findings discovered by Lv et al., (2005), Miyasako (2002), Vela (2015), and Wang (2005), who argue that

L1 glosses are more beneficial to learners' incidental vocabulary acquisition through reading for those with lower language proficiency. In addition, Vela (2015) believes that both L1 glosses and L2 glosses are facilitative to learners' incidental vocabulary acquisition for those with higher language proficiency.

In summary, compared with the differences between these two vocabulary tests, the learners with different language proficiency perform significantly differently. For the learners with higher language proficiency, they perform significantly better in the immediate vocabulary test than in the delayed test, however, significant differences are only found under the condition of Chinese plus English glosses and null glosses. For those with lower language proficiency, they conduct significantly better in the immediate vocabulary test, and so do they under each glossing condition. In brief, Chinese plus English glosses are significantly the most beneficial to learners' incidental vocabulary acquisition through reading.

4.3 Discussion

From the data analysis mentioned above, some conclusions can be made briefly. To begin with, with regard to learners' reading comprehension under four glossing conditions, glosses can be employed to facilitate learners' reading comprehension, especially Chinese plus English glosses. The result is consistent with the findings discovered by Davis (1989), Elekaei et al. (2015), Farvardin and Biria (2012), Meng and Chen (2015), and Rott (2005), who all argue that glosses can help to improve learners' reading comprehension, However, Cheng and Good (2009), Holley and King (1971), Johnson (1982), as well as Wu et al. (2012), who hold that glosses do not have any help to the learners in their reading comprehension. As for the languages employed in glosses, Farvardin and Biria (2012) hold that L2 glosses are more conducive to learners' reading comprehension. Nevertheless, Meng and Chen (2015) argue that L1 glosses are more facilitative to learners' reading comprehension.

According to the participants' interview about their attitudes toward English reading, some participants hold that English reading is really difficult, especially for the learners with lower language proficiency. In fact, reading comprehension is not only involved in reading itself. It is the comprehensive use of English knowledge, including English grammar and vocabulary. Sometimes, it may be rather difficult to get the main idea of the reading text, because of some unfamiliar words. However, at times, the reading difficulty may lie in the understanding of the text. It means that the combination of specified English knowledge counts with the understanding ability of language learners. Some participants have mentioned that they only read English in class. After class, they seldom read English, even though English teachers have told them many times that reading is of great importance in English learning, especially in varieties of English proficiency tests. However, more time is needed in English reading to deal with the unfamiliar words and the problems of text understanding. At the same time, progress in English reading comprehension is so slow that most of the learners are not willing to spend their time on English reading. In short, on one hand, English reading is of great significance in English learning; on the other hand, because of some reasons the learners do not want to spend their time on English reading. This is one of the serious problems existing in our current English reading teaching.

Nevertheless, some learners think English reading is quite interesting. They may know more from English reading than those who do not like English reading. We cannot deny the fact that English is the most widely used language in the world. Accordingly, some latest information is provided in English. With the constant expansion of international communication, English is also frequently seen in our daily lives. Therefore, the learners can know more about what is happening in the world through English reading. In addition, reading can be employed as a facilitative method to foster English learning. Just as what has been mentioned above, English reading is actually the comprehensive use of English knowledge. In the course of reading, English grammar is tested. All of us many encounter this situation, in which we know all the words in a given sentence, however, we cannot figure out what it really means. At this time, grammar counts. With the help of grammar, we can divide the sentence into different segments, and then get its accurate meaning. With regard to English vocabulary, it is rather difficult to memorize English words, because we seldom use them in our daily lives. But in reading, we may encounter an unfamiliar word more than two or three times, which can help us memorize the word and with the help of the context, we may also know its usage clearly. In a word, reading can help the learners to learn English vocabulary. Finally, English reading can give the learners a sense of achievements. According to the participants' interview, almost all the learners with higher language proficiency have got fairly better reading performance in tests, which is confirmed in this empirical study. The scores of reading comprehension for the learners with higher language proficiency under each glossing condition are higher than those with lower language proficiency. Even for the learners with lower language proficiency, they may get higher scores in a test because of their better performance in English reading. Hence, the opinion that a student who does well in reading will get higher points in the English test is widely accepted in English teaching and learning.

Therefore, even if the learners with higher language proficiency and those with lower language proficiency have different points of view about English reading, there is a consensus that English reading is of great importance in English learning.

As for glosses, in this empirical study, four different glossing conditions are involved, that is, Chinese glosses, English glosses, Chinese plus English glosses, as well as null glosses. According to the interview, all the participants agree that glosses can help them better understand the text. This may indicate that the learners tend to know as many words as possible while reading. However, in reading, it is really not necessary to know all the words. We may choose what should be known according to their importance in the sentence understanding. For those important unfamiliar words, some guessing strategies may be employed. We may guess the meanings of the words, according to the context, the formation of the words, as well as their relationship to the other words. Of course, with the help of glosses, we may easily figure out the meanings of some unknown words. However, this may lead to the loss of the opportunity to use some reading strategies. In any case, glosses can aid the learners to better comprehend the text, which is confirmed in this empirical study.

With regard to the languages used in glosses, the learners with different language proficiency have different standpoints. In total, 40 participants are involved in the interview, 20 with higher language proficiency and 20 with lower language proficiency. 28 learners (8 with higher language proficiency and 20 with lower language proficiency) are in favor of Chinese glosses. 26 learners

(18 with higher language proficiency and 8 with lower language proficiency) would like to receive English glosses. 34 learners (20 with higher language proficiency and 14 with lower language proficiency) prefer to have Chinese plus English glosses. For null glosses, only 4 learners with higher language proficiency choose this type. Every day, we are surrounded in the Chinese-speaking context. Even though English is widely seen in our daily lives, it is actually seldom used. All the participants have been learning English for at least 7 years. However, out of class, they hardly use English. Even for the learners with higher language proficiency, they only get higher points in English tests, having less to do with the actual use of English. Therefore, they like to have Chinese glosses. However, their views are partially supported in this empirical study.

For English glosses, the learners with higher language proficiency think that the best way of learning English is to be immersed in the English context, even though there are not many chances for them to use English. After all, practice makes perfect. This may also help to explain why all the learners with higher language proficiency tend to choose Chinese plus English glosses. For the learners with lower language proficiency, although they may have some difficulty in understanding glosses, they still think that it is better to learn L2 under the target language environment. They also hold that their native language may also have some positive assistance with English learning.

Therefore, most of them choose Chinese plus English glosses and some of them pick out English glosses. The learners' opinions about Chinese plus English glosses are supported in this empirical study.

Why do 4 learners choose null glosses? They report that they only want to see how much they can understand the text and how well they can perform in reading without any glosses. This also implies that the learners are inclined to have glosses in reading.

Concerning the effects of language proficiency, the learners with higher language proficiency perform significantly better than those with lower language proficiency in the empirical study. The learners' language proficiency with their attitudes toward different types of glossing may account for this result. Reading ability is one of the indicators of English learners' language proficiency. Especially, in the empirical study, the learners' language proficiency is evaluated by means of their vocabulary size. A larger vocabulary size really helps in English reading. It may aid the learners to better comprehend the text. Meanwhile, in the teaching practice, it is often discovered that the learners who have higher English language proficiency usually have relatively higher Chinese language proficiency. This may indicate that there are some similarities in language learning. Together with the learners' opinions about different types of glosses mentioned above, the learners with higher language proficiency perform significantly better than those with lower language proficiency.

In addition, in the immediate vocabulary test, there are significant differences in vocabulary gain under four different glossing conditions. To be precise, significant differences are found between Chinese plus English glosses and English glosses, Chinese plus English glosses and null glosses, as well as between Chinese glosses and null glosses. What's more, in the delayed test, significant differences also exist in learners' vocabulary retention under four different glossing conditions. To be exact, there are significant differences between Chinese plus English glosses and Chinese glosses, and between Chinese plus English glosses and null glosses. From these two vocabulary tests, we may come to a conclusion that Chinese plus English glosses can significantly improve learners' incidental vocabulary acquisition through reading. This result is consistent with the findings obtained by Chen (2013), Shi (2010) and Xu (2010), who all argue that Chinese plus English glosses are the most facilitative to learners' incidental vocabulary acquisition through reading. However, some scholars (Chen and Leung, 1989; Cheng and Good, 2009; Farvardin and Biria, 2012; Hulstijn et al., 1996; Ko, 2005; Kroll, 1993; Lv et al., 2005; Meng and Chen, 2015; Miyasako, 2002; Vela, 2015; Wu and Xu, 2009, etc.) hold that L1 glosses or L2 glosses are more helpful.

With regard to the effects of learners' language proficiency, there are significant differences in their vocabulary gain under four different glosses, except under the condition of Chinese glosses. In the delayed vocabulary test, significant differences exist in learners' vocabulary retention under each glossing condition.

Compared with the differences between two vocabulary tests, learners' performance in vocabulary gain and vocabulary retention is significantly different under each glossing condition. As to the effects of language proficiency, learners' vocabulary gain and vocabulary retention are significantly different for the learners with higher language proficiency. However, significant differences only exist under the condition of Chinese plus English glosses and null glosses. For the learners with lower language proficiency, significant differences are found under each glossing condition between two vocabulary tests. However, Lv et al. (2005), Miyasako (2002), Vela (2015), and Wang (2005) argue that L1 glosses are more beneficial to learners' incidental vocabulary acquisition through reading for those with lower language proficiency. In addition, Vela (2015) believes that both L1 glosses and L2 glosses are facilitative to learners' incidental vocabulary acquisition for those with higher language proficiency.

Generally speaking, no matter what language proficiency the learners have, and no matter when the vocabulary test is given, Chinese plus English glosses are significantly the most facilitative to learners' incidental vocabulary acquisition through reading.

Based on the Noticing Hypothesis, Chinese plus English glosses may attract more attention from the learners in the course of reading. Meanwhile, this kind of glosses combines two languages together, Chinese and English. No matter how long the learners have learnt English, it is rather difficult for them to completely get rid of the Chinese thinking mode. Meanwhile, English glosses may help them better understand the words. It is quite common that the Chinese meanings of two given English words are really similar in that there are so many synonymous words in English. However, English explanations may help the learners to differentiate them from each other. Taking into consideration the learners' reading habit that they tend to figure out the meaning of each word in the text, they have to spend more time on the Chinese plus English gloss given to a certain word, resulting in deeper processing of the word, according to the Depth of Processing Hypothesis. In other words, this type of glosses requires more involvement loads from the learners. Therefore, reading under the condition of Chinese plus English glosses, the learners can better understand the target words, so as to keep them longer in their memory.

What's more, in the immediate vocabulary test, Chinese glosses can significantly help learners' vocabulary gain than null glosses, while significant differences disappear in learners' vocabulary retention. This result may indicate that Chinese language may help the learners to learn English, to some extent. But it only has a limited effect on their English learning. After all, most of the learners desire to learn English in the immersion learning environment, just as what has been mentioned in the interview.

Furthermore, one point needs to be mentioned. For vocabulary gain, the learners with lower language proficiency perform slightly better than those with higher language proficiency under the condition of Chinese glosses, even though there are not significant differences between these two groups of the learners. According to the interview, among four different glossing conditions, all the learners with lower language proficiency are in favor of Chinese glosses. And they actually perform better in vocabulary gain than those with higher language proficiency under this glossing condition. Two reasons may account for this result. For one thing, the learners with lower language proficiency are more dependent on Chinese in English learning, even though they know the immersion learning is greatly important. Meanwhile, they have also been accustomed to reading English with the help of Chinese to comprehend the text. For another, the evaluation of vocabulary gain employs the format of Vocabulary Knowledge Scale, in which the word meaning carries greater weight. To some extent, this testing method may be advantageous for the learners with lower language proficiency. Maybe, the luck in the test also works.

After all, the score of the learners with lower language proficiency is only .067 higher than that of those with higher language proficiency.

4.4 Summary

This chapter mainly concentrates on the first empirical study, investigating the relationship between learners' language proficiency and their reading comprehension, together with their incidental vocabulary acquisition through reading under four different glossing conditions, that is, Chinese glosses, English glosses, Chinese plus English glosses and null glosses.

To begin with, the methodology employed in the empirical study is introduced, including research questions, the participants, the target words and the data collection. What is followed is learners' performance in reading comprehension under four different glossing conditions. Meanwhile the effects of learners' language proficiency on their reading comprehension under each glossing condition are illustrated, as well.

In the following, the results of the immediate vocabulary test and the delayed vocabulary test are reported, together with language proficiency differences in these two vocabulary tests under each glossing condition. Finally, the differences between vocabulary gain and vocabulary retention are compared, along with the effects of learners' language proficiency on incidental vocabulary acquisition through reading.

Finally, some reasons which account for the results in the empirical study are provided. Chinese plus English glosses are significantly the most facilitative type of glosses not only for learners' reading comprehension, but also for their vocabulary gain and vocabulary retention through reading. This general conclusion supports the Involvement Load Hypothesis and the Theory of Depth Processing. In other words, the information which requires greater involvement loads results in deeper processing, so as to make it stored longer in memory.

Chapter Five Empirical Study II

This chapter is chiefly concerned with the second empirical study. From the first empirical study, it is known that Chinese plus English glosses can significantly improve learners' reading comprehension and their incidental vocabulary acquisition through reading. The topic about the number of the options provided to glosses for the unfamiliar words in reading has been discussed in detail in Section 2.6.2. If too many options are provided to glosses, the nature of incidental vocabulary acquisition is likely to get changed. It means that intentional vocabulary acquisition may take place. Meanwhile, Hulstijn (1992) argues that for multiple-choice glosses, two options will be better. Therefore, two options at the most are provided to glosses. Consequently, the second empirical study attempts to investigate the effects of single Chinese plus English glosses and multiple-choice Chinese plus English glosses with two options on reading comprehension and incidental vocabulary acquisition through reading for the learners with different language proficiency.

5.1 Methodology

5.1.1 Research Questions

In this empirical study, there are 3 questions involved.

1. Which type of glosses is more facilitative to learners' reading comprehension? Are there significant differences in reading comprehension between the learners with different languagc proficiency under different glossing conditions?

2. Which type of glosses is more beneficial to learners' incidental vocabulary acquisition through reading? Are there significant differences in vocabulary gain and vocabulary retention between the learners with different language proficiency under different glossing conditions?

3. Are there significant differences between learners' vocabulary gain and vocabulary retention under each glossing condition? Are there significant differences between vocabulary gain and vocabulary retention for the learners with different language proficiency?

5.1.2 Participants

215 first-year non-English majors from 4 classes were chosen. They were asked to take two vocabulary tests, one with the 3,000 word level, and the other with the 5,000 word level. According to Qin's (2003: 37) method, the participants whose scores were

equal or higher than 44 belonged to the higher language proficiency group, while those whose scores were equal or lower than 34 belonged to the lower language proficiency group. In each group, there were 53 participants. These participants were subdivided into two groups, each group with 40 learners. One group were requested to read the passage with 10 target words explained with single Chinese plus English glosses, and the other group to read the same passage with the same target words explained with multiple-choice Chinese plus English glosses with two options.

Table 5.1 Differences between the learners of two groups

Group	Proficiency	N	Mean	SD	t	Sig.(2-tailed)
SCEG	HLP	20	47.200	3.054	19.734	.000
	LLP	20	32.950	1.050		
MCEG	HLP	20	46.550	3.316	17.843	.000
	LLP	20	32.150	1.424		
Total	HLP	40	46.875	3.164	29.871	.000
	LLP	40	32.550	1.300		

Note: SCEG: single Chinese plus English glosses; MCEG: multiple-choice Chinese plus English glosses with two options; HLP: higher language proficiency; LLP: lower language proficiency.

According to the above table, it is clearly seen that there are significant differences between the learners with higher language proficiency and those with lower language proficiency ($t=29.871$, $p=.000<.01$). In addition, significant differences are also found under two different glossing conditions (under the condition of single Chinese plus English glosses, $t=19.734$, $p=.000<.01$; under multiple-choice Chinese plus English glosses with two options, $t=17.843$, $p=.000<.01$).

5.1.3 Target Words

Two groups of the first-year non-English majors were involved in this empirical study. There were 53 learners in each group. In addition, in each group, 40 learners were subdivided into two groups to deal with the reading passage with the target words explained with different options of Chinese plus English glosses. That means the rest, 135 learners out of 215 participants did not actually participate in the study. These learners would be required to read the passage, and then pick out which words were unfamiliar to them.

In total, they identified 22 unknown words, among which 10 were chosen as the target words in this empirical study. Exactly speaking, there were 6 adjectives (equivalent, tough, grueling, enthusiastic, blazing, and fierce), 2 nouns (testament and shelter), as well as 2 verbs (combat and abandon). These words were explained with either single Chinese plus English glosses or multiple-choice Chinese plus English glosses with two options.

What's more, the grammatical categories of the words were also offered to the participants. Glosses provided referred to Oxford Advanced Learners' English-Chinese Dictionary (2009). Glosses were presented to all the participants on a separate paper (refer to Appendix Ⅵ to Ⅶ).

5.1.4 Date Collection

In all, 80 participants were divided into 2 groups, each of which had 40 learners. They were then subdivided into 2 groups, according to their language proficiency. In each subgroup, there were 20 learners with higher language proficiency and 20 with lower language proficiency. The participants in each subgroup were asked to read the same passage with the same reading comprehension tasks as the one mentioned in Chapter Four. The participants in each subgroup were required to finish reading the passage and completing the reading comprehension tasks within 20 minutes with the help of glosses provided to the target words. After 10 minutes of a short break, they would be requested to take an immediate vocabulary test with the format of the Vocabulary Knowledge Scale, to evaluate learners' vocabulary gain through reading. In each subgroup, 10 participants (5 with higher language proficiency and 5 with lower language proficiency) were asked to have a semi-structured interview about their attitudes towards the options of glosses presented to the target words in reading. In all, 20 learners were concerned. Two weeks later, a delayed vocabulary test, which had the same vocabulary items as those in the immediate vocabulary test, but in a different order, was given to the same group of the participants, to value learners' vocabulary retention under two different glossing conditions. All the participants did not know that after reading, two vocabulary tests would be given, in advance.

All the data collected was analyzed with the help of SPSS 20.0.

5.2 Data Analysis and Results

This part is to report the results of the effects of two different glossing conditions on reading comprehension and incidental vocabulary acquisition through reading for the learners with different language proficiency. One is to provide single Chinese plus English glosses, and the other is to offer multiple-choice Chinese plus English glosses with two options. In the following, the effects of two different glossing conditions on learners' reading comprehension will be presented, first of all.

5.2.1 Relationship between Learners' Language Proficiency and Reading Comprehension

This section concentrates on learners' reading comprehension under two different glossing conditions. Meanwhile, the effects of learners' language proficiency on reading comprehension under two different glossing conditions are also illustrated.

5.2.1.1 Reading Comprehension under Two Glossing Conditions

The following table shows the results of learners' reading comprehension under two different glossing conditions, that is, single Chinese plus English glosses and multiple-choice Chinese plus English glosses with two options.

Table 5.2 Results of learners' reading comprehension under two glossing conditions

Group	N	Minimum	Maximum	Mean	SD
SCEG	40	8.000	15.000	11.950	1.753
MCEG	40	8.000	15.000	11.050	1.840
Total	80	8.000	15.000	11.500	1.842

Table 5.2 shows clearly that for learners' reading comprehension, they get the higher score under the condition of single Chinese plus English glosses (M=11.950) than under multiple-choice Chinese plus English glosses with two options (M=11.050). In addition, the average score of the participants under two different glossing conditions is 11.500, beyond the required passing score.

Table 5.3 Differences in learners' reading comprehension under two glossing conditions

	Sum of Squares	df	Mean Square	F	Sig.
Between Groups	16.200	1	16.200	5.018	.028
Within Groups	251.800	78	3.228		
Total	268.000	79			

The above table demonstrates that there are significant differences in learners' reading comprehension under two different glossing conditions ($F=5.018$, $p=.028<.05$).

Concerning the results revealed in Table 5.2, learners' reading comprehension is significantly better under the condition of single Chinese plus English glosses than under multiple-choice Chinese plus English glosses with two options. Therefore, it can be concluded that between two different glossing conditions, single Chinese plus English glosses can be significantly facilitative to learners' reading comprehension. This result is contrary to the findings discovered by Rott (2005), who claims that multiple - choice glosses are more conducive to learners' reading comprehension. It also indirectly demonstrates that glosses provided in L2 reading can help the learners to better comprehend the text.

5.2.1.2 Effects of Learners' Language Proficiency on Reading Comprehension

The following table demonstrates the effects of language proficiency on learners' reading comprehension under two different glossing conditions.

Table 5.4 Proficiency differences in learners' reading comprehension under two glossing conditions

Group	Proficiency	N	Mean	SD	F	t	Sig.
SCEG	HLP	20	13.050	1.050	3.729	5.072	.000
	LLP	20	10.850	1.631			
MCEG	HLP	20	12.250	1.618	2.528	5.428	.000
	LLP	20	9.850	1.136			
Total	HLP	40	12.650	1.406	.087	7.133	.000
	LLP	40	10.350	1.477			

It is obviously seen from the above table that there are significant differences in reading comprehension between the learners with higher language proficiency and those with lower language proficiency (F=.087, t=7.133, p=.000<.01).

As for glossing conditions, significant differences in reading comprehension are also found under the condition of both single

Chinese plus English glosses ($F=3.729$, $t=5.072$, $p=.000<.01$) and multiple-choice Chinese plus English glosses with two options ($F=2.528$, $t=5.428$, $p=.000<.01$) between the learners with different language proficiency.

In terms of the mean scores, under the condition of single Chinese plus English glosses, the mean score for the learners with higher language proficiency is 13.050, while the mean score for those with lower language proficiency is 10.850; under multiple-choice Chinese plus English glosses with two options, the mean score for the learners with higher language proficiency is 12.250, while the mean score for those with lower language proficiency is 9.850. Under these two different glossing conditions, the mean score for the learners with higher language proficiency is 12.650, while the mean score for those with lower language proficiency is 10.350. From the perspective of the mean scores, it may be safe to draw a conclusion that single Chinese plus English glosses are significantly more beneficial to learners' reading comprehension, compared with multiple-choice Chinese plus English glosses with two options. This result is against the findings discovered by Rott (2005), who holds that multiple-choice glosses can greatly facilitate learners' reading comprehension.

In summary, the number of glosses provided in reading has a significant effect on learners' reading comprehension. To be exact, the learners perform significantly better under the condition of single Chinese plus English glosses in reading comprehension than under multiple-choice Chinese plus English glosses with two options. What's more, significant differences are also found between the learners with different language proficiency under the condition of both single Chinese plus English glosses and multiple-choice Chinese plus English glosses with two options. Taking into consideration the mean scores of learners' reading comprehension in each group, to be brief, we may come to a conclusion that single Chinese plus English glosses are significantly more advantageous to learners' reading comprehension.

5.2.2 Relationship between Learners' Language Proficiency and Incidental Vocabulary Acquisition

This section is chiefly concerned with the effects of the number of glosses (single Chinese plus English glosses and multiple-choice Chinese plus English glosses with two options) on learners' vocabulary gain and vocabulary retention through reading. At the same time, it is involved in whether learners' language proficiency has a significant effect on their vocabulary gain and vocabulary retention under two different glossing conditions.

5.2.2.1 Results of the Immediate Vocabulary Test

The following table displays the results of learners' vocabulary gain in the immediate vocabulary test after reading the passage under two different glossing conditions.

Table 5.5 Results of learners' vocabulary gain

Group	N	Minimum	Maximum	Mean	SD
SCEG	40	30.000	45.000	36.325	3.970
MCEG	40	28.000	43.000	34.600	3.410
Total	80	28.000	45.000	35.463	3.779

From Table 5.5, it is clearly seen that in the immediate vocabulary test, the mean score of learners' vocabulary gain is 35.463, which is higher than the required passing score. With the help of single Chinese plus English glosses in reading, the average score of learners' vocabulary gain is 36.325, while under the condition of multiple-choice Chinese plus English glosses with two options, the mean score is 34.600. It may be concluded that the learners perform better in vocabulary gain through reading under the condition of single Chinese plus English glosses than under multiple-choice Chinese plus English glosses with two options.

Table 5.6 Differences in learners' vocabulary gain under two glossing conditions

	Sum of Squares	df	Mean Square	F	Sig.
Between Groups	5.000	1	5.000	.317	.004
Within Groups	1231.00	78	15.782		
Total	1236.00	79			

Table 5.6 clearly demonstrates that the number of glosses provided in reading has a significant effect on learners' vocabulary gain through reading ($F=.317$, $p=.004<.01$). Considering the mean scores of learners' vocabulary gain under two different glossing conditions provided in Table 5.5, it may be safe to come to a conclusion that single Chinese plus English glosses are significantly more conducive to learners' vocabulary gain through reading than multiple-choice Chinese plus English glosses with two options. This result agrees with the one found by Jasteh and Akbarpour (2011), who claim that single glosses are more facilitative to learners' vocabulary gain through reading.

The following table presents the differences between the learners with higher language proficiency and those with lower language proficiency in vocabulary gain under two different glossing conditions.

Table 5.7　Proficiency differences in learners' vocabulary gain under two glossing conditions

Group	Proficiency	N	Mean	SD	F	t	Sig.(2-tailed)
SCEG	HLP	20	36.600	3.747	.247	.433	.007
	LLP	20	36.050	4.261			
MCEG	HLP	20	34.750	4.633	19.825	.275	.035
	LLP	20	34.450	1.538			
Total	HLP	40	35.675	4.573	7.682	.563	.043
	LLP	40	35.250	3.264			

According to the above table, it is evident that the learners with different language proficiency perform significantly differently in terms of vocabulary gain through reading (F=7.682, t=.563, p=.043<.05). To be exact, there are significant differences between the learners with higher language proficiency and those with lower language proficiency under the condition of both single Chinese plus English glosses (F=.247, t=.433, p=.007<.01) and multiple - choice Chinese plus English glosses with two options (F=19.825, t=.275, p=.035<.05).

It is clearly seen from the above table that the learners with higher language proficiency (M=35.675) perform significantly better than those with lower language proficiency (M=35.250). Even though significant differences in vocabulary gain between the learners with different language proficiency are found under the condition of both single Chinese plus English glosses and multiple - choice Chinese plus English glosses with two options, in terms of the mean scores of vocabulary gain in each subgroup for the learners with different language proficiency, it may be safe to arrive at a conclusion that single Chinese plus English glosses (the mean scores of vocabulary gain for the learners with different language proficiency are 36.600 and 36.050, respectively) are significantly more facilitative to learners' vocabulary gain through reading than multiple - choice Chinese plus English glosses with two options (the mean scores of vocabulary gain for the learners with different language proficiency are 34.750 and 34.450, respectively).

In summary, there are significant differences in vocabulary gain between the learners with different language proficiency under two different glossing conditions, that is, single Chinese plus English glosses and multiple- choice Chinese plus English glosses with two options. To be exact, the learners with higher language proficiency perform significantly better than those with lower language proficiency under both glossing conditions. What's more, in terms of the mean scores of vocabulary gain for the learners with different language proficiency, single Chinese plus English glosses are significantly more beneficial to learners' vocabulary gain through reading.

5.2.2.2 Results of the Delayed Vocabulary Test

Table 5.8 shows the results of learners' vocabulary retention under two different glossing conditions. The average score of the learners in the delayed vocabulary test is 32.125, just beyond the score required to pass the test. Under the condition of single Chinese plus English glosses, the mean score of the learners in the delayed vocabulary test is 32.850, while under multiple-choice Chinese plus English glosses with two options, the mean score is 31.400. It seems that compared with the mean scores under two different glossing conditions, the learners get higher marks under the condition of single Chinese plus English glosses.

Table 5.8 Results of learners' vocabulary retention

Group	N	Minimum	Maximum	Mean	SD
SCEG	40	26.000	43.000	32.850	4.216
MCEG	40	26.000	42.000	31.400	4.528
Total	80	26.000	43.000	32.125	4.408

Table 5.9 demonstrates that in the delayed vocabulary test, there are not any significant differences in vocabulary retention between two different glossing conditions ($F=2.197$, $p=.142>.05$),

even though the learners perform better under the condition of single Chinese plus English glosses (M=32.850) than under multiple - choice Chinese plus English glosses with two options (M=31.400). The result confirms the ones found by Jasteh and Akbarpour (2011), Lei (2011), Shi (2010) and Watanabe (1997), who hold that there are not any significant differences in learners' vocabulary retention between single glosses and multiple - choice glosses. However, it is inconsistent with the findings discovered by Duan and Yan (2004) and Nagata (1999), who believe that there are significant differences between these two different glossing conditions.

Table 5.9 Differences in learners' vocabulary retention under two glossing conditions

	Sum of Squares	df	Mean Square	F	Sig.
Between Groups	42.050	1	42.050	2.197	.142
Within Groups	1492.700	78	19.137		
Total	1534.75	79			

The following table indicates the results of vocabulary retention for the learners with different language proficiency under two different glossing conditions.

Table 5.10 Proficiency differences in learners' vocabulary retention under two glossing conditions

Group	Proficiency	N	Mean	SD	F	t	Sig.(2-tailed)
SCEG	HLP	20	33.900	3.712	2.378	1.607	.116
	LLP	20	31.800	4.514			
MCEG	HLP	20	32.200	5.258	4.363	1.121	.269
	LLP	20	30.600	3.619			
Total	HLP	40	33.050	4.574	.024	1.908	.060
	LLP	40	31.200	4.084			

Based on the data provided in the above table, it indicates that there are not any significant differences in vocabulary retention between the learners with different language proficiency under two different glossing conditions (F=.024, t=1.908, p=.060>.05). Significant differences do not exist in vocabulary retention between the learners with different language proficiency under the condition of either single Chinese plus English glosses (F=2.378, t=1.607, p=.116>.05) or multiple-choice Chinese plus English glosses with two options (F=4.363, t=1.121, p=.269>.05).

In summary, even though learners' vocabulary retention is better under the condition of single Chinese plus English glosses than under multiple - choice Chinese plus English glosses with two options, significant differences in learners' vocabulary retention are not found under these two different glossing conditions. In terms of language proficiency, learners' language proficiency does not have a significant effect on their vocabulary retention under two different glossing conditions.

5.2.2.3 Differences between Two Vocabulary Tests

The following table exhibits the differences between learners' incidental vocabulary acquisition in the immediate vocabulary test and in the delayed vocabulary test under two different glossing conditions.

Table 5.11 Differences between learners' vocabulary gain and vocabulary retention under two glossing conditions

Group	Test	N	Mean	SD	t	df	Sig.(2-tailed)
SCEG	IVT	40	36.325	3.970	8.416	39	.000
	DVT	40	32.850	4.216			
MCEG	IVT	40	34.600	3.410	7.026	39	.000
	DVT	40	31.400	4.528			
Total	IVT	80	35.463	3.779	10.925	79	.000
	DVT	80	32.125	4.408			

Note: IVT: the immediate vocabulary test; DVT: the delayed vocabulary test

It is evident that in Table 5.11 there are significant differences in learners' incidental vocabulary acquisition between two vocabulary tests (t=10.925, df=79, p=.000<.01). In addition, under two different glossing conditions, significant differences are also found between learners' vocabulary gain and vocabulary retention (under the condition of single Chinese plus English glosses, t=8.416, df=39, p=.000<.01, under multiple-choice Chinese plus English glosses with two options, t=7.026, df=39, p=.000<.01).

What is worth mentioning is that learners' incidental vocabulary acquisition is significantly better in the immediate vocabulary test than in the delayed vocabulary test. Learners' mean score in the immediate vocabulary test is 35.463, while in the delayed vocabulary test, it is 32.125. To be exact, under the condition of single Chinese plus English glosses, learners' mean score in the immediate vocabulary test is 36.325, while in the delayed vocabulary test, it is 32.850; under multiple - choice Chinese plus English glosses with two options, the mean score in the immediate vocabulary test is 34.600, while in the delayed vocabulary test, it is 31.400. From the perspective of the mean scores of learners' vocabulary gain and vocabulary retention, it may be safe to reach a conclusion that single glosses are significantly more facilitative to learners' incidental vocabulary acquisition through reading. This result is consistent with the ones found by Jasteh and Akbarpour (2011) and Watanabe (1997), while it is contrary to the findings discovered by Cao and Song (2014), Duan and Yan (2004), Hulstijn (1992), Lei (2011), Nagata (1999), Rott (2005), Rott and Williams (2003), and Shi (2010), who all hold that multiple-choice glosses are more facilitative to learners' incidental vocabulary acquisition through reading.

Table 5.12 reveals the differences between vocabulary gain and vocabulary retention for the learners with higher language proficiency. It is clear that for the learners with higher language proficiency, significant differences exist between two vocabulary tests under two different glossing conditions ($t=8.483$, $df=39$, $p=.000<.01$). There are also significant differences between learners' vocabulary gain and vocabulary retention under the condition of both single Chinese plus English glosses ($t=7.285$, $df=19$, $p=.000<.01$) and multiple - choice Chinese plus English glosses with two options ($t=5.048$, $df=19$, $p=.000<.01$).

Table 5.12 Differences between vocabulary gain and vocabulary retention for the learners with higher language proficiency

Group	Test	N	Mean	SD	t	df	Sig.(2-tailed)
SCEG	IVT	20	36.600	3.747	7.285	19	.000
	DVT	20	33.900	3.712			
MCEG	IVT	20	34.750	4.633	5.048	19	.000
	DVT	20	32.200	5.258			
Total	IVT	40	35.675	4.573	8.483	39	.000
	DVT	40	33.050	4.574			

It is also discovered that the learners with higher language proficiency get the significantly higher score in the immediate vocabulary test (M=35.675) than in the delayed vocabulary test (M=33.050). To be precise, under the condition of single Chinese plus English glosses, the learners with higher language proficiency perform significantly better in the immediate vocabulary test (M=36.600) than in the delayed vocabulary test (M=33.900), and so it is the same with the learners under multiple-choice Chinese plus English glosses with two options (M=34.750 in the immediate vocabulary test and M=32.200 in the delayed vocabulary test).

Table 5.13 demonstrates the differences in learners' incidental vocabulary acquisition between the immediate vocabulary test and the delayed vocabulary test for the learners with lower language proficiency.

Table 5.13 Differences between vocabulary gain and vocabulary retention for the learners with lower language proficiency

Group	Test	N	Mean	SD	t	df	Sig.(2-tailed)
SCEG	IVT	20	36.050	4.261	6.014	19	.000
	DVT	20	31.800	4.514			
MCEG	IVT	20	34.450	1.538	5.148	19	.000
	DVT	20	30.600	3.619			
Total	IVT	40	35.250	3.264	7.959	39	.000
	DVT	40	31.200	4.084			

From the above table, it manifests clearly that for the learners with lower language proficiency, there are significant differences between the immediate vocabulary test and the delayed vocabulary test under two different glossing conditions ($t=7.959$, $df=39$, $p=.000<.01$). To be exact, under the condition of single Chinese plus English glosses, significant differences are found between the immediate vocabulary test and the delayed vocabulary test for the learners with lower language proficiency (t=6.014, df=19, p=.000<.01). Meanwhile, there are also significant differences between vocabulary gain and vocabulary retention under multiple - choice Chinese plus English glosses with two options (t=5.148, df=19, p=.000<.01).

In addition, it is discovered again that the average score of the learners with lower language proficiency is significantly higher in the immediate vocabulary test (M=35.250) than in the delayed vocabulary test (M=31.200). Exactly speaking, the learners with lower language proficiency perform significantly better in the immediate vocabulary test (M=36.050) than in the delayed vocabulary test (M=31.800) under the condition of single Chinese plus English glosses. At the same time, under multiple-choice Chinese plus English glosses with two options, the learners conduct significantly better in the immediate vocabulary test (M=34.450) than in the delayed vocabulary test (M=30.600).

In summary, the participants perform significantly differently between the immediate vocabulary test and the delayed vocabulary test under two different glossing conditions. In terms of the differences in learners' language proficiency, the learners with higher language proficiency and those with lower language proficiency both conduct significantly differently in their vocabulary gain and vocabulary retention under two different glossing conditions. What should be noted is that all the participants behave significantly better in the immediate vocabulary test than in the delayed vocabulary test under two different glossing conditions.

5.3 Discussion

First of all, a brief conclusion will be made about the results of this empirical study, in which the effects of the number of the options provided to Chinese plus English glosses are investigated on learners' reading comprehension and their vocabulary gain and vocabulary retention through reading for the learners with different language proficiency. First of all, as for the effects of glosses on learners' reading comprehension, it is found that significant differences exist under two different glossing conditions between the learners with different language proficiency. To be exact, under the condition of single Chinese plus English glosses, the learners conduct significantly better than they do under multiple-choice Chinese plus English glosses with two options. With regard to learners' vocabulary gain, the learners perform significantly differently under two different glossing conditions. Meanwhile, significant differences are also found between the learners with different language proficiency under each glossing condition. To be precise, the learners with higher language proficiency get significantly higher scores under the condition of both single Chinese plus English glosses and multiple - choice Chinese plus English glosses with two options than those with lower language proficiency. Concerning the results of learners' vocabulary retention, there are not any significant differences under two different glossing conditions. In addition, significant differences are not discovered between the learners with different language proficiency under each glossing condition, either. Compared with the differences between learners' vocabulary gain and vocabulary retention, it is found that there are significant differences under two different glossing conditions. As to the learners with different language proficiency, the learners with higher language proficiency behave significantly better in the immediate vocabulary test than those with lower language proficiency in the delayed vocabulary test. In short, single Chinese plus English glosses can significantly help to facilitate learners' reading comprehension and their vocabulary gain through reading. However, Rott (2005) discovers that multiple - choice glosses are more facilitative to learners' reading comprehension. In addition, Jasteh and Akbarpour (2011) and Watanabe (1997) find that single glosses are more beneficial to learners' incidental vocabulary acquisition through reading, while Cao and Song (2014), Duan and Yan (2004), Hulstijan (1992), Lei (2011), Nagata (1999), Rott (2005), Rott and Williams (2003) and Shi (2010) hold that multiple-choice glosses are more helpful to learners' incidental vocabulary acquisition.

In the following, to begin with, the results of the semi-structured interview are explored about the participants' points of view toward two different glossing conditions provided in reading. Just as what has been found in the interview in Chapter Four, all the participants hold the view that glosses provided to the unfamiliar words help to improve their reading comprehension in that it is not necessary for them to take time to figure out the meanings of the unknown words. With the help of glosses, they may spend more time comprehending the passage. At the same time, 45% of the participants acknowledge that providing glosses may not help them develop good reading strategies about inferring the meanings of the unknown words. What's more, as for the options provided to glosses, the learners with different language proficiency have different opinions. 80% of the learners with higher language proficiency prefer to have multiple-choice Chinese plus English glosses. It is reported that this type of glosses can not only improve their reading comprehension, but also facilitate their vocabulary learning. One of the two options provides the proper meaning to the unknown word in reading. In order to figure out the exact meaning, the learners have to understand the meaning of the sentence containing the target word, even several sentences before or after the target word at times. Processing the sentence in this way may greatly help the learners to have a better understanding of the reading passage. Having finished getting the proper meaning of the specific sentence, the learners have to make a choice between the two options. They have to figure out both meanings provided to a certain target word, and then a proper choice may be made. In this way, the target word is processed more than once. For some sophisticated words, several attempts will be made, deepening the processing of the words, so as to foster learners' vocabulary learning and memorization.

On the contrary, 90% of the learners with lower language proficiency would like to have single Chinese plus English glosses provided to the unknown words. For the learners of this group, when required to finish reading the passage, they only want to finish the task as soon as possible. All their attention is paid to reading only. They focus little on the unknown words themselves, except getting the proper meanings. Furthermore, glosses with two options will increase their cognitive loads in terms of the inference of the word meanings, so as to negatively influence their reading process and the results. This may explain why the learners with lower language proficiency perform significantly worse in vocabulary gain than those with higher language proficiency.

From the results of this empirical study, it is known that single Chinese plus English glosses can significantly facilitate learners' reading performance and their vocabulary gain through reading, compared with multiple-choice Chinese plus English glosses with two options. This result is consistent with Jasteh and Akbarpour's (2011) research, in which single glosses are more facilitative to learners' vocabulary gain through reading. Actually, in comparison with multiple-choice Chinese plus English glosses with two options, it is much easier for the learners to process single Chinese plus English glosses. Consequently, the learners may work out the proper meanings of the target words promptly, without spending some extra time making the choice between the options. This may account for the fact that single Chinese plus English glosses can significantly facilitate learners' reading comprehension, compared with multiple-choice Chinese plus English glosses with two options. Even though most of the learners with higher language proficiency would like to have multiple-choice Chinese plus English glosses with two options in reading, they really conduct significantly better under the condition of single Chinese plus English glosses. This may lead to a common phenomenon in foreign language learning that for most of the time, the learners do not have a clear picture of what they really need or what lever they actually reach.

The learners' good performance in reading continues in their vocabulary gain. From what has actually happened in reading, it has been discovered that the learners who received single Chinese plus English glosses finished reading earlier than those who got multiple-choice Chinese plus English glosses with two options. Moreover, they have been told many times by their teachers that the papers should be checked again and again before handed in. During this process, the learners who got single Chinese plus English glosses might obtain the opportunity to encounter the target words once again, and even more. This may indirectly aid the learners to deepen the processing of the target words. In addition, greatly influenced by the traditional foreign language teaching methods, the teachers tend to focus their foreign language teaching on grammar and vocabulary learning. Having been trained under this teaching context, the learners will be inclined to concentrate on the given target words, as a result. Therefore, the learners will make full use of the time left to check the reading comprehension and process the target words. Due to these two reasons, the learners conduct significantly better under the condition of single Chinese plus English glosses than under multiple-choice Chinese plus English glosses with two options, especially for the learners with higher language proficiency.

Despite the advantages of single Chinese plus English glosses for learners' reading comprehension and their vocabulary gain, its positive effect is not showed in the delayed vocabulary test. The result agrees with those found by Jasteh and Akbarpour (2011), Lei (2011), Shi (2010) and Watanabe (1997), who also discover that there are not any significant differences in learners' vocabulary retention between single glosses and multiple-choice glosses. However, Duan and Yan (2004) and Nagata (1999) find out that there are significant differences between two different glossing conditions.

This may be caused by their learning styles, to some greater extent. From the interview of the learners and their teachers, the learners in these four classes are relatively lazier. After class, they are not willing to spend some extra time reviewing what has been learnt in class. The most obvious proof is that only a few of the learners get higher scores in dictation. In addition, only some of them have a strong desire to learn English better. They greatly lack English learning motivation. This phenomenon has been noticed by some Chinese scholars (Tang, 2012; Zhou and Wang, 2012). The learners' bad learning styles may also explicate why the learners perform significantly better in the immediate vocabulary test than in the delayed vocabulary test. On the other hand, it also implies the importance of the timely practice.

On the basis of the Involvement Load Hypothesis, the words which are processed deeper will be stored in a relatively longer time in memory. However, based on the options provided to glosses, it may be safe to conclude that more cognitive loads are needed in processing multiple - choice Chinese plus English glosses with two options, compared with single Chinese plus English glosses. Consequently, the words with multiple - choice Chinese plus English glosses with two options ought to be kept longer in memory. However, the results demonstrate that as for learners' vocabulary retention, no significant differences are found between the learners with different language proficiency under two different glossing conditions. This may lead to some doubts thrown to the Involvement Load Hypothesis. The depth of the word processing is only based on the difficulty of the tasks involved in the words. In other words, it is barely calculated from the perspective of cognitive loads perceived by the researchers, without taking into consideration the learners' actual performance in the process of completing the given tasks. This may have some implications for the revision of the theory. The problems in the theory have been noticed by some scholars, such as Huang (2004), Wu (2010), Wu et al. (2010), Zhou (2008), and so on. They all agree that some other factors should be taken into consideration, in order to make the theory more practical.

5.4 Summary

This chapter is mainly to investigate the effects of the options provided to Chinese plus English glosses on learners' reading comprehension as well as on their vocabulary gain and vocabulary retention through reading.

To start with, the methodology employed in this empirical study is introduced. The research questions are raised, first. Then the choice of the participants and the identification of the target words are explicated in detail. In the end, the execution of the empirical study is presented.

In the following, the results of the empirical study are reported. First of all, learners' reading performance under two different glossing conditions is showed, that is, single Chinese plus English glosses and multiple-choice Chinese plus English glosses with two options. At the same time, the effects of learners' language proficiency on reading are examined under these two different glossing conditions.

What will be mentioned next are the results of the immediate vocabulary test and the delayed vocabulary test. Learners' vocabulary gain and vocabulary retention are calculated under two different glossing conditions, based on the analysis of the collected data. The factor of learners' language proficiency is also taken into account. Finally, a comparison is made between learners' vocabulary gain and vocabulary retention.

In the end, some possible reasons are proposed to account for the results of this empirical study. In brief, single Chinese plus English glosses can be significantly beneficial to learners' reading comprehension and their vocabulary gain, compared with multiple - choice Chinese plus English glosses. However, this positive effect is not displayed in learners' vocabulary retention through reading. This leads to the need for the revision of the Involvement Load Hypothesis.

Chapter Six　Empirical Study III

This empirical study is mainly to investigate the effects of glossing positions on learners' reading comprehension, and their incidental vocabulary acquisition through reading. In Chapter Five, it has been confirmed that compared with multiple-choice Chinese plus English glosses with two options, single Chinese plus English glosses are significantly more facilitative to learners' reading comprehension and their incidental vocabulary acquisition through reading. In addition, as for the positions of glosses provided in reading, generally speaking, four positions are involved, that is, in the interlinear position, on the marginal side of the text, at the bottom of the page, and at the end of the text. These four positions of glosses respond to four types of glosses, that is to say, in-text glosses, marginal glosses, footnote glosses and endnote glosses. Therefore, this empirical study attempts to probe into the effects of four different positions of single Chinese plus English glosses on learners' reading comprehension and their incidental vocabulary acquisition through reading.

6.1 Methodology

6.1.1 Research Questions

This empirical study is to investigate the effects of different positons of single Chinese plus English glosses (in-text glosses, marginal glosses, footnote glosses and endnote glosses) on learners' reading comprehension, and their vocabulary gain and vocabulary retention through reading. Consequently, the following questions are involved.

1. Which type of glosses is more facilitative to learners' reading comprehension? Are there significant differences in reading comprehension between the learners with different language proficiency under different glossing conditions?

2. Which type of glosses is more beneficial to learners' incidental vocabulary acquisition through reading? Are there significant differences in vocabulary gain and vocabulary retention between the learners with different language proficiency under different glossing conditions?

3. Are there significant differences between learners' vocabulary gain and vocabulary retention under each glossing condition? Are there significant differences between vocabulary gain and vocabulary retention for the learners with different language proficiency?

6.1.2 Participants

The participants were from first-year non-English majors of four classes. In total, there were 267 participants. They were required to take two vocabulary tests with 3,000 word level and 5,000 word level, respectively. Based on the method provided by Qin (2003: 37), the learners whose scores were equal or higher than 43 belonged to the higher language proficiency group, while those whose scores were equal or higher than 35 belonged to the lower language proficiency group. There were 66 learners in each group. Then the participants were subdivided into four groups to read the passage with the target words explained with in-text glosses, marginal glosses, footnote glosses and endnote glosses, according to their language proficiency. In each subgroup, there were 30 participants, 15 with higher language proficiency and 15 with lower language proficiency.

Table 6.1 displays the proficiency differences between the participants in four subgroups. It is found that there are significant differences between the learners with higher language proficiency and those with lower language proficiency ($t=2.723$, $p=.007<.01$). Under each glossing condition, significant differences also exist between the learners with different language proficiency (under the condition of in-text glosses, $t=1.900$, $p=.006<.01$; under marginal glosses, $t=1.898$, $p=.037<.05$; under footnote glosses, $t=.613$, $p=.045<.05$; under endnote glosses, t=1.182, p=.024<.05).

Table 6.1 Differences between the learners of four groups

Group	Proficiency	N	Mean	SD	t	Sig.(2-tailed)
ITG	HLP	15	34.733	4.350	1.900	.006
	LLP	15	32.267	2.520		
MG	HLP	15	34.400	3.719	1.898	.037
	LLP	15	32.400	1.682		
FG	HLP	15	32.800	4.601	.613	.045
	LLP	15	31.933	2.963		
EG	HLP	15	32.867	3.441	1.182	.024
	LLP	15	31.600	2.324		
Total	HLP	60	33.700	4.048	2.723	.007
	LLP	60	32.050	2.375		

Note: ITG: in - text glosses; MG: marginal glosses; FG: footnote glosses; EG: endnote glosses; HLP: higher language proficiency; LLP: lower language proficiency

6.1.3 Target Words

In total, there were 267 participants involved in this empirical study. However, only 120 of them actually engaged in the experiment. The rest, 147 of them were required to pick out the unknown words from the given text. In all, 24 unfamiliar words were identified, from which 10 words were chosen as the target words in this empirical study. To be exact, there were 3 verbs (combat, dehydrate and appeal), 3 nouns (testament, shelter and urine) and 4 adjectives (equivalent, tough, grueling and fierce). The target words were explained with single Chinese plus English glosses, including their grammatical categories. Glosses appear in four different positions, that is, in the interlinear position, on the marginal side of the text, at the bottom of the page and at the end of the text. The given glosses referred to Oxford Advanced Learners' English-Chinese Dictionary (2009) (refer to Appendix Ⅷ to Ⅺ).

6.1.4 Data Collection

The text with the target words glossed in four different ways was provided to each of the four groups. The participants in each group were required to finish two reading tasks within 20 minutes. After 10 minutes of a short break, all the participants were asked to complete the immediate vocabulary test with the format of the Vocabulary Knowledge Scale, to assess learners' vocabulary gain through reading under each glossing condition. In each subgroup, 10 participants (5 with higher language proficiency and 5 with lower language proficiency) were asked to have a semi-structured interview about their opinions of glossing positions. In total, 40 learners were concerned. Two weeks later, a delayed vocabulary test was given, with the same testing items, but in a different order. It was employed to evaluate learners' vocabulary retention through reading. All the participants did not know that two vocabulary tests would be given, in advance.

All the date collected was processed by SPSS 20.0.

6.2 Data Analysis and Results

This part is to report the effects of glossing positions on reading comprehension and incidental vocabulary acquisition through reading for the learners with different language proficiency. There are four single Chinese plus English glossing positions involved, that is to say, in - text glosses, marginal glosses, footnote glosses and endnote glosses. In the following, the effects of glossing positions on reading comprehension are examined for the learners with different language proficiency.

6.2.1 Relationship between Learners' Language Proficiency and Reading Comprehension

This section is to examine the relationship between learners' language proficiency and their reading comprehension under each glossing condition. To begin with, the results of learners' reading comprehension are reported under four glossing conditions. Then the effects of language proficiency on reading comprehension are investigated under four different glossing conditions.

6.2.1.1 Reading Comprehension under Four Glossing Conditions

Table 6.2 shows the results of learners' reading comprehension under four different glossing conditions, that is, in-text glosses, marginal glosses, footnote glosses and endnote glosses. It is clearly seen that the learners' average reading score is 10.625, just beyond the required passing score. They get the highest score in reading under the condition of marginal glosses (M=11.300), followed by endnote glosses (M=10.567), and in-text glosses (M=10.400). The lowest score is got under footnote glosses (M=10.234). It seems that under marginal glosses and endnote glosses, the participants conduct better in reading comprehension.

Table 6.2 Results of learners' reading comprehension under four glossing conditions

Group	N	Minimum	Maximum	Mean	SD
ITG	30	7.000	13.000	10.400	1.905
MG	30	8.000	14.000	11.300	1.915
FG	30	7.000	13.000	10.234	1.716
EG	30	7.000	13.000	10.567	1.960
Total	120	7.000	14.000	10.625	1.900

The following table indicates that there are significant

differences in learners' reading comprehension under four different glossing conditions (F=2.713, p=.048<.05). This result is for the study performed by Elekaei et al. (2015). However, it is inconsistent with the findings discovered by Cheng and Good (2009), Holley and King (1971), Johnson (1982), and Wu et al. (2012), who all claim that the positions where glosses are presented do not have any significant effects on learners' reading comprehension.

Concerning the mean scores of learners' reading comprehension under each glossing condition provided in Table 6.2, it may be safe to conclude that marginal glosses are significantly the most facilitative to learners' reading comprehension.

Table 6.3 Differences in learners' reading comprehension under four glossing conditions

	Sum of Squares	df	Mean Square	F	Sig.
Between Groups	19.892	3	6.631	2.713	.048
Within Groups	408.233	116	3.519		
Total	428.125	119			

The following table demonstrates the differences in learners' reading comprehension between four different glossing conditions.

Table 6.4 Differences in learners' reading comprehension between four glossing conditions

(I) Group	(J) Group	Mean Difference (I-J)	Std. Error	Sig.	95% Confidence Interval Lower Bound	Upper Bound
ITG	MG	-.900*	.484	.025	-2.163	.363
	FG	.167	.484	.986	-1.096	1.429
	EG	-.825**	.484	.008	-1.429	1.096
MG	ITG	.900*	.484	.025	-.363	2.163
	FG	1.067*	.484	.019	-.196	2.329
	EG	.733*	.484	.032	-.529	1.996
FG	ITG	-.167	.484	.986	-1.429	1.096
	MG	-.1.067*	.484	.019	-2.329	.196
	EG	-.333	.484	.901	-1.596	.929
EG	ITG	.825**	.484	.008	-1.096	1.429
	MG	-.733*	.484	.032	-1.996	.529
	FG	.333	.484	.901	-.929	1.596

Note: *<.05; **<.01

It is clearly shown in Table 6.4 that there are significant differences in learners' reading comprehension between marginal glosses and in-text glosses (Mean difference=.900, p=.025<.05), endnote glosses and in - text glosses (Mean difference=.825, p=.008<.01), marginal glosses and footnote glosses (Mean difference=1.067, p=.019<.05), as well as between marginal glosses and endnote glosses (Mean difference=.733, p=.032<.05). However, significant differences are not found in learners' reading comprehension between in - text glosses and footnote glosses (Mean difference=.167, p=.986>.05), or between endnote glosses and footnote glosses (Mean difference=.333, p=.901>.05).

Taking into consideration the mean scores of learners' reading comprehension under each glossing condition mentioned in Table 6.2, it is safe to conclude that in terms of glossing positions, marginal glosses are significantly the most beneficial to learners' reading comprehension. This result is partially supported by Davis (1989) and Meng and Chen (2015), who argue that marginal L1 glosses are facilitative to learners' reading comprehension. The similarity lies in the fact that marginal glosses are conducive to learners' reading comprehension, while the difference is that in this empirical study, Chinese plus English glosses are more helpful, but not L1 glosses.

In addition, compared with in-text glosses, endnote glosses are significantly more facilitative to learners' reading comprehension. However, Elekaei et al. (2015) hold that in-text glosses are more beneficial to learners' reading comprehension. They believe that the result is caused by the convenience brought by in-text glosses, because they are the closest to the target words, compared with the other glosses.

6.2.1.2 Effects of Learners' Language Proficiency on Reading Comprehension

Table 6.5 illustrates the differences in reading comprehension between the learners with different language proficiency under four different glossing conditions. It is evident that there are significant differences in reading comprehension between the learners with higher language proficiency and those with lower language proficiency ($F=19.340$, $t=2.822$, $p=.006<.01$), which means that the learners with higher language proficiency ($M=11.100$) get the significantly higher score in reading than those with lower language proficiency ($M=10.150$). To be exact, significant differences are found in reading comprehension between the learners with different language proficiency under the condition of both marginal glosses ($F=.301$, $t=2.613$, $p=.014<.05$) and endnote glosses ($F=3.774$, $t=1.026$, $p=.023<.05$). It is also seen clearly that the mean score of reading comprehension for the learners with higher language proficiency is 12.133 under the condition of marginal glosses, while the mean score of reading comprehension is 10.467 for those with lower language proficiency; under endnote glosses, the mean score of reading comprehension for the learners with higher language proficiency is 10.933, while the mean score of reading comprehension is 10.200 for those with lower language proficiency. Therefore, we may arrive at a conclusion that the learners with higher language proficiency perform significantly better in reading under the condition of marginal glosses and endnote glosses than those with lower language proficiency.

Table 6.5 Proficiency differences in learners' reading comprehension under four glossing conditions

Group	Proficiency	N	Mean	SD	F	t	Sig.
ITG	HLP	15	10.933	2.219	7.305	1.572	.127
	LLP	15	9.867	1.407			
MG	HLP	15	12.133	1.922	.301	2.613	.014
	LLP	15	10.467	1.552			
FG	HLP	15	10.400	2.028	7.822	.525	.603
	LLP	15	10.067	1.387			
EG	HLP	15	10.933	2.282	3.774	1.026	.023
	LLP	15	10.200	1.567			
Total	HLP	60	11.100	2.161	19.340	2.822	.006
	LLP	60	10.150	1.460			

However, there are not any significant differences in reading comprehension between the learners with different language proficiency under the condition of in-text glosses ($F=7.305$, $t=1.572$, $p=.127>.05$), or footnote glosses ($F=7.822$, $t=.525$, $p=.603>.05$).

In summary, glossing positions have a significant effect on

reading comprehension for the learners with different language proficiency. Exactly speaking, the learners with higher language proficiency get significantly higher scores in reading under the condition of marginal glosses and endnote glosses than those with lower language proficiency.

6.2.2 Relationship between Learners' Language Proficiency and Incidental Vocabulary Acquisition

This section is to report the results of vocabulary gain and vocabulary retention for the learners with different language proficiency under four different glossing conditions. The comparison is made between vocabulary gain and vocabulary retention, as well.

6.2.2.1 Results of the Immediate Vocabulary Test

Table 6.6 demonstrates the results of learners' vocabulary gain under four different glossing positions. It can be discovered from the table that the average score of learners' vocabulary gain is 32.892. Under the condition of marginal glosses, the learners get the highest score (M=33.367), while under endnote glosses, they get the lowest score (M=32.634). The scores are in between under in-text glosses (M=32.867) and under footnote glosses (M= 32.700).

Table 6.6 Results of learners' vocabulary gain

Group	N	Minimum	Maximum	Mean	SD
ITG	30	26.000	39.000	32.867	3.540
MG	30	28.000	42.000	33.367	2.906
FG	30	28.000	38.000	32.700	3.196
EG	30	27.000	41.000	32.634	3.479
Total	120	26.000	42.000	32.892	3.261

Table 6.7 demonstrates the differences in learners' vocabulary gain under four different glossing conditions. It is shown clearly in the table that there are significant differences in learners' vocabulary gain under four different glossing conditions (F=.305, t=.028<.05).

Table 6.7 Differences in learners' vocabulary gain under four glossing conditions

	Sum of Squares	df	Mean Square	F	Sig.
Between Groups	9.892	3	3.297	.305	.028
Within Groups	1255.700	116	10.825		
Total	1265.592	119			

Table 6.8 demonstrates the differences in learners' vocabulary gain between four glossing conditions. It is discovered that in learners' vocabulary gain, there are significant differences between marginal glosses and in-text glosses (Mean Difference=.500, $t=.035<.05$), footnote glosses and marginal glosses (Mean Difference=.667, $t=.016<.05$), as well as between marginal glosses and endnote glosses (Mean Difference=.733, $t=.024<.05$). At the same time, significant differences are also found in learners' vocabulary gain between in-text glosses and endnote glosses (Mean Difference=.233, $t=.039<.05$), and between endnote glosses and footnote glosses (Mean Difference=.067, $t=.001<.01$). Concerning the mean scores of learners' vocabulary gain under each glossing condition provided in Table 6.6, it may be safe to reach a conclusion that marginal glosses are significantly the most facilitative to learners' vocabulary gain through reading. This result is consistent with the findings discovered by Davis (1989), Hulstijn et al. (1996), and Wu et al. (2012). However, it is inconsistent with the results found by Chen et al. (2013), Cheng and Good (2009), Elekaei et al. (2015), and Lan and Zhang (2013), who argue that in-text glosses are more beneficial to learners' vocabulary gain through reading. In addition, it is also found that endnote glosses are significantly the least conducive to learners' vocabulary gain among these four glossing conditions.

Table 6.8 Differences in learners' vocabulary gain between four glossing conditions

(I) Group	(J) Group	Mean Difference (I-J)	Std. Error	Sig.	95% Confidence Interval	
					Lower Bound	Upper Bound
ITG	MG	-.500*	.850	.035	-2.714	1.714
	FG	.167	.850	.097	-2.048	2.381
	EG	.233*	.850	.039	-1.981	2.448
MG	ITG	.500*	.850	.035	-1.714	2.714
	FG	-.667*	.850	.016	-1.548	2.881
	EG	.733*	.850	.024	-1.481	2.948
FG	ITG	-.167	.850	.097	-2.381	2.048
	MG	.667*	.850	.016	-2.881	1.548
	EG	-.067**	.850	.001	-2.148	2.281
EG	ITG	-.233*	.850	.039	-2.448	1.981
	MG	-.733*	.850	.024	-2.948	1.481
	FG	.067**	.850	.001	-2.281	2.148

Note: *<.05; **<.01

Nevertheless, significant differences are not found in learners' vocabulary gain between in-text glosses and footnote glosses (Mean Difference=.167, t=.097>.05).

Table 6.9 demonstrates the proficiency differences in learners' vocabulary gain under each glossing condition. It is found that there are significant differences in learners' vocabulary gain between the learners with higher language proficiency and those with lower language proficiency ($F=10.938$, $t=3.811$, $p=.000<.01$). Exactly speaking, there are significant differences in vocabulary gain through reading between the learners with different language proficiency under the condition of both marginal glosses ($F=1.165$, $t=2.597$, $p=.016<.05$), and endnote glosses ($F=7.147$, $t=1.677$, $p=.015<.05$). However, significant differences in vocabulary gain through reading are not found between the learners with different language proficiency under the condition of in-text glosses ($F=6.772$, $t=1.902$, $p=.067>.05$), or footnote glosses ($F=.145$, $t=1.331$, $p=.194>.05$).

It is shown clearly in Table 6.9, under the condition of marginal glosses, the mean score of vocabulary gain is 34.333 for the learners with higher language proficiency, while the mean score is 32.400 for those with lower language proficiency; under endnote glosses, the mean score is 33.667 for the learners with higher language proficiency, while the mean score is 31.600 for those with lower language proficiency. Therefore, it may be safe to reach a conclusion that the higher the learners' language proficiency is, the better their vocabulary gain through reading is under the condition of marginal glosses and endnote glosses. However, compared with marginal glosses, endnote glosses are significantly less beneficial to learners' vocabulary gain through reading.

Table 6.9 Proficiency differences in learners' vocabulary gain under four glossing conditions

Group	Proficiency	N	Mean	SD	F	t	Sig.(2-tailed)
ITG	HLP	15	34.400	3.851	6.772	1.902	.067
	LLP	15	31.333	2.469			
MG	HLP	15	34.333	3.559	1.165	2.597	.016
	LLP	15	32.400	1.682			
FG	HLP	15	33.467	3.335	.145	1.331	.194
	LLP	15	31.933	2.963			
EG	HLP	15	33.667	4.169	7.147	1.677	. 015
	LLP	15	31.600	2.323			
Total	HLP	60	33.967	3.668	10.938	3.811	.000
	LLP	60	31.817	2.376			

To sum up, glossing positions have a significant effect on learners' vocabulary gain through reading. To be specific, marginal glosses are significantly the most facilitative to learners' vocabulary gain through reading, while endnote glosses are significantly the least beneficial to learners' vocabulary gain through reading. With regard to learners' proficiency differences, the learners with higher language proficiency perform significantly better in vocabulary gain under the condition of marginal glosses and endnote glosses than those with lower language proficiency.

6.2.2.2 Results of the Delayed Vocabulary Test

Table 6.10 displays the results of learners' vocabulary retention through reading under four different glossing conditions. It is obvious that the average score of learners' vocabulary retention is 31.784. Under four different glossing conditions, the learners get the highest score in vocabulary retention under the condition of marginal glosses (M=32.600), followed by endnote glosses (M=31.867) and footnote glosses (M=31.400). The learners get the lowest score in vocabulary retention under in-text glosses (M=31.267). It seems that marginal glosses are the most facilitative to learners' vocabulary retention through reading.

Table 6.10 Results of learners' vocabulary retention

Group	N	Minimum	Maximum	Mean	SD
ITG	30	25.000	38.000	31.267	4.417
MG	30	27.000	41.000	32.600	3.519
FG	30	26.000	38.000	31.400	3.635
EG	30	26.000	39.000	31.867	3.711
Total	120	25.000	41.000	31.784	3.824

Table 6.11 demonstrates that glossing conditions have a significant effect on learners' vocabulary retention through reading (F=.739, p=.031<.05).

Table 6.11 Differences in learners' vocabulary retention under four glossing conditions

	Sum of Squares	df	Mean Square	F	Sig.
Between Groups	32.633	3	10.878	.739	.031
Within Groups	1707.733	116	14.722		
Total	1740.367	119			

Table 6.12 shows the differences in learners' vocabulary retention between four glossing positions. It is found that there are significant differences in learners' vocabulary retention through reading between marginal glosses and in - text glosses (Mean Difference=1.333, p=.036<.05), marginal glosses and footnote glosses (Mean Difference=1.200, p=.021<.05), as well as between marginal glosses and endnote glosses (Mean Difference=.733, p=.018<.05). However, significant differences are not found in learners' vocabulary retention through reading between footnote glosses and in - text glosses (Mean Difference=.133, p=.999>.05), endnote glosses and in - text

glosses (Mean Difference=.600, p=.930>.05), as well as between endnote glosses and footnote glosses (Mean Difference=.467, p=.965>.05).

Table 6.12 Differences in learners' vocabulary retention between four glossing conditions

(I) Group	(J) Group	Mean Difference (I-J)	Std. Error	Sig.	95% Confidence Interval Lower Bound	95% Confidence Interval Upper Bound
ITG	MG	-1.333*	.991	.036	-3.916	1.249
	FG	-.133	.991	.999	-2.716	2.449
	EG	-.600	.991	.930	-3.182	1.982
MG	ITG	1.333*	.991	.036	-1.249	3.916
	FG	1.200*	.991	.021	-1.382	3.782
	EG	.733*	.991	.018	-1.849	3.316
FG	ITG	.133	.991	.999	-2.449	2.716
	MG	-1.200*	.991	.021	-3.782	1.382
	EG	-.467	.991	.965	-3.049	2.116
EG	ITG	.600	.991	.930	-1.982	3.182
	MG	-.733*	.991	.018	-3.316	1.849
	FG	.467	.991	.965	-2.116	3.049

Note: *<.05

Concerning the mean scores of learners' vocabulary retention under each glossing condition provided in Table 6.10, it is safe to conclude that marginal glosses are significantly the most conducive to learners' vocabulary retention through reading among four different glossing positions. This result is consistent with the findings discovered by Davis (1989), Hulstijn et al. (1996), Meng and Chen (2015), and Wu et al. (2012), who hold that marginal glosses are more facilitative to learners' vocabulary retention through reading, while Watanabe (1997) considers that marginal glosses are not beneficial to learners' vocabulary retention through reading. In addition, it is inconsistent with the results obtained by Chen et al. (2013), Cheng and Good (2009), Elekaei et al. (2015), Lan and Zhang (2013), and Zarei and Hasani (2011), who argue that in-text glosses are more conducive to learners' vocabulary retention through reading.

Table 6.13 shows the proficiency differences in learners' vocabulary retention under each glossing condition. It is clearly displayed that there are significant differences in learners' vocabulary retention through reading under different glossing conditions ($F=52.109$, $t=3.116$, $p=.002<.01$). It means that the learners with higher language proficiency ($M=32.833$) conduct significantly better than those with lower language proficiency ($M=30.734$). However, significant differences in vocabulary retention through reading between the learners with different language proficiency only exist under the condition of marginal glosses ($F=5.795$, $t=1.482$, $p=.049<.05$). There are not any significant differences in vocabulary retention between the learners with higher language proficiency and those with lower language proficiency under the condition of in-text glosses (F=13.707, t=1.341, p=.191>.05), footnote glosses (F=29.934, t=1.769, p=.088>.05), as well as endnote glosses (F=24.705, t=1.617, p=.117>.05).

Table 6.13 Proficiency differences in learners' vocabulary retention under four glossing conditions

Group	Proficiency	N	Mean	SD	F	t	Sig.(2-tailed)
ITG	HLP	15	32.333	5.192	13.707	1.341	.191
	LLP	15	30.200	3.321			
MG	HLP	15	33.533	4.138	5.795	1.482	.049
	LLP	15	31.667	2.582			
FG	HLP	15	32.533	4.518	29.934	1.769	.088
	LLP	15	30.267	2.052			
EG	HLP	15	32.933	4.511	24.705	1.617	.117
	LLP	15	30.800	2.396			
Total	HLP	60	32.833	4.511	52.109	3.116	.002
	LLP	60	30.734	2.629			

Under the condition of marginal glosses, the mean score of vocabulary retention through reading is 33.533 for the learners with higher language proficiency, while the mean score is 31.667 for those with lower language proficiency. Therefore, the higher language proficiency the learners have, the better their vocabulary retention through reading will be.

In summary, there are significant differences in learners' vocabulary retention through reading under different glossing conditions. Meanwhile, marginal glosses are significantly the most facilitative to learners' vocabulary retention through reading. In terms of learners' language proficiency, the learners with higher language proficiency perform significantly better in vocabulary retention through reading under the condition of marginal glosses than those with lower language proficiency.

6.2.2.3 Differences between Two Vocabulary Tests

The results of the immediate vocabulary test and the delayed vocabulary test are reported in the above two subsections. The following is involved in the comparison between learners' vocabulary gain and their vocabulary retention. Learners' language proficiency differences between two vocabulary tests are also taken into account.

Table 6.14 displays the differences between vocabulary gain and vocabulary retention under each glossing condition. There are significant differences between learners' vocabulary gain and their vocabulary retention under four different glossing conditions ($t=2.505$, $df=119$, $p=.014<.05$). In other words, the learners perform significantly better in the immediate vocabulary test (M=32.892) than in the delayed vocabulary test (M=31.784). To be exact, there are significant differences between learners' vocabulary gain and their vocabulary retention under the condition of in-text glosses ($t=1.971$, $df=29$, $p=.048<.05$), marginal glosses ($t=.918$, $df=29$, $p=.036<.05$), footnote glosses ($t=1.321$, $df=29$, $p=.017<.05$), as well as endnote glosses ($t=1.311$, $df=29$, $p=.020<.05$).

Table 6.14 Differences between learners' vocabulary gain and vocabulary retention under four glossing conditions

Group	Test	N	Mean	SD	t	df	Sig.(2-tailed)
ITG	IVT	30	32.867	3.540	1.971	29	.048
	DVT	30	31.267	4.417			
MG	IVT	30	33.367	2.906	.918	29	.036
	DVT	30	32.600	3.519			
FG	IVT	30	32.700	3.196	1.321	29	.017
	DVT	30	31.400	3.635			
EG	IVT	30	32.634	3.479	1.311	29	.020
	DVT	30	31.867	3.711			
Total	IVT	120	32.892	3.261	2.505	119	.014
	DVT	120	31.784	3.824			

Note: IVT: the immediate vocabulary test; DVT: the delayed

vocabulary test

It is clearly displayed in Table 6.14 that under the condition of marginal glosses, the mean scores of learners' vocabulary gain (M=33.367) and vocabulary retention (M=32.600) are the highest among the scores under the other three glossing conditions (under in-text glosses, the mean scores of vocabulary gain and vocabulary retention are 32.867 and 31.267; under footnote glosses, the mean scores are 32.700 and 31.400; under endnote glosses, the mean scores are 32.634 and 31.867, respectively). This demonstrates that marginal glosses are significantly the most facilitative to learners' incidental vocabulary acquisition through reading. The result is consistent with the findings discovered by Davis (1989), Hulstijn et al. (1996), Meng and Chen (2015), and Wu et al. (2012). However, Chen et al. (2013), Cheng and Good (2009), Elekaei et al. (2015), Lan and Zhang (2013), and Zarei and Hasani (2011) believe that in-text glosses are more beneficial to learners' incidental vocabulary acquisition through reading.

Table 6.15 demonstrates the differences between vocabulary gain and vocabulary retention through reading for the learners with higher language proficiency under each glossing condition. It is found that there are significant differences between vocabulary gain and vocabulary retention through reading under different glossing conditions for the learners with higher language proficiency (t=1.640, df=59, p=.016<.05). To be exact, significant differences are found between vocabulary gain and vocabulary retention through reading for the learners with higher language proficiency under the condition of marginal glosses (t=.536, df=14, p=.046<.05), and endnote glosses (t=.728, df=14, p=.048<.05). For the learners of this group, under the condition of marginal glosses, the mean score of vocabulary gain through reading is 34.333, while the mean score of vocabulary retention is 33.533; under endnote glosses, the mean score of vocabulary gain is 33.667, while the mean score of vocabulary retention is 32.933. It is safe to arrive at a conclusion that the learners with higher language proficiency perform significantly better in the immediate vocabulary test (M=33.967) than in the delayed vocabulary test (M=32.833), especially under the condition of marginal glosses and endnote glosses. Compared with endnote glosses, marginal glosses are significantly more facilitative to learners' incidental vocabulary acquisition through reading for the learners with higher language proficiency. However, significant differences do not exist between vocabulary gain and vocabulary retention through reading for the learners with higher language proficiency under the condition of in-text glosses (t=1.585, df=14, p=.638>.05), or footnote glosses (t=.537, df=14, p=.600>.05).

Table 6.15 Differences between vocabulary gain and vocabulary retention for the learners with higher language proficiency

Group	Test	N	Mean	SD	t	df	Sig.(2-tailed)
ITG	IVT	15	34.400	3.851	1.585	14	.638
	DVT	15	32.333	5.192			
MG	IVT	15	34.333	3.559	.536	14	. 046
	DVT	15	33.533	4.138			
FG	IVT	15	33.467	3.335	.537	14	. 600
	DVT	15	32.533	4.518			
EG	IVT	15	33.667	4.169	.728	14	.048
	DVT	15	32.933	4.511			
Total	IVT	60	33.967	3.668	1.640	59	. 016
	DVT	60	32.833	4.511			

Table 6.16 demonstrates the differences between vocabulary gain and vocabulary retention through reading for the learners with lower language proficiency under different glossing conditions. It is found that significant differences exist between vocabulary gain and vocabulary retention through reading for the learners with lower language proficiency ($t=2.539$, $df=59$, $p=.014<.05$). It means that the learners with lower language proficiency conduct significantly better in the immediate vocabulary test ($M=31.817$) than in the delayed vocabulary test ($M=30.734$). However, significant differences between

vocabulary gain and vocabulary retentions are only found under the condition of endnote glosses (t=1.262, df=14, p=.028<.05). Under the other three glossing conditions, there are not any significant differences between vocabulary gain and vocabulary retention through reading for the learners with lower language proficiency (under the condition of in-text glosses, t=1.134, df=14, p=.276>.05; under marginal glosses, t=.902, df=14, p=.383>.05; under footnote glosses, t=1.649, df=14, t=.112>.05).

Under the condition of endnote glosses, the mean score of vocabulary gain through reading for the learners with lower language proficiency is 31.600, while the mean score of vocabulary retention is 30.800. It shows that for the learners with lower language proficiency, they perform significantly better in the immediate vocabulary test than in the delayed vocabulary test, especially under the condition of endnote glosses.

In summary, there are significant differences between learners' vocabulary gain and vocabulary retention through reading under four different glossing conditions. With regard to the language proficiency, there are significant differences between vocabulary gain and vocabulary retention through reading for the learners with higher language proficiency and for those with lower language proficiency. The difference is that there are significant differences between vocabulary gain and vocabulary retention through reading for the learners with higher language proficiency under the condition of both marginal glosses and endnote glosses, while for the learners with lower language proficiency, significant differences between vocabulary gain and vocabulary retention only exist under the condition of endnote glosses.

Table 6.16 Differences between vocabulary gain and vocabulary retention for the learners with lower language proficiency

Group	Test	N	Mean	SD	t	df	Sig.(2-tailed)
ITG	IVT	15	31.333	2.469	1.134	14	.276
	DVT	15	30.200	3.321			
MG	IVT	15	32.400	1.682	.902	14	.383
	DVT	15	31.667	2.582			
FG	IVT	15	31.933	2.963	1.649	14	.112
	DVT	15	30.267	2.052			
EG	IVT	15	31.600	2.323	1.262	14	.028
	DVT	15	30.800	2.396			
Total	IVT	60	31.817	2.376	2.539	59	.014
	DVT	60	30.734	2.629			

6.3 Discussion

The above part is mainly related to the results of this empirical study about the effects of glossing positions on reading comprehension and incidental vocabulary acquisition through reading for the learners with different language proficiency. To start with, the results obtained in this empirical study are summarized.

As for the effects of glossing positions on learners' reading comprehension, it is found that there are significant differences in learners' reading comprehension under different glossing conditions. This result is consistent with the one found by Elekaei et al. (2015). However, Cheng and Good (2009), Holley and King (1971), Johnson (1982), and Wu et al. (2012) discover that glossing positions do not have any significant effects on learners' reading comprehension. To be exact, learners' reading comprehension is significantly different between marginal glosses and in-text glosses, footnote glosses and marginal glosses, marginal glosses and endnote glosses, as well as between endnote glosses and in-text glosses. Therefore, it can be concluded that marginal glosses are significantly the most beneficial to learners' reading comprehension. The result is for the studies performed by Davis (1989), as well as Meng and Chen (2015). However, Elekaei et al. (2015) argue that in-text glosses are more beneficial to learners' reading comprehension. Compared with in-text glosses, endnote glosses are significantly more facilitative to learners' reading comprehension. Taking learners' language proficiency into consideration, it is discovered that there are significant differences in learners' reading comprehension under different glossing conditions. Exactly speaking, the higher the learners' language proficiency is, the better their reading comprehension is under the condition of marginal glosses and endnote glosses.

With regard to learners' vocabulary gain through reading, there are significant differences in learners' vocabulary gain under different glossing positions. Briefly speaking, significant differences do not exist in learners' vocabulary gain only between footnote glosses and in - text glosses. At the same time, a conclusion can be made that marginal glosses are significantly the most conducive to learners' vocabulary gain, while endnote glosses are significantly the least beneficial to learners' vocabulary gain. Davis (1989), Hulstijn et al. (1996), and Wu et al. (2012) all hold that marginal glosses are facilitative to learners' vocabulary gain through reading, while Chen et al. (2013), Cheng and Good (2009), Elekaei et al. (2015), as well as Lan and Zhang (2013) argue that in - text glosses are more beneficial to learners' vocabulary gain. As to learners' language proficiency differences, it is found that there are significant differences in learners' vocabulary gain between the learners with different language proficiency. To be exact, the higher the learners' language proficiency is, the better their vocabulary gain is under the condition of marginal glosses and endnote glosses.

As to learners' vocabulary retention, significant differences are found in learners' vocabulary retention under different glossing conditions. To be specific, learners' vocabulary retention through reading is significantly different between marginal glosses and in-text glosses, footnote glosses and marginal glosses, as well as between endnote glosses and marginal glosses. In other words, marginal glosses are significantly the most beneficial to learners' vocabulary retention through reading. Davis (1989), Hulstijn et al. (1996), Meng and Chen (2015), and Wu et al. (2012) have the same findings, while Watanabe (1997) considers that marginal glosses are not beneficial to learners' vocabulary retention. In addition, Chen et al. (2013), Cheng and Good (2009), Elekaei et al. (2015), Lan and Zhang (2013), and Zarei and Hasani (2011) hold that in-text glosses are more conducive to learners' vocabulary retention through reading. Taking learners' language proficiency into consideration, significant differences are also found in their vocabulary retention under different glossing conditions. To be detailed, the higher the learners' language proficiency is, the better their vocabulary retention is under the condition of marginal glosses.

In regard to the differences between the immediate vocabulary test and the delayed vocabulary test, it is found that significant differences exist between vocabulary gain and vocabulary retention under different glossing conditions. In addition, significant differences between vocabulary gain and vocabulary retention are also found for the learners with higher language proficiency and for those with lower language proficiency between the two tests. To be exact, for the learners with higher language proficiency, there are significant differences between vocabulary gain and vocabulary retention under the condition of both marginal glosses and endnote glosses, while for the learners with lower language proficiency, significant differences only exist under endnote glosses.

A brief conclusion may be made in this empirical study that marginal glosses are significantly the best to facilitate learners' reading comprehension and their incidental vocabulary acquisition through reading.

In the following, the participants' opinions about different glossing positions will be reported, first of all. Among four different positions, 90% of the learners feel that marginal glosses are the best; 85% choose endnote glosses; 70% opt for footnote glosses and only 40% consider in-text glosses to be helpful. The learners' opinions about glossing conditions can help to explicate the results in this empirical study.

As to reading comprehension, the learners feel that marginal glosses are closer to the target words in reading. Therefore, it is much easier for them to move their eyes between glosses and the target words. However, for in-text glosses, the learners feel much confused. It may be caused by the facts that in this study, Chinese plus English glosses are provided, and that some glosses have more than 10 words, resulting in greater difficulty for the learners to distinguish glosses from the text. Even though in-text glosses are the closest to the target words, the boundaries between the text and glosses are not clear, to some extent, leading to some reading difficulty, and increasing learners' cognitive loads. As for endnote glosses, because of the distances between the target words and their corresponding glosses, it may be quite difficult for the learners to locate the target words again after referring to their given glosses. Finally, for endnote glosses, the learners have been accustomed to them while reading. These differences among four glossing conditions may account for the reasons why marginal glosses are the most beneficial to learners' reading comprehension, and why endnote glosses are more helpful than in-text glosses.

For learners' language proficiency differences in reading, the learners with higher language proficiency perform significantly better under the condition of marginal glosses and endnote glosses than those with lower language proficiency. There may be three reasons to account for this result. The first one is closely related to their language proficiency. Endnote glosses are the most popular glossing method in the textbooks. Reading comprehension under this glossing condition is really common to the learners. Therefore, their language proficiency definitely becomes an important factor to determine their performance in reading. Another reason is that the learners with higher language proficiency are inclined to adopt something new more easily than those with lower language proficiency. They like to do with something challenging. In addition to these two reasons, the distances between marginal glosses and their corresponding target words are really helpful to learners' reading comprehension. These reasons lead to better reading comprehension for the learners with higher language proficiency under the condition of marginal glosses and endnote glosses.

In terms of vocabulary gain of the learners, marginal glosses are significantly the most beneficial, while endnote glosses are significantly the least conducive. Marginal glosses are the closest to the target words, except in-text glosses. However, in-text glosses in this empirical study are too complicated and long, resulting in some interference for learners' noticing resources. Because of the distances between marginal glosses and their corresponding target words, it is quite convenient for the learners to connect the words with their Chinese plus English meanings, which will be easier for the learners to store the relevant information in memory, resulting in their better vocabulary gain through reading. On the other hand, endnote glosses are far from the target words. The learners need to move their eyes between endnote glosses and their corresponding target words, which makes their cognitive loads heavier. In addition, the learners may have some difficulty relating the target words to their corresponding glosses. Therefore, endnote glosses are significantly the least beneficial to learners' vocabulary gain through reading.

Taking learners' language proficiency differences into consideration, the learners with higher language proficiency perform significantly better in vocabulary gain through reading under the condition of marginal glosses and endnote glosses. It is generally held that the learners with higher language proficiency have higher degrees of the automatic knowledge (Anderson, 1992). They can make full use of their noticing resources, and make some necessary changes, according to the given circumstances. The advantages of marginal glosses have been mentioned in the above analysis. As to endnote glosses, in order to understand the text, the learners with higher language proficiency may use more noticing resources, because of the distances between endnote glosses and the target words, resulting in better memorization of the words.

As for learners' vocabulary retention, marginal glosses are significantly the most facilitative, especially for the learners with higher language proficiency. Just as what has been mentioned above, because of the distances between marginal glosses and their corresponding target words, it is quite convenient for the learners to combine the words with their glosses, resulting in the quick access to the word forms and their meanings. In addition, the contexts and the given grammatical categories provide some clues to the actual use of the words. Therefore, the learners may easily get the proper meanings of the target words, on one hand. On the other hand, the meanings may be checked in the text, leading to the deeper processing of the combined information between the word meanings and the word forms.

Concerning the comparison between learners' vocabulary gain and vocabulary retention, there are significant differences for the learners with higher language proficiency under the condition of marginal glosses and endnote glosses, while significant differences are found for the learners with lower language proficiency only under the condition of endnote glosses. Marginal glosses not only provide the learners with chances to quickly check the word meanings without interrupting the text reading, but also require less noticing resources of the learners to figure out the word meanings, leading to more noticing resources required to process some related information. However, because the learners with lower language proficiency are restricted by their limited vocabulary size and grammatical knowledge, they don't possess as many noticing resources as the learners with higher language proficiency. As to endnote glosses, because of the distances between the target words and their corresponding glosses, the learners have to move their eyes frequently between the words and their given glosses. In other words, more noticing resources are required to process the word meanings and the word forms, thus resulting in better memory of the relevant information.

From the perspective of the Involvement Load Hypothesis, the information which is processed deeper or requires more involvement loads to deal with tends to be kept in the long-term memory longer. However, in this empirical study, the hypothesis is partially supported. To some extent, compared with endnote glosses, fewer noticing resources are needed in marginal glosses. It means that the target words with endnote glosses should be kept longer in memory. Nevertheless, in the delayed vocabulary test, this effect is not manifested in learners' vocabulary retention through reading.

On the other hand, based on the comparison between learners' vocabulary gain and vocabulary retention, the learners with different language proficiency perform significantly differently in the immediate vocabulary test and the delayed vocabulary test under the condition of endnote glosses. Among four types of glossing conditions, endnote glosses are the farthest from the target words. That is to say, more noticing resources are needed to process the information related to the target words, resulting in better memory of the words. This point gets confirmed in this study.

Therefore, the Involvement Load Hypothesis is partially confirmed in this empirical study. It also demonstrates that this theory needs to be revised. This result is consistent with those found by Huang (2004), Wu (2010), Wu et al. (2010) and Zhou (2008), who all consider that some factors in the theory need to be quantified more precisely.

6.4 Summary

This chapter mainly attempts to investigate the effects of glossing positions on reading comprehension and incidental vocabulary acquisition through reading for the learners with different language proficiency.

First of all, the methodology exploited in this empirical study is introduced in detail. The research questions are put forward first, followed by how the participants are chosen and how the target words are identified. In the end, how the empirical study is executed is explicated.

In the following, the results of this empirical study are reported. First, learners' reading comprehension under four glossing conditions is showed. At the same time, the effects of language proficiency on learners' reading comprehension are investigated. The results show that marginal glosses are significantly the most facilitative to learners' reading comprehension and that the higher the learners' language proficiency is, the better their reading performance is under the condition of marginal glosses and endnote glosses.

What is followed is to probe into the effects of language proficiency on learners' vocabulary gain and vocabulary retention through reading under four glossing conditions. First, the results of learners' vocabulary gain and vocabulary retention under each glossing condition are demonstrated. Then the effects of language proficiency on learners' vocabulary gain and vocabulary retention are examined. In the end, a comparison is made between vocabulary gain and vocabulary retention for the learners with different language proficiency under each glossing condition.

Finally, some possible reasons are given to account for the results of this empirical study. To sum up, marginal glosses can be employed to significantly facilitate learners' reading comprehension and their incidental vocabulary acquisition through reading. The results also imply that the Involvement Load Hypothesis needs to be revised.

Chapter Seven Conclusion

This chapter is the conclusion of the current research. It is composed of four sections. To begin with, the results of the research are summarized in detail. Next, the implications of the results gained in the current research are illustrated. The following are the limitations existing in the research. Finally, some suggestions will be made for the future research.

7.1 Major Findings of the Research

The current research is composed of three empirical studies. The first is involved in the relationship between the languages employed in glosses and learners' reading comprehension, together with their incidental vocabulary acquisition for the learners with diverse language proficiency. Another one is concerned with the effects of the number of the options provided to glosses on learners' reading comprehension, as well as their vocabulary gain and vocabulary retention for the learners with different language proficiency. The other one is related to the effects of glossing positions on learners' reading comprehension, and their vocabulary gain and vocabulary retention for the learners with varying language proficiency. The major findings obtained in these three empirical studies will be provided in detail.

To begin with, the effects of the languages employed in glosses on learners' reading comprehension and their incidental vocabulary acquisition through reading will be summarized. As for the effects of glosses in different languages on learners' reading comprehension, it is found that among four different glosses, that is, Chinese glosses, English glosses, Chinese plus English glosses, together with null glosses, there are significant differences in learners' reading comprehension under four different glossing conditions. To be exact, significant differences exist in learners' reading comprehension between Chinese glosses and Chinese plus English glosses, Chinese glosses and null glosses, English glosses and Chinese plus English glosses, English glosses and null glosses, as well as between null glosses and Chinese plus English glosses. To be simple, Chinese plus English glosses are significantly the most beneficial to learners' reading comprehension, while null glosses are significantly the least conducive to learners' reading comprehension. Concerning the learners with different language proficiency, significant differences in learners' reading comprehension are discovered between the learners with higher language proficiency and those with lower language proficiency under each glossing condition. This indirectly demonstrates that glosses can be employed to significantly facilitate learners' reading comprehension, especially Chinese plus English glosses. This result is consistent with the findings discovered by Davis (1989), Elekaei et al. (2015), Farvardin and Biria (2012), Meng and Chen (2015), and Rott (2005), who argue that glosses are helpful to learners' reading comprehension, while Cheng and Good (2009), Holley and King (1971), Johnson (1982), as well as Wu et al. (2012) hold that glosses do not have any help to learners' reading comprehension. In addition, Farvardin and Biria (2012) believe that L2 glosses are more conducive to learners' reading comprehension, while Meng and Chen (2015) consider that L1 glosses are more facilitative.

With regard to learners' vocabulary gain through reading under four glossing conditions, it is found that there are significant differences in learners' vocabulary gain under four different glossing conditions. To be precise, significant differences are found in learners' vocabulary gain between Chinese glosses and null glosses, English glosses and Chinese plus English glosses, as well as between null glosses and Chinese plus English glosses. In addition, there are significant differences in learners' vocabulary gain through reading between the learners with different language proficiency under each glossing condition, except under the condition of Chinese glosses. The results indirectly illustrate that Chinese plus English glosses are significantly the most helpful to learners' vocabulary gain through reading. This result confirms the studies carried out by

Chen (2013), Shi (2010) and Xu (2010). However, Cao and Song (2014), and Ko (2005) argue that L2 glosses are more conducive. In addition, Jacobs et al. (1994), Lv et al. (2005) and Miyasako (2002) hold that both L1 glosses and L2 glosses are conducive to learners' vocabulary gain.

As to learners' vocabulary retention, it is found that there are significant differences in learners' vocabulary retention under four different glossing conditions. Exactly speaking, significant differences are found in learners' vocabulary retention between Chinese glosses and Chinese plus English glosses, as well as between null glosses and Chinese plus English glosses. Meanwhile, under each glossing condition, there are also significant differences in vocabulary retention through reading between the learners with different language proficiency. In other words, Chinese plus English glosses are significantly the most conducive to learners' vocabulary retention through reading. This result agrees with the findings discovered by Chen (2013), Shi (2010) and Xu (2010). However, it is against the findings obtained by Meng and Chen (2015), who argue that Chinese glosses are more helpful to learners' vocabulary retention. In addition, Jocobs et al. (1994), and Lv et al. (2005) hold that both L1 glosses and L2 glosses are significantly facilitative to learners' vocabulary retention.

In comparison with the differences between learners' vocabulary gain and vocabulary retention, it is found that for the learners with higher language proficiency, there are significant differences in learners' incidental vocabulary acquisition between their vocabulary gain and vocabulary retention. However, significant differences only exist between Chinese plus English glosses and null glosses. Nevertheless, for the learners with lower language proficiency, significant differences in learners' incidental vocabulary acquisition are found under each glossing condition. However, Lv et al., (2005), Miyasako (2002), Vela (2015), and Wang (2005) hold that L1 glosses are more beneficial to incidental vocabulary acquisition through reading for the learners with lower language proficiency. In addition, Vela (2015) argues that both L1 glosses and L2 glosses are facilitative to incidental vocabulary acquisition for the learners with higher language proficiency.

To be simple, for the effects of different languages employed in glosses on learners' reading comprehension and their incidental vocabulary acquisition, glosses are significantly beneficial to learners' reading compression and their incidental vocabulary acquisition, especially Chinese plus English glosses.

The following is involved in the effects of the number of the options provided to glosses on learners' reading comprehension and their incidental vocabulary acquisition through reading. In this empirical study, two types of glossing are concerned, that is, single Chinese plus English glosses and multiple-choice Chinese plus English glosses with two options. It is found that learners' reading comprehension is significantly different under these two glossing conditions. At the same time, it is found that there are significant differences in reading comprehension under both glossing conditions between the learners with higher language proficiency and those with lower language proficiency. This result shows that single Chinese plus English glosses are significantly more beneficial to learners' reading comprehension. However, Rott (2005) discovers that multiple-choice glosses are more conducive to learners' reading comprehension.

As to learners' vocabulary gain through reading, it is found that there are significant differences in learners' vocabulary gain under these two glossing conditions. In addition, significant differences are also found in learners' vocabulary gain under two glossing conditions between the learners with different language proficiency. In other words, the higher the learners' language proficiency is, the better their vocabulary gain will be under the condition of both single Chinese plus English glosses and multiple-choice Chinese plus English glosses with two options. It implies that single Chinese plus English glosses are significantly more helpful to learners' vocabulary gain through reading. The result is consistent with the one found by Jasteh and Akbarpour (2011), who hold that single glosses are more facilitative to learners' vocabulary gain through reading.

As for learners' vocabulary retention, it is found that there are not any significant differences in learners' vocabulary retention under these two glossing conditions. In addition, significant differences in learners' vocabulary retention are not found under either glossing condition betweenr the learners with higher language proficiency and those with lower language proficiency. To put it another way, these two different glossing conditions don't have any significant effects on learners' vocabulary retention through reading. The result is consistent with the findings found by Jasteh and Akbarpour (2011), Lei (2011), Shi (2010) and Watanabe (1997), who argue that there are not any significant differences in learners' vocabulary retention between single glosses and multiple-choice glosses. However, it is against the findings discovered by Duan and Yan (2004) and Nagata (1999), who hold that there are significant differences between these two different glossing conditions.

Compared with the differences between learners' vocabulary gain and vocabulary retention, it is found that there are significant differences between learners' vocabulary gain and vocabulary retention under either glossing condition. Meanwhile, significant differences in learners' vocabulary acquisition through reading are also found under either glossing condition for the learners with higher language proficiency and those with lower language proficiency.

In short, single Chinese plus English glosses are significantly more facilitative to learners' reading comprehension and their incidental vocabulary acquisition through reading.

Jasteh and Akbarpour (2011), and Watanabe (1997) also hold that single glosses are more beneficial to learners' incidental vocabulary acquisition through reading, while Cao and Song (2014), Duan and Yan (2004), Hulstijn (1992), Lei (2011), Nagata (1999), Rott (2005), Rott and Williams (2003), and Shi (2010) believe that multiple-choice glosses are more helpful to learners' incidental vocabulary acquisition through reading.

The last empirical study is concerned with the effects of glossing positions on learners' reading comprehension and their incidental vocabulary acquisition through reading. There are four types of glosses are involved, that is, in-text glosses, marginal glosses, footnote glosses and endnote glosses. It is found that there are significant differences in learners' reading comprehension under four different glossing conditions. This result confirms the study conducted by Elekaei et al. (2015). However, it is against the findings found by Cheng and Good (2009), Holley and King (1971), Johnson (1982), and Wu et al. (2012), who all hold that glossing positions do not have any significant effects on learners' reading comprehension. Exactly speaking, significant differences exist in learners' reading comprehension between in-text glosses and marginal glosses, in-text glosses and endnote glosses, marginal glosses and footnote glosses, as well as between marginal glosses and endnote glosses. It means that marginal glosses are significantly the most facilitative to learners' reading comprehension. In addition, compared with in-text glosses, endnote glosses are significantly more helpful to learners' reading comprehension. As to learners' language proficiency differences, it is found that there are significant differences in learners' reading comprehension under four glossing conditions between the learners with different language proficiency. To be exact, significant differences are found in reading comprehension under the condition of marginal glosses and endnote glosses between the learners with higher language proficiency and those with lower language proficiency. In other words, the higher the learners' language proficiency is, the better their reading comprehension is under the condition of marginal glosses and endnote glosses. In a word, marginal glosses are significantly the most beneficial to learners' reading comprehension. This result confirms the studies performed by Davis (1989), and Meng and Chen (2015). However, Elekaei et al. (2015) hold that in-text glosses are more beneficial to learners' reading comprehension.

As for vocabulary gain, there are significant differences in learners' vocabulary gain through reading under four different glossing conditions. To be precise, significant differences exist in learners' vocabulary gain between in-text glosses and marginal glosses, in-text glosses and endnote glosses, marginal glosses and footnote glosses, marginal glosses and endnote glosses, as well as between footnote glosses and endnote glosses. That is, marginal glosses are significantly the most beneficial to learners' vocabulary gain, while endnote glosses are significantly the least facilitative. Concerning learners' language proficiency differences, significant differences in vocabulary gain are found between the learners with different language proficiency under four glossing conditions. However, significant differences only exist under the condition of marginal glosses and endnote glosses. It means that the higher the learners' language proficiency is, the better their vocabulary gain through reading is under the condition of marginal glosses and endnote glosses. The results indirectly illustrate that marginal glosses are significantly the most conducive to learners' vocabulary gain, while endnote glosses are the least beneficial. This result is consistent with the findings obtained by Davis (1989), Hulstijn et al. (1996), and Wu et al. (2012). However, Chen et al. (2013), Cheng and Good (2009), Elekaei et al. (2015), and Lan and Zhang (2013) argue that in-text glosses are more beneficial to learners' vocabulary gain through reading.

As to vocabulary retention, it is found that significant differences are found in learners' vocabulary retention under four glossing conditions. Exactly speaking, there are significant differences in learners' vocabulary retention between marginal glosses and in-text glosses, marginal glosses and footnote glosses, as well as between marginal glosses and endnote glosses. At the same time, significant differences are also found in vocabulary retention under each glossing condition between the learners with different language proficiency. However, significant differences in vocabulary retention only exist under the condition of marginal glosses between the learners with higher language proficiency and those with lower language proficiency. It shows that marginal glosses are significantly the most facilitative to learners' vocabulary retention through reading. This result is consistent with the findings discovered by Davis (1989), Hulstijn et al. (1996), Meng and Chen (2015), and Wu et al. (2012), while Watanabe (1997) argues that marginal glosses are not beneficial to learners' vocabulary retention through reading. In addition, Chen et al. (2013), Cheng and Good (2009), Elekaei et al. (2015), Lan and Zhang (2013), and Zarei and Hasani (2011) hold that in-text glosses are more conducive to learners' vocabulary retention through reading.

In terms of the comparison between vocabulary gain and vocabulary retention, it is discovered that there are significant differences between learners' vocabulary gain and vocabulary retention under each glossing condition. To be specific, for the learners with higher language proficiency, there are significant differences between learners' vocabulary gain and vocabulary retention under four glossing conditions. However, significant differences only exist under the condition of marginal glosses and endnote glosses. For the learners with lower language proficiency, significant differences are also found between learners' vocabulary gain and vocabulary retention under four glossing conditions. However, significant differences only exist under the condition of endnote glosses. The results indirectly display that marginal glosses are significantly the most beneficial to learners' incidental vocabulary acquisition through reading. The result supports the studies conducted by Davis (1989), Hulstijn et al. (1996), Meng and Chen (2015), and Wu et al. (2012). Nevertheless, Chen et al. (2013), Cheng and Good (2009), Elekaei et al. (2015), Lan and Zhang (2013), and Zarei and Hasani (2011) hold that in-text glosses are more beneficial to learners' incidental vocabulary acquisition.

In brief, marginal glosses are significantly the most facilitative to learners' reading comprehension and their incidental vocabulary acquisition through reading.

Generally speaking, according to the findings discovered in the above three empirical studies, it is safe to conclude that single marginal Chinese plus English glosses are the best way to facilitate learners' reading comprehension and their incidental vocabulary acquisition through reading.

This general result is partially consistent with the Involvement Load Hypothesis. According to this hypothesis, the information that is processed deeper tends to be stored longer in memory. Among glosses in different languages, Chinese plus English glosses require more cognitive loads. As for the number of the options provided to glosses, multiple-choice Chinese plus English glosses with two options need more involvement loads.

With regard to the positions of glosses, because of the distances between glosses and the target words, more resources are needed to process endnote glosses. However, the general conclusion of the current research is that single marginal Chinese plus English glosses are significantly beneficial to learners' reading comprehension and their incidental vocabulary acquisition through reading. Therefore, the Involvement Load Hypothesis needs to be revised.

7.2 Implications of the Research

Just as what has been mentioned above, single marginal Chinese plus English glosses are significantly facilitative to learners' reading comprehension and their incidental vocabulary acquisition through reading. This general conclusion has some practical implications for foreign language vocabulary teaching and theoretical implications for the relevant theory reconstruction.

In terms of practical implications, to begin with, the current research throws some insights into the edition of the English textbooks. It is generally found that most of the published textbooks provide glosses of the unfamiliar words either in Chinese or in English. Only a few of them provide Chinese plus English glosses. The editors of the textbooks may think that it is quite direct and convenient for the learners to have access to Chinese glosses of the unfamiliar words. After all, for most of our Chinese English learners, we don't have so many opportunities to use English in our daily lives, except in class. Therefore, Chinese glosses may offer great help to learners' English learning. Nevertheless, even though we cannot completely get rid of the influence of our native language, we should try to use English we are learning as much as possible, which has proved to be greatly helpful to foreign language learning. As for English learning, it is generally held that the best way to learn English is to adopt the immersion learning approach. The learners should contact their native language as less as possible. Of course, the intention is quite good. However, under the foreign language learning context, it is quite difficult to operate in practice. And it has been confirmed in English teaching practice. When the teachers only provide English glosses to the unknown words, it is likely that they may not write down English glosses, but they may note down Chinese glosses, after referring to the dictionaries. Meanwhile, only a few students who have strong motivation to learn English may take note of English glosses or Chinese plus English glosses. Consequently, the compromise is to provide Chinese plus English glosses to the unknown words. In addition, the interview in the first empirical study has confirmed that most of the learners prefer to have Chinese plus English glosses.

As for the positions of the unfamiliar words, most of the textbooks take the form of endnote glosses, at the end of the text, arranged in the order of their appearance in the text. The learners can easily find all glosses of the unfamiliar words in the text in the same position. To some extent, this glossing method may bring some convenience to the learners. However, what cannot be ignored is that the distances between glosses and the new words may lead to some inconvenience to the learners, as well, which has been discussed in Chapter Six.

Based on the above analysis, it may be better for our English learners to be provided with single marginal Chinese plus English glosses to the unfamiliar words in the textbooks. On the other hand, this general conclusion also helps us to choose proper reading materials for the learners. Reading extensively can aid the learners to incidentally acquire some vocabulary knowledge. However, it is known from the practice that not all the reading materials work. When choosing reading materials, we should pick out those that provide proper glosses. Only in this way can learners' incidental vocabulary acquisition through reading be improved.

In addition, this current research also has some implications for foreign language vocabulary teaching. Even though it has been testified that foreign language learners can acquire some vocabulary knowledge through reading, the effect is not always satisfactory. In three empirical studies, no other clues are given to the target words, except their corresponding glosses. In order to strengthen learners' vocabulary acquisition through reading, some related exercises should be complemented. For example, the learners are required to do some exercises directed at the target words, such as filling in the blanks with the target words, or making up sentences using the target words, after they have finished reading the text. The exercises may help the learners to use the target words in the given context, so as to help them process the words deeply, resulting in better memorization of the words. In other words, in our vocabulary teaching, explaining how to use the words is only one of the steps for vocabulary acquisition. Some complementary exercises targeting the target words should be offered.

At the same time, vocabulary teaching should also take into consideration learners' language proficiency differences. For example, in the first empirical study, significant differences between vocabulary gain and vocabulary retention are found under the condition of Chinese plus English glosses and null glosses for the learners with higher language proficiency, while there are significant differences between vocabulary gain and vocabulary retention under each glossing condition for the learners with lower language proficiency. It means that the learners with different language proficiency should be provided with different glossing conditions in reading, so as to facilitate their incidental vocabulary acquisition through reading.

In terms of theoretical reconstruction, it is mainly concerned with the Involvement Load Hypothesis. It is held by the hypothesis that three factors determine the quantity of the involvement loads, that is, need, search and evaluation (Laufer and Hulstijn, 2001). To be simple, need refers to whether it is necessary for the learners to figure out the meanings of the target words. Search means how the learners figure out the word meanings. Evaluation requires the learners to make a choice about which meaning is appropriate in the given context. Generally speaking, need can be decided by learners' vocabulary size. However, it may be quite difficult to quantify the involvement loads required by search and evaluation, which may account for the fact that in the current research, the findings partially support the Involvement Load Hypothesis. In other words, some other factors should be integrated into the hypothesis.

7.3 Limitations of the Research

Every research has some flaws, including the current research. The limitations of the research are demonstrated in the following three aspects.

To begin with, there is only one method employed to examine the results of learners' incidental vocabulary acquisition through reading. In order to make the results compatible with those found in other studies, the Vocabulary Knowledge Scale (Paribakht and Wesche, 1997: 181) is adopted to test learners' vocabulary gain and vocabulary retention through reading. Even though the actual use of the target words is involved, there are some problems existing in this method (Wang, 2010: 80-82). To test learners' vocabulary acquisition is quite complicated. One method is not sufficient to demonstrate the actual vocabulary acquisition of the learners.

In addition, exercises employed to improve learners' incidental vocabulary acquisition are not provided. In order to demonstrate the incidental feature of vocabulary acquisition through reading, only two reading tasks are supplied. And on some occasions, some questions in the tasks are not related to the target words. Even though this approach may reveal some aspects of learners' incidental vocabulary acquisition through reading, the learning results are far from satisfactory.

The last limitation existing in the current research lies in the number of the participants. In these three empirical studies, there are 20 participants involved at the most in each subgroup of the learners with different language proficiency. If more participants were recruited to take part in the empirical studies, the results obtained in the current research would be more reliable.

7.4 Suggestions for the Future Research

Based on the limitations mentioned in Section 7.3, some suggestions will be made for the future research.

The first suggestion is concerned with the methodology related to the empirical studies. It is generally acknowledged that the more participants there are in the empirical study, the more reliable the results will be by means of SPSS analyzing the data. In addition, in order to demonstrate the various aspects of learners' incidental vocabulary acquisition, more methods should be adopted to test learners' incidental vocabulary acquisition. Finally, more exercises related to the target words should be provided to the learners, so as to improve their incidental vocabulary acquisition through reading.

The second suggestion is that the sources of language learners should be expanded. Just as the situation in the current research, most of the relevant studies are involved in college or university learners. Even though the learners in the middle school or in the primary school have a limited vocabulary size, there is no doubt that they may incidentally acquire some vocabulary knowledge through reading. However, few studies are involved in such language learners.

References

[1] Aljabri, S. S. (2011). The effect of pictorial annotations on Saudi EFL students' incidental vocabulary learning. Journal of Arabic and Human Sciences, 2(2): 43-52.

[2] Anderson, J. R. (1992). Automaticity and the ACT theory. American Journal of Psychology, 105(2): 165-180.

[3] Arnaud, P. J. L., & Savignon, S. J. (1997). Rare words, complex lexical units and the advanced learners. In Coady, J., & Huckin, T. (Eds.), Second Language Vocabulary Acquisition (pp. 157-173). Cambridge: Cambridge University Press.

[4] Chen, H. C., & Leung, Y. S. (1989). Patterns of lexical processing in a non-native language. Journal of Experimental Psychology: Learning, Memory and Cognition. 15(2): 316-325.

[5] Cheng, Y. H., & Good, R. L. (2009). L1 glosses: Effects on EFL learners' reading comprehension and vocabulary retention. Reading in a Foreign Language, 21(2): 119-142.

[6] Chern, C. L. (1993). Chinese learners' word - solving strategies in reading in English. In Huckin, T., Haynes, M.,

& Coady, J. (Eds.), Second Language Reading and Vocabulary Acquisition (pp. 67-85). Norwood: Ablex Publishing.

[7] Chun, D. M., & Plass, J. L. (1996). Effects of multimedia annotations on vocabulary acquisition. The Modern Language Journal, 80(2): 183-198.

[8] Craik, F. I. M., & Lockhart, R. S. (1972). Levels of processing: A framework for memory research. Journal of Verbal Learning and Verbal Behavior. 11(6): 671-684.

[9] Davis, J. N. (1989). Facilitating effects of marginal glosses on foreign language reading. The Modern Language Journal, 73 (1): 41-18.

[10] Ebbinghaus, H. (1913). Memory: A Contribution to Experimental Psychology. New York: Columbia University Press.

[11] Elekaei, A., Faramarzi, S., & Koosha, M. (2015). The impact of gloss types on reading comprehension, vocabulary gain and vocabulary retention: A comparative study. International Journal of Applied Linguistics & English Literature, 4(5): 97-103.

[12] Ellis, R. (1999). The Study of Second Language Acquisition. Shanghai: Shanghai Foreign Language Education Press.

[13] Farvardin, M. T., & Biria, R. (2012). The impact of gloss types on Iranian EFL students' reading comprehension and

lexical retention. International Journal of Instruction, 5(1): 99-114.

[14] Gardner, D. (2004). Vocabulary input through extensive reading: A comparison of words found in children's narrative and expository reading materials. Applied Linguistics, 25(1): 1-37.

[15] Gass, S. (1999). Discussion: Incidental vocabulary acquisition. Studies in Second Language Acquisition, 21 (2): 319-333.

[16] Ghafouri, A., & Masoomi, M. (2016). The effect of visual and auditory input enhancement on vocabulary acquisition of Iranian EFL university students. International Journal of English Linguistics, 6(7): 81-86.

[17] Grabe, W., & Stoller, F. (1997). Reading and vocabulary development in a second language: A case study. In Coady, J., & Huckin, T. (Eds.), Second Language Vocabulary Acquisition (pp. 98-112). Cambridge: Cambridge University Press.

[18] Haastrup, K. (1991). Lexical Inferring Procedures or Talking about Words. Tubingen, Germany: Gunter Narr.

[19] Hatch, E., & Brown, C. (2001). Vocabulary, Semantics and Language Education. Cambridge: Cambridge University Press.

[20] Holley, E., & King, J. (1971). Vocabulary glosses in foreign

language reading materials. Language Learning, 21(2): 213-219.

[21] Huckin, T., & Bloch, J. (1993). Strategies for inferring word meanings in context: A cognitive model. In Huckin, T., Haynes, M., & Coady, J. (Eds.), Second Language Reading and Vocabulary Acquisition (pp. 130-152). Norwood: Ablex Publishing.

[22] Huckin, T., & Coady, J. (1999). Incidental vocabulary acquisition in a second language. Studies in Second Language Acquisition, 21(2), 181-193.

[23] Hüllen, W. (1989). Their Manner of Discourse: Nachdenken über Sprache in Umkreis der Royal Society. Tübingen: Gunter Narr.

[24] Hulstijn, J. H. (1992). Retention of inferred and given word meanings: Experiments in incidental vocabulary learning. In. Arnaud, P. J. L., & Bejoint, H. (Eds.), Vocabulary and Applied Linguistics (pp.113-125). London: Macmillan.

[25] Hulstijn, J. H., Hollander, M., & Greidanus, T. (1996). Incidental vocabulary learning by advanced foreign language students: The influence of marginal glosses, dictionary use, and reoccurrence of unknown words. The Modern Language Journal, 80(3): 327-339.

[26] Jacobs, G. M. (1994). What lurks in the margin: Use of vocabulary glosses as a strategy in second language

reading. Issues in Applied Linguistics, 5(1): 115-137.

[27] Jacobs, G. M., Dufon, P., & Fong, C. H. (1994). L1 and L2 vocabulary glosses in L2 reading passages: Their effectiveness for increasing comprehension and vocabulary knowledge. Journal of Research in Reading, 17(1): 19-28.

[28] Jasteh, L., & Akbarpour, R. (2011). The comparative effect of single and multiple gloss conditions on EFL learners' vocabulary retention and production. Journal of English Language Teaching, 1(2): 57-70.

[29] Joe, A. (1998). What effects do text-based tasks promoting generation have on incidental vocabulary acquisition. Applied Linguistics, 19(3): 357-377.

[30] Johnson, P. (1982). Effects on reading comprehension of building background knowledge. TESOL Quarterly, 16(4): 503-516.

[31] Judd, E. L. (1978). Vocabulary teaching and TESOL: A need for reevaluation of existing assumptions. TESOL Quarterly, 12(1): 71-76.

[32] Ke, Y. (2003). The effects of input modification on incidental vocabulary learning. Selected papers from the Twelfth International Symposium on English Teaching and Learning. Taipei: Crane: 208-209.

[33] Kern, R. G. (1989). Second language reading strategy instruction: Its effects on comprehension and word

inference ability. The Modern Language Journal, 73(2): 135-149.

[34] Ko, M. H. (2005). Glosses, comprehension and strategy use. Reading in a Foreign Language, 17(2): 125-143.

[35] Ko, M. H. (2012). Glossing and second language vocabulary learning. TESOL Quarterly, 46(1): 56-79.

[36] Krashen, S. (1985). The Input Hypothesis: Issues and Implications. Beverly Hills, CA: Laredo Publishing Company.

[37] Krashen, S. (1989). We acquire vocabulary and spelling by reading: Additional evidence for the input hypothesis. The Modern Language Journal, 73(4): 440-464.

[38] Kroll, J. F. (1993). Accessing conceptual representation for words in a second language. In Schreuder, R., & Weltens, B. (Eds.), The Bilingual Lexicon (pp. 58-81). Amsterdam: John Benjamins.

[39] Laufer, B. (2003). Vocabulary acquisition in a second language: Do learners really acquire most vocabulary by reading? Some empirical evidence. Canadian Modern Language Review, 59(4): 567-587.

[40] Laufer, B. (2009). Second language vocabulary acquisition from language input and from form-focused activities. Language Teaching, 42(3): 341-354.

[41] Laufer, B., & Hill, M. (2000). What lexical information do

L2 learners select in a CALL dictionary and how does it affect retention? Language Learning and Technology, 3(2): 58-76.

[42] Laufer, B., & Hulstijn, J. H. (2001). Incidental vocabulary acquisition in a second language: The construct of task-induced involvement. Applied Linguistics, 22(1): 1-26.

[43] Lee, J. F., & Vanpatten, B. (1995). Making Communicative Language Teaching Happen. New York: McGraw-Hill.

[44] Li, J. (2014). Effect of task-induced online learning behavior on incidental vocabulary acquisition by Chinese learners: Revisiting Involvement Load Hypothesis. Theory and Practice in Language Studies, 4(7): 1385-1394.

[45] Li, X. L. (1988). Effects of contextual cues on inferring and remembering meanings of new words. Applied Linguistics, 9 (4): 402-413.

[46] Lomicka, L. (1998). To gloss or not to gloss: An investigation of reading comprehension online. Language Learning and Technology, 1(2): 41-50.

[47] Miyasako, N. (2002). Does text-glossing have any effects on incidental vocabulary learning through reading for Japanese senior high school students? Language Education and Technology, 39, 1-20.

[48] Mondria, J. R., & Wit de Boer, M. (1991). The effects of contextual richness on the guessability and the retention of

words in a foreign language. Applied Linguistics, 12(3): 249-267.

[49] Nagata, N. (1999). The effectiveness of computer- assisted interactive glosses. Foreign Language Annals, 32(4): 469-479.

[50] Nagy, W. (1997). On the role of context in first and second language vocabulary learning. In Schmitt, N., & McCarthy, M. (Eds.), Vocabulary: Description, Acquisition and Pedagogy (pp. 64-83). Cambridge: Cambridge University Press.

[51] Nagy, W., Herman, P., & Anderson, R. (1985). Learning words from context. Reading Research Quarterly, 20(2), 233-253.

[52] Nation, I. S. P. (1983). Testing and teaching vocabulary. Guidelines, 5(1): 12-25.

[53] Nation, I. S. P. (1990). Teaching and Learning Vocabulary. New York: Newbury House.

[54] Nation, I. S. P. (2001). Learning Vocabulary in Another Language. Cambridge: Cambridge University Press.

[55] Oxford Advanced Learners' English-Chinese Dictionary. (2009). Beijing: The Commercial Press.

[56] Oxford, R. L. (1990). Language Learning Strategies: What Every Teacher Should Know. Rowley, Mass: Newbury House.

[57] Paribakht, T. S., & Wesche, M. (1993). Reading comprehension and second language development in a comprehension-based ESL program.TESL Canada Journal, 11(1):9-29.

[58] Paribakht, T. S., & Wesche, M. (1997). Vocabulary enhancement activities and reading for meaning in second language vocabulary acquisition. In Coady, J., & Huckin, T. (Eds.), Second Language Vocabulary Acquisition (pp. 174-200). Cambridge: Cambridge University Press.

[59] Parry, K. (1993). Too many words: Learning the vocabulary of an academic subject. In Huckin, T., Haynes, M., & Coady, J. (Eds.), Second Language Reading and Vocabulary Acquisition (pp. 109-127). Norwood: Ablex Publishing.

[60] Parry, K. (1997). Vocabulary and comprehension: Two portraits. In Coady, J., & Huckin, T. (Eds.), Second Language Vocabulary Acquisition (pp. 55-68). Cambridge: Cambridge University Press.

[61] Pasternak, M., & Wrangell, E. (2008). Well Read 3: Skills and Strategies for Reading. New York: Oxford University Press.

[62] Pulido, D. (2003). Modeling the role of L2 proficiency and topic familiarity in L2 incidental vocabulary acquisition through reading. Language Learning, 53(2): 233-284.

[63] Pulido, D. (2004a). The effect of cultural familiarity on

incidental vocabulary acquisition through reading. The Reading Matrix: An International Online Journal, 4(2): 20-53.

[64] Pulido, D. (2004b). The relationship between text comprehension and second language incidental vocabulary acquisition: A matter of topic familiarity? Language Learning, 54(3): 469-523.

[65] Pulido, D. (2007). The effects of topic familiarity and passage sight vocabulary on L2 lexical inferencing and retention through reading. Applied Linguistics, 28(1): 66-86.

[66] Rieder, A. (2002). A cognitive view of incidental vocabulary acquisition: From text meaning to word meaning. Views, 11 (2): 53-71.

[67] Roby, W. (1999). What's in a gloss. Language Learning and Technology, 2(2): 94-101.

[68] Rott, S. (1999). The effect of exposure frequency on intermediate language learners' incidental vocabulary acquisition and retention through reading. Studies in Second Language Acquisition, 21(4): 589-619.

[69] Rott, S. (2005). Processing glosses: A qualitative exploration of how form-meaning connections are established and strengthened. Reading in a Foreign Language, 17(2): 95-124.

[70] Rott, S., & Williams, J. (2003). Making form-meaning

connections while reading: A qualitative analysis of word processing. Reading in a Foreign Language, 15(1): 45-75.

[71] Rouhi, A., & Mohebbi, H. (2012). Glosses, spatial intelligence, and L2 vocabulary learning in multimedia context. 3L: The Southeast Asian Journal of English Language Studies, 19(2): 75-87.

[72] Rubin, J. (1987). Learner strategies: Theoretical assumptions, research history and typology. In Wenden, A. L., & Rubin, J. (Eds.), Learner Strategies in Language Learning (pp. 15-30). Englewood Cliffs: Prentice Hall.

[73] Schmidt, R. (1990). The role of consciousness in second language learning. Applied Linguistics, 11(2): 129-158.

[74] Schmidt, R. (1995). Consciousness and foreign language learning: A tutorial on the role of attention and awareness in learning. In Schmidt, R. (Ed.), Attention and Awareness in Foreign Language Learning (pp. 1 - 64). Honolulu: University of Hawaii Press.

[75] Schmidt, R. (2001). Attention. In Robinson, P. (Ed.), Cognition and Second Language Instruction (pp. 3-32). Cambridge: Cambridge University Press.

[76] Schmitt, N. (1994). Vocabulary testing: Questions for test development with six examples of tests of vocabulary size and depth. Thai TESOL Bulletin, 6(2): 9-16.

[77] Schmitt, N. (2015). Researching Vocabulary: A Vocabulary Research Manual. Beijing: Foreign Language Teaching and

Research Press.

[78] Schmitt, N., Schmitt, D., & Clapham. C. (2001). Developing and exploring the behavior of two new versions of the Vocabulary Levels Test. Language Testing, 18(1): 55-88.

[79] Segler, T. M., Pain, H., & Sorace, A. (2002). Second language vocabulary acquisition and learning strategies in ICALL environments. Computer Assisted Language Learning, 15(4): 409-422.

[80] Shahrokni, S. A. (2009). Second language incidental vocabulary learning: The effect of online textual, pictorial and textual pictorial glosses. TESL-EJ, 13(3): 1-17.

[81] Shelton, D., & Newhouse, R. C. (1981). Incidental learning in a paired-associate task. The Journal of Experimental Education, 50(1): 36-38.

[82] Singleton, D. (1999). Exploring the Second Language Mental Lexicon. Cambridge: Cambridge University Press.

[83] Stanovich, K. (1986). Matthew effects in reading: Some consequences of individual differences in the acquisition of literacy. Reading Research Quarterly, 21(4): 360-407.

[84] Stewart, R. A., & Cross, T. L. (1991). The effect of marginal glosses on reading comprehension and retention. Journal of Reading, 35(1): 4-12.

[85] Swain, M. (1985). Communicative competence: Some roles of comprehensible input and comprehensible output in its

development. In Gass, S., & Madden, C. (Eds.), Input in Second Language Acquisition (pp. 235-256). New York: Newbury House.

[86] Swain, M. (1995). Three functions of output in second language learning. In Cook, G., & Seidlhofer, B. (Eds.), Principles and Practice in Applied Linguistics (pp. 125-144). Oxford: Oxford University Press.

[87] Taylor, A. (2006). The effects of CALL versus traditional L1 glosses on L2 reading comprehension. CALICO Journal, 23 (2): 309-318.

[88] Tomlin, R., & Villa, V. (1994). Attention in cognitive science and SLA. Studies in Second Language Acquisition, 16(2): 183-203.

[89] Truscott, J. (1998). Noticing in second language acquisition: A critical review. Second Language Research, 14(2): 103-135.

[90] Vela, V. (2015). Using glosses for incidental vocabulary acquisition. Procedia-Social and Behavioral Sciences, 199: 305-310.

[91] Watanabe, Y. (1997). Input, intake, and retention: Effects of increased processing on incidental learning of foreign language vocabulary. Studies in Second Language Acquisition, 19(3): 287-307.

[92] Wesche, M., & Paribakht, T. S. (1996). Assessing second

language vocabulary knowledge: Depth versus breadth. Canadian Modern Language Review, 53(1): 13-40.
[93] Widdowson, H. G. (1978). Teaching Language as Communication. Oxford: Oxford University Press.
[94] Wilkins, D. (1972). Linguistics in Language Teaching. London: Edward Arnold.
[95] Xu, X. (2010). The effects of glosses on incidental vocabulary acquisition in reading. Journal of Language Teaching and Research, 1(2): 117-120.
[96] Yoshii, M. (2006). L1 and L2 glosses: Their effects on incidental vocabulary learning. Language Learning and Technology, 10(3): 85-101.
[97] Zahar, R., Cobb, T., & Spada, N. (2001). Acquiring vocabulary through reading: Effects of frequency and context richness. Canadian Modern Language Review, 57 (4): 541-572.
[98] Zarei, A. A., & Hasani, S. (2011). The effects of glossing conventions on L2 vocabulary recognition and production. The Journal of Teaching Language Skills, 3(2): 209-233.
[99] 曹佳学, 宋娇. (2014). 不同注释方式对词汇附带习得的影响. 外语学刊, (1): 117-120.
[100] 常乐, 李家坤. (2009). 元认知策略、听力理解和附带词汇习得的相关性研究. 外语界, (6): 50-57, 90.
[101] 陈毅萍, 兰国帅, 杨胜楠. (2013). 超媒体注释的不同位

置对大学生英语阅读理解及词汇习得效果的影响. 电化教育研究, 34(5): 85-90, 96.

[102] 陈玉珍. (2013). CALL环境下词典查阅行为与词汇习得的相关性研究. 外语与外语教学, (5): 46-51.

[103] 段士平, 严辰松. (2004). 多项选择注释对英语词汇附带习得的作用. 外语教学与研究, 36(3): 213-218.

[104] 盖淑华. (2003). 英语专业学生词汇附带习得实证研究. 外语教学与研究, 35(4): 282-286.

[105] 干红梅, 何清强. (2015). 伴随性词汇习得研究发展三十年. 四川师范大学学报(社会科学版), 42(3): 106-114.

[106] 高照, 刘翊. (2009). 国外伴随性词汇习得中注释的实证研究综述. 西南民族大学学报(人文社科版), 30(5): 272-277.

[107] 龚兵. (2009). 阅读附带词汇习得中的频率效应. 解放军外国语学院学报, 32(4): 61-66.

[108] 顾琦一, 臧传云. (2011). 输入模态对第二语言理解和附带词汇习得的影响. 解放军外国语学院学报, 34(3): 55-59, 68.

[109] 顾曰国. (2007). 多媒体、多模态学习剖析. 外语电化教学, (4): 3-12.

[110] 黄燕. (2004). 检验"投入量假设"的实证研究——阅读任务对中国学生词汇记忆的影响. 现代外语, 27(4): 386-398.

[111] 兰国帅, 张一春. (2013). 合理利用超媒体注释技术促进

英语阅读理解及词汇习得——梅耶多媒体信息设计“临近原则”的实验验证.中国远程教育, (9): 40-45.

[112] 雷蕾. (2011). 词汇强化条件和语言水平对词汇附带习得的影响研究. 外语研究, 28(1): 75-79.

[113] 李红, 田秋香. (2005). 第二语言词汇附带习得研究. 外语教学, 26(3): 52-56.

[114] 李思萦, 高原. (2016). 移动技术辅助外语教学对英语词汇习得有效性的实证研究.外语界, (4): 73-81.

[115] 李燕. (2008). 不同投入量任务对产出性词汇知识附带习得的作用. 外语教学理论与实践, (2): 6-9, 22.

[116] 刘凌, 秦晓晴. (2014). 词汇呈现方式对英语词汇学习影响的实证研究. 外语界, (2): 67-75.

[117] 刘文慧. (2011). 多媒体呈现方式对成人外语词汇习得的影响. 外语与外语教学, (6): 41-46.

[118] 吕红梅, 姚梅林, 杜煜旻. (2005). 英语阅读中单词注释对词汇学习的影响研究. 心理科学, 28(6): 1415-1417.

[119] 马丽亚. (2013). 外语词汇刻意习得研究. 北京: 国防工业出版社.

[120] 孟春国, 陈莉萍. (2015). 生词注释对限时阅读理解与词汇附带习得的影响. 外语与外语教学, (1): 50-56.

[121] 秦晓晴. (2003). 外语教学研究中的定量数据分析. 武汉: 华中科技大学出版社.

[122] 邵艳春. (2006). 不同阅读目的对词汇附带习得的影响——一项基于SPSS统计分析的调查研究. 外语电化教

学, (3): 60-64.
[123] 时敬霞. (2010). 注释方式对词汇附带习得的影响. 北京航空航天大学学报(社会科学版), 23(2): 93-96.
[124] 汤闻励. (2012). 非英语专业大学生英语学习"动机缺失"研究分析. 外语教学, 33(1): 70-75.
[125] 王改燕. (2009). 二语自然阅读词汇附带习得研究. 解放军外国语学院学报, 32(5): 48-53.
[126] 王改燕. (2013). 第二语言阅读中词汇附带习得研究. 北京: 北京大学出版社.
[127] 王同顺, 姚禹, 徐莹莹. (2012). 听说输入模态下二语词汇附带习得的对比研究. 外语与外语教学, (6): 1-5.
[128] 王哲希. (2010). 英语阅读中词汇习得研究. 上海: 上海交通大学出版社.
[129] 汪徽. (2005). 字幕对伴随性词汇习得的影响.外语电化教学, (4): 47-52.
[130] 吴建设, 郎建国, 党群. (2010). 词汇附带习得与"投入量假说". 外语教学与研究, 42(5): 360-366.
[131] 吴旭东. (2010). 学习任务能影响词汇附带习得吗? ——"投入量假说"再探. 外语教学与研究, 42(2): 109-116.
[132] 武卫, 许洪. (2009). 多媒体环境下不同形式的注释对二语词汇附带学习的影响. 解放军外国语学院学报, 32(1): 44-49.
[133] 武卫, 周榕, 许洪. (2012). 注释呈现方式对二语阅读理

解和词汇附带习得的影响. 外国语言文学, 29(4): 267-273.

[134] 许洪, 武卫. (2007). 通过阅读附带学习英语词汇的实证研究. 外国语言文学, 24(2): 113-117, 122.

[135] 寻明. (2006). 二语词汇习得途径探究. 外语界, (1): 22-27, 39.

[136] 易红波, 穆凤英. (2013). 国内二语词汇附带习得研究综述. 重庆文理学院学报(社会科学版), 31(6): 153-158.

[137] 张萍. (2004). 学习者词汇策略对成绩的预测规律. 外语与外语教学, (12): 21-23.

[138] 张宪, 亓鲁霞. (2009). 自然阅读中词汇附带习得研究. 外语教学与研究, 41(4): 303-308.

[139] 张艳, 任爱军. (2013). 二语词汇习得机制探微——"输入+输出"任务组合效应. 外国语文, 29(6): 147-152.

[140] 张云勤, 许洪. (2014). 多媒体注释对英语词汇附带习得和阅读理解作用的实证研究. 中国外语, 11(4): 69-74.

[141] 赵龙武. (2012). 阅读文本、词汇注释与显性猜词策略——第二语言词汇附带习得研究. 外语学刊, (5): 129-131.

[142] 周慈波, 王文斌. (2012). 大学英语学习者负动机影响因子调查研究. 中国外语, 9(1): 48-55.

[143] 周浩. (2008). 基于投入量假设的一项实证性研究. 外语教学理论与实践, (1): 19-25.

Appendix I
Original Reading
Material with Two Reading Tasks

The Marathon des Sables is a seven - day, 149 - mile (240 kilometer) ultramarathon and a testament to the human ability to endure. It is equivalent to 5 1/2 regular marathons, and what makes it even tougher is that it is held in the deathly hot, 120-degree (Fahrenheit) Moroccan desert. It is considered to be not only the world's most difficult foot race, but also one of the most grueling athletic tests on Earth. As tough as it is for all of its participants, it was the toughest on Mauro Prosperi, an Italian police officer who lost his way in a sandstorm during the 1994 race.

Mauro Prosperi is an Olympic gold medal - winning pentathlete and an enthusiastic endurance runner. The Marathon des Sables appealed to his sense of personal challenge and competition. The race started out well enough, but on the third day of the race, there was a fierce sandstorm. Prosperi became completely disoriented, but he didn't want to stop the race, and continued to run. Unfortunately, he started running in the wrong direction, and he kept running further and further from the race route.

Competitors in the race must carry all their personal belongings and food for the race in their own rucksack. Organizers of the race provide water (9 liters a day) at various points in the race, and tents for runners to sleep in at night. When Prosperi became lost, he had only one-day's worth of dried food and a few gulps of water with him; he also had no shelter to protect him from the blazing sun. After 36 hours, his food supplies ran out. To combat starvation and thirst, he caught and ate some bats he found in an abandoned mosque, and some snakes in the desert. He also drank his own urine. And he kept running.

When race organizers realized that Prosperi was lost, they sent out a helicopter and people on foot to find him. The searchers found his shoelaces and gave him up for dead. Prosperi saw the helicopter, but the pilot did not see him, and flew away. Prosperi had heard that to die of thirst was a slow, painful death, so that night, he decided to take his own life. He took his pocketknife, cut his wrists, and lay down to die. But he didn't die. Because he was so dehydrated, his blood had thickened and wouldn't flow, and the wounds clotted. When he woke up the next day, he was determined to live to see his family again, and continued to move through the desert.

After 9 days, Prosperi had unknowingly wandered into

Algeria. He was found by a nomadic family, blindfolded, and taken to an Algerian military camp, and then a hospital. He was 186 miles off-route. He had lost 30 pounds, on the verge of liver failure, but he had survived.

Four years later, Prosperi was back at the Marathon des Sables. As Prosperi, said, "I am a competitor, and I love the desert." Today, Prosperi is a hero in his native Italy, and to all those who admire his survival spirit.

I. Multiple Choice

____ 1. What is the main topic of the passage?

a. the Moroccan desert c. a story of survival

b. a marathon d. survival tips

____ 2. Where does the Marathon des Sables take place?

a. during the Olympics c. Italy

b. the Moroccan desert d. Algeria

____ 3. Who is Mauro Prosperi?

a. a helicopter pilot c. an Algerian nomad

b. an Olympic marathoner d. an Italian police officer

____ 4. What did Prosperi find that helped him survive in the desert?

a. dried food b. bats and snakes c. water d. a tent

____ 5. Who found Prosperi?

a. a nomadic family c. searchers on foot

b. a helicopter pilot d. race organizers

____ 6. How long is the Marathon des Sables?

a. 120 miles c. 149 miles

b. 5 1/2 miles d. 240 miles

____ 7. How hot is the Moroccan desert?

a. 149 degrees b. 120 degrees

c. 240 degrees d. 36 degrees

____ 8. How long was Prosperi lost in the desert?

a. 5 1/2 days b. 36 hours c. 7 days d. 9 days

____ 9. How much weight did Prosperi lose?

a. 7 pounds b. 30 pounds c. 9 liters d. 36 pounds

____ 10. How far was Prosperi off route when he was found?

a. 30 miles b. 149 miles

c. 120 kilometers d. 186 miles

II. True / False

____ 11. Race organizers provide all food and water for runners.

____ 12. The Marathon des Sables is the same distance as 5 1/2 regular marathons.

____ 13. Prosperi got lost on the third day of the race.

____ 14. Prosperi had a tent with him.

____ 15. Someone in a helicopter found him.

Appendix Ⅱ
Target Words with Chinese Glosses

1. testament	*n.* 证明
2. equivalent	*a.* 相等的
3. grueling	*a.* 使人筋疲力尽的
4. disoriented	*a.* 迷失方向的
5. blazing	*a.* 酷热的
6. combat	*v.* 减轻
7. mosque	*n.* 清真寺
8. urine	*n.* 尿
9. dehydrate	*v.* (使)脱水
10. verge	*n.* 边缘

Appendix Ⅲ
Target Words with English Glosses

1. testament	*n*. a thing that shows that sth. else exists or is true
2.equivalent	*a*. equal in value, amount, meaning, importance, etc.
3. grueling	*a*. very difficult and tiring
4. disoriented	*a*. be lost
5. blazing	*a*. extremely hot
6. combat	*v*. to stop something unpleasant from getting worse
7. mosque	*n*. a building in which Muslims worship
8. urine	*n*. the waste liquid that you pass from your body
9. dehydrate	*v*. to make a person's body lose too much water
10. verge	*n*. edge or rim

Appendix Ⅳ
Target Words with
Chinese plus English Glosses

1. testament	*n.*	a thing that shows that sth. else exists or is true 证明
2. equivalent	*a.*	equal in value, amount, meaning, importance, etc. 相等的
3. grueling	*a.*	very difficult and tiring 使人筋疲力尽的
4. disoriented	*a.*	be lost 迷失方向的
5. blazing	*a.*	extremely hot 酷热的
6. combat	*v.*	to stop something unpleasant from getting worse 减轻
7. mosque	*n.*	a building in which Muslims worship 清真寺
8. urine	*n.*	the waste liquid that you pass from your body 尿
9. dehydrate	*v.*	to make a person's body lose too much water (使)脱水
10. verge	*n.*	edge or rim 边缘

Appendix Ⅴ
Target Words with Null Glosses

1. testament *n.*
2. equivalent *a.*
3. grueling *a.*
4. disoriented *a.*
5. blazing *a.*
6. combat *v.*
7. mosque *n.*
8. urine *n.*
9. dehydrate *v.*
10. verge *n.*

Appendix Ⅵ
Target Words with Single Chinese plus English Glosses

1. testament — *n.* a thing that shows that sth. else exists or is true 证明

2. equivalent — *a.* equal in value, amount, meaning, importance, etc. 相等的

3. tough — *a.* having or causing problems or difficulties 艰难的

4. grueling — *a.* very difficult and tiring 使人筋疲力尽的

5. enthusiastic — *a.* feeling or showing a lot of excitement and interest about ab. / sth. 热情的

6. fierce — *a.* (of weather conditions or temperatures) very strong in a way that could cause damage 恶劣的

7. shelter — *n.* protection from rain, danger or attack 遮蔽

8. blazing — *a.* extremely hot 酷热的

9. combat — *v.* to stop something unpleasant from

getting worse 减轻

10. abandon *v.* to leave a thing or a place, especially because it is impossible or dangerous to stay 舍弃

Appendix Ⅶ
Target Words with Multiple-choice Chinese plus English Glosses with Two Options

1. testament — *n.* a thing that shows that sth. else exists or is true 证明
an experiment to discover whether or how well sth. works, or to find out more information about it 试验

2. equivalent — *a.* equal in value, amount, meaning, importance, etc. 相等的
having a great or severe effect on sth. 等效的

3. tough — *a.* having or causing problems or difficulties 艰难的
demanding that particular rules be obeyed and showing a lack of sympathy for any problems or suffering that this may cause 严厉的

4. grueling — *a.* very difficult and tiring 使人筋疲力尽的

		very unpleasant and filling you with horror, usually because it is connected with death or injury 令人厌恶的
5. enthusiastic	*a.*	feeling or showing a lot of excitement and interest about ab. / sth. 热情的 interesting and amusing 有趣的
6. fierce	*a.*	(of weather conditions or temperatures) very strong in a way that could cause damage 恶劣的 (especially of people or animals) angry and aggressive in a way that is frightening 凶猛的
7. shelter	*n.*	protection from rain, danger or attack 遮蔽 the fact of having a place to live or stay, considered as a basic human need 居所
8. blazing	*a.*	extremely hot 酷热的 extremely angry or full of strong emotion 极其愤怒的
9. combat	*v.*	to stop something unpleasant from getting worse 减轻 to fight against an enemy 与…搏斗
10. abandon	*v.*	to leave a thing or a place, especially because it is impossible or dangerous to

stay 舍弃

to leave sb., especially sb. you are responsible for, with no intention of returning 离弃

Appendix Ⅷ
Target Words with In-text Glosses

The Marathon des Sables is a seven - day, 149 - mile (240 kilometer) ultramarathon and a testament (n. a thing that shows that sth. else exists or is true 证明) to the human ability to endure. It is equivalent (a. equal in value, amount, meaning, importance, etc. 相等的) to 5 1/2 regular marathons, and what makes it even tougher (a. having or causing problems or difficulties 艰难的) is that it is held in the deathly hot, 120-degree (Fahrenheit) Moroccan desert. It is considered to be not only the world's most difficult foot race, but also one of the most grueling (a. very difficult and tiring 使人筋疲力尽的) athletic tests on Earth. As tough as it is for all of its participants, it was the toughest on Mauro Prosperi, an Italian police officer who lost his way in a sandstorm during the 1994 race.

Mauro Prosperi is an Olympic gold medal - winning pentathlete and an enthusiastic endurance runner. The Marathon des Sables appealed (v. to attract or interest sb. 有吸引力) to his sense of personal challenge and competition. The race started out well enough, but on the third day of the race, there was a fierce (a. (of weather conditions or temperatures) very strong in a way that could cause damage 恶劣的) sandstorm. Prosperi became completely disoriented, but he didn't want to stop the race, and continued to run. Unfortunately, he started running in the wrong direction, and he kept running further and further from the race route.

Competitors in the race must carry all their personal belongings and food for the race in their own rucksack. Organizers of the race provide water (9 liters a day) at various points in the race, and tents for runners to sleep in at night. When Prosperi became lost, he had only one-day's worth of dried food and a few gulps of water with him; he also had no shelter (n. protection from rain, danger or attack 遮蔽) to protect him from the blazing sun. After 36 hours, his food supplies ran out. To combat (v. to stop something unpleasant from getting worse 减轻) starvation and thirst, he caught and ate some bats he found in an abandoned mosque, and some snakes in the desert. He also drank his own urine (n. the waste liquid that you pass from your body 尿). And he kept running.

When race organizers realized that Prosperi was lost, they sent out a helicopter and people on foot to find him. The searchers found his shoelaces and gave him up for dead. Prosperi saw the helicopter, but the pilot did not see him, and flew away. Prosperi had heard that to die of thirst was a slow, painful death, so that night, he decided to take his own life. He took his pocketknife, cut his wrists, and lay down to die. But he didn't die. Because he was so dehydrated (v. to make a person's body lose too much water 使脱水), his blood had thickened and wouldn't flow, and the wounds clotted. When he woke up the next day, he was determined to live to see his family again, and continued to move through the desert.

After 9 days, Prosperi had unknowingly wandered into Algeria. He was found by a nomadic family, blindfolded, and taken to an Algerian military camp, and then a hospital. He was 186 miles off-route. He had lost 30 pounds, on the verge of liver failure, but he had survived.

Four years later, Prosperi was back at the Marathon des Sables. As Prosperi, said, "I am a competitor, and I love the desert." Today, Prosperi is a hero in his native Italy, and to all those who admire his survival spirit.

Appendix Ⅸ
Target Words with Marginal Glosses

The Marathon des Sables is a seven-day, 149-mile (240 kilometer) ultramarathon and a testament to the human ability to endure. It is equivalent to 5 1/2 regular marathons, and what makes it even tougher is that it is held in the deathly hot, 120-degree (Fahrenheit) Moroccan desert. It is considered to be not only the world's most difficult foot race, but also one of the most grueling athletic tests on Earth. As tough as it is for all of its participants, it was the toughest on Mauro Prosperi, an Italian police officer who lost his way in a sandstorm during the 1994 race.

Mauro Prosperi is an Olympic gold medal-winning pentathlete and an enthusiastic endurance runner. The

1. testament: *n.* a thing that shows that sth. else exists or is true 证明
2. equivalent: *a.* equal in value, amount, meaning, importance, etc. 相等的
3. tough: *a.* having or causing problems or difficulties 艰难的
4. grueling: *a.* very difficult and tiring 使人筋疲力尽的

Marathon des Sables appealed to his sense of personal challenge and competition. The race started out well enough, but on the third day of the race, there was a fierce sandstorm. Prosperi became completely disoriented, but he didn't want to stop the race, and continued to run. Unfortunately, he started running in the wrong direction, and he kept running further and further from the race route.

Competitors in the race must carry all their personal belongings and food for the race in their own rucksack. Organizers of the race provide water (9 liters a day) at various points in the race, and tents for runners to sleep in at night. When Prosperi became lost, he had only one-day's worth of dried food and a few gulps of water with him; he also had no shelter to protect him from the blazing sun. After 36 hours, his food supplies ran out. To combat starvation

5. appeal: *v.* to attract or interest sb. 有吸引力

6. fierce: *a.* (of weather conditions or temperatures) very strong in a way that could cause damage 恶劣的

7. shelter: *n.* protection from rain, danger or attack 遮蔽

and thirst, he caught and ate some bats he found in an abandoned mosque, and some snakes in the desert. He also drank his own urine. And he kept running.

When race organizers realized that Prosperi was lost, they sent out a helicopter and people on foot to find him. The searchers found his shoelaces and gave him up for dead. Prosperi saw the helicopter, but the pilot did not see him, and flew away. Prosperi had heard that to die of thirst was a slow, painful death, so that night, he decided to take his own life. He took his pocketknife, cut his wrists, and lay down to die. But he didn't die. Because he was so dehydrated, his blood had thickened and wouldn't flow, and the wounds clotted. When he woke up the next day, he was determined to live to see his family again, and continued to move through the desert.

After 9 days, Prosperi had

8. combat: *v.* to stop something unpleasant from getting worse 减轻

9. urine: *n.* the waste liquid that you pass from your body 尿

10. dehydrate: *v.* to make a person's body lose too much water 使脱水

unknowingly wandered into Algeria. He was found by a nomadic family, blindfolded, and taken to an Algerian military camp, and then a hospital. He was 186 miles off-route. He had lost 30 pounds, on the verge of liver failure, but he had survived.

Four years later, Prosperi was back at the Marathon des Sables. As Prosperi, said, "I am a competitor, and I love the desert." Today, Prosperi is a hero in his native Italy, and to all those who admire his survival spirit.

Appendix X
Target Words with Footnote Glosses

The Marathon des Sables is a seven - day, 149 - mile (240 kilometer) ultramarathon and a testament to the human ability to endure. It is equivalent to 5 1/2 regular marathons, and what makes it even tougher is that it is held in the deathly hot, 120-degree (Fahrenheit) Moroccan desert. It is considered to be not only the world's most difficult foot race, but also one of the most grueling athletic tests on Earth. As tough as it is for all of its participants, it was the toughest on Mauro Prosperi, an Italian police officer who lost his way in a sandstorm during the 1994 race.

Mauro Prosperi is an Olympic gold medal - winning pentathlete and an enthusiastic endurance runner. The Marathon des Sables appealed to his sense of personal challenge and competition. The race started out well enough, but on the third

---

1. testament: *n.* a thing that shows that sth. else exists or is true 证明
2. equivalent: *a.* equal in value, amount, meaning, importance, etc. 相等的
3. tough: *a.* having or causing problems or difficulties 艰难的
4. grueling: *a.* very difficult and tiring 使人筋疲力尽的
5. appeal: *v.* to attract or interest sb. 有吸引力

day of the race, there was a fierce sandstorm. Prosperi became completely disoriented, but he didn't want to stop the race, and continued to run. Unfortunately, he started running in the wrong direction, and he kept running further and further from the race route.

Competitors in the race must carry all their personal belongings and food for the race in their own rucksack. Organizers of the race provide water (9 liters a day) at various points in the race, and tents for runners to sleep in at night. When Prosperi became lost, he had only one-day's worth of dried food and a few gulps of water with him; he also had no shelter to protect him from the blazing sun. After 36 hours, his food supplies ran out. To combat starvation and thirst, he caught and ate some bats he found in an abandoned mosque, and some snakes in the desert. He also drank his own urine. And he kept running.

When race organizers realized that Prosperi was lost, they sent out a helicopter and people on foot to find him. The searchers found his shoelaces and gave him up for dead. Prosperi saw the helicopter, but the pilot did not see him, and flew away.

---

6. fierce: *a.* (of weather conditions or temperatures) very strong in a way that could cause damage 恶劣的

7. shelter: *n.* protection from rain, danger or attack 遮蔽

8. combat: *v.* to stop something unpleasant from getting worse 减轻

9. urine: *n.* the waste liquid that you pass from your body 尿

Prosperi had heard that to die of thirst was a slow, painful death, so that night, he decided to take his own life. He took his pocketknife, cut his wrists, and lay down to die. But he didn't die. Because he was so dehydrated, his blood had thickened and wouldn't flow, and the wounds clotted. When he woke up the next day, he was determined to live to see his family again, and continued to move through the desert.

After 9 days, Prosperi had unknowingly wandered into Algeria. He was found by a nomadic family, blindfolded, and taken to an Algerian military camp, and then a hospital. He was 186 miles off-route. He had lost 30 pounds, on the verge of liver failure, but he had survived.

Four years later, Prosperi was back at the Marathon des Sables. As Prosperi, said, "I am a competitor, and I love the desert." Today, Prosperi is a hero in his native Italy, and to all those who admire his survival spirit.

10. dehydrate: *v.* to make a person's body lose too much water 使脱水

Appendix XI
Target Words with Endnote Glosses

The Marathon des Sables is a seven - day, 149 - mile (240 kilometer) ultramarathon and a testament to the human ability to endure. It is equivalent to 5 1/2 regular marathons, and what makes it even tougher is that it is held in the deathly hot, 120-degree (Fahrenheit) Moroccan desert. It is considered to be not only the world's most difficult foot race, but also one of the most grueling athletic tests on Earth. As tough as it is for all of its participants, it was the toughest on Mauro Prosperi, an Italian police officer who lost his way in a sandstorm during the 1994 race.

Mauro Prosperi is an Olympic gold medal - winning pentathlete and an enthusiastic endurance runner. The Marathon des Sables appealed to his sense of personal challenge and competition. The race started out well enough, but on the third day of the race, there was a fierce sandstorm. Prosperi became completely disoriented, but he didn't want to stop the race, and continued to run. Unfortunately, he started running in the wrong direction, and he kept running further and further from the race route.

Competitors in the race must carry all their personal belongings and food for the race in their own rucksack. Organizers of the race provide water (9 liters a day) at various points in the race, and tents for runners to sleep in at night. When Prosperi became lost, he had only one-day's worth of dried food and a few gulps of water with him; he also had no shelter to protect him from the blazing sun. After 36 hours, his food supplies ran out. To combat starvation and thirst, he caught and ate some bats he found in an abandoned mosque, and some snakes in the desert. He also drank his own urine. And he kept running.

When race organizers realized that Prosperi was lost, they sent out a helicopter and people on foot to find him. The searchers found his shoelaces and gave him up for dead. Prosperi saw the helicopter, but the pilot did not see him, and flew away. Prosperi had heard that to die of thirst was a slow, painful death, so that night, he decided to take his own life. He took his pocketknife, cut his wrists, and lay down to die. But he didn't die. Because he was so dehydrated, his blood had thickened and wouldn't flow, and the wounds clotted. When he woke up the next day, he was determined to live to see his family again, and continued to move through the desert.

After 9 days, Prosperi had unknowingly wandered into Algeria. He was found by a nomadic family, blindfolded, and taken to an Algerian military camp, and then a hospital. He was

186 miles off-route. He had lost 30 pounds, on the verge of liver failure, but he had survived.

Four years later, Prosperi was back at the Marathon des Sables. As Prosperi, said, "I am a competitor, and I love the desert." Today, Prosperi is a hero in his native Italy, and to all those who admire his survival spirit.

1. testament	*n.* a thing that shows that sth. else exists or is true 证明
2. equivalent	a. equal in value, amount, meaning, importance, etc. 相等的
3. tough	a. having or causing problems or difficulties 艰难的
4. grueling	*a.* very difficult and tiring 使人筋疲力尽的
5. appeal	*v.* to attract or interest sb. 有吸引力
6. fierce	*a.* (of weather conditions or temperatures) very strong in a way that could cause damage 恶劣的
7. shelter	*n.* protection from rain, danger or attack 遮蔽
8. combat	*v.* to stop something unpleasant from getting worse 减轻
9. urine	*n.* the waste liquid that you pass from your body 尿
10. dehydrate	*v.* to make a person's body lose too much water 使脱水